"Let's pretend that never happened," Rosemary suggested.

Feeling vaguely angry, Paul strode through her apartment. There was no need to pretend. Nothing *had* happened. "I guess the elevator should go here," he said, getting control.

She gasped. "An elevator? What on earth for?"

"It's code in Tyler for a two-story office building."

"Over my dead body!"

"We could arrange something along those lines," he replied cheerfully.

She leveled a steely gaze on him. "Am I a problem for you?"

"Yes, Rosemary. You are." He smiled ruefully, shaking his head. "You know you are."

She went very still. "Maybe I should go, then." Her voice was soft, her eyes luminous in the dusky room. "Maybe I should find another place to live.".

He said nothing, but very slowly he shook his head. The gesture was answer enough.

Helen Conrad is acknowledged as the author of this work.

ISBN 0-373-82553-6

THOSE BABY BLUES

HELEN CONRAD

Those Baby Blues

He'd ruined her life once,
and now he was back.

Harlequin Books

TORONTO • NEW YORK • LONDON
AMSTERDAM • PARIS • SYDNEY • HAMBURG
STOCKHOLM • ATHENS • TOKYO • MILAN
MADRID • WARSAW • BUDAPEST • AUCKLAND

WELCOME TO A
HOMETOWN REUNION

Twelve books set in Tyler.
Twelve unique stories. Together they form a
colorful patchwork of triumphs and trials—
the fabric of America's favorite hometown.

Around the quilting circle...

"Martha Bauer, that is the most stunning quilt you've ever made," Tessie Finklebaum said.

"Do you like it?" Martha stood back and stared critically at her own handiwork stretched on the wooden quilting frame. "I wanted to work in the history of Tyler. I got the idea from those history reenactors at Timberlake Lodge."

Bea Ferguson nodded. "I see where you used that bright orange fabric to represent the fire at the F&M. And the blue and gold for the pioneers. You will enter that in the contest, won't you?"

Martha hesitated. "I'm not sure—"

"You might as well enter it in the contest, Martha," Annabelle Scanlon said in an exasperated tone. "You certainly won't have time to put together any other idea on that scale. The way things are going, we'll just be churning out baby quilts from now on. Seems like every woman in Tyler between eighteen and forty is incubating a new citizen."

Tessie let out a snort of laughter. "Maybe it's something in the water supply."

Bea settled back in her wheelchair and exchanged a glance with Martha. "More likely it's this new crop of gorgeous men we've been seeing around here lately. What do you think, Martha?"

Martha smiled but didn't answer. Right now her mind was on Rosemary Dusold, her physical therapist, and Paul Chambers, the handsome new pediatrician. He'd bought the lovely old Victorian house where Rosemary lived, and then moved in. Something was going on there. She'd bet her masterpiece quilt on it.

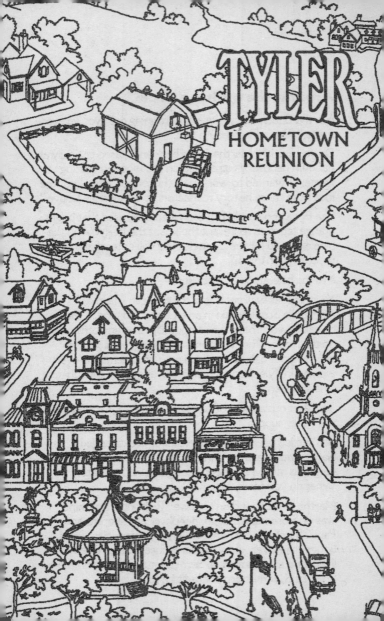

CHAPTER ONE

SPRING WAS BURSTING OUT in crisp green buds all through the park, and children were dressed in brightly colored shorts and playsuits, their bare legs and arms pale against the stiff, new fabric. Paul Chambers settled down at the picnic table with his hamburger and looked about him with a sense of wonder. Was this for real? Could there truly be a place so peaceful, so normal?

Too many years spent close to the action in war zones all over the world had left him slightly shell-shocked, and he took in the scene hungrily. This was what he'd been dreaming about for a long time. This was home—or at least a place to make the home he'd never really had before. This was where he would put down roots.

Tall, with muscles that had length rather than bulk, he moved with a grace and athleticism that made him look like a college swim star, though it was a good twenty years since he'd been on a college campus. His dark hair tended to catch the breeze and fall over his forehead, and at first glance, his bright blue eyes always seemed to be laughing at something just beyond the horizon. Only with closer observation did one see the deep shadows he just couldn't shake.

But all that was going to change. He was here in Tyler to start a new life. After all his years surviving like a no-mad, living out of a suitcase and hopping from one troubled country to another, he was finally going to settle down. His game plan included falling in love, a white picket fence, two kids in the yard. It was time he grabbed himself a piece of the American Dream.

Taking another bite of his juicy hamburger, he watched the young mothers pushing toddlers on the swings, talking softly to one another, laughing at the delighted cries from their children. Like a film shot through a filter, the light on their hair seemed golden, as though they had a special glow.

Paul loved it, every bit of it. His gaze traveled over two little boys arguing about baseball, over a young woman setting out picnic supplies on a neighboring table, over two older men throwing a Frisbee back and forth, over dogs and babies and a couple in love, and he sighed happily. Yes, this was what he'd come to Tyler for. This was what he wanted—a normal life.

He let the dream surface, the one that had sustained him lately—the one where the freckle-faced little boy called him "Dad" and the toddler in the pinafore reached her chubby little arms up to him, waiting to be held. That was what he wanted. Time was passing, and he'd begun to wonder if it was too late for him. He wanted a wife and he wanted a family. The question was could he get them?

Of course, he had to find the right woman first. Finding women had never been a problem for him. But this was different. This time he needed to look beyond a pretty face and a great body. This woman was going to be the mother of his children.

The park was full of women, but he barely glanced at any of them until his attention was caught by a statuesque blonde who was obviously preparing for a trip into the woods.

The park was a trailhead area, and she was putting things into a backpack, leading him to believe she was planning quite an expedition. Taking a last bite of the hamburger he'd picked up at the Dairy King, he admired her for a moment. Her light hair was tied back in a ponytail and her pretty face was set with concentration on the task at hand. A pair of faded denim shorts fit snugly around her trim but sturdy figure. Her legs were muscular in a very sexy way, somehow made even more intriguing by the heavy hiking boots and thick socks she wore. His gaze moved appreciatively up the sinuous line of her long legs to her trim waist and was sliding higher when he became aware that she'd stopped working on her supplies and was staring right at him, her hands on her hips and her silver-blue eyes stormy.

He smiled.

She didn't smile back. Nor did she waste much time on him, instead clipping her canteen onto her belt and turning away with a toss of her head. He'd been about to say something, but before he had a chance, she was gone, striding off through the brush, heading for the woods.

"Sorry," he mouthed, laughing to himself.

But seeing the young woman heading out reminded him of his childhood visits to Tyler. His grandfather had taken him out on those wilderness trails, usually with a fishing pole in hand, and suddenly Paul wanted to splash in that icy stream again, lose himself among the towering trees and catch the cry of a red-tailed hawk. He glanced down at his leather shoes and knew he wouldn't get far in them. But he might be able to go a little way, enough to detect that smell, that taste. Tossing the hamburger wrapper in the trash can provided, he started out along the same path the backpacker had taken, his heart light, his mind full of memories.

ROSEMARY DUSOLD SHIFTED the weight of her backpack and grimaced. There was something in her boot, something rubbing, and she was going to have to get rid of it. Here she was, barely five minutes away from the park, and already she'd run into problems.

"Drat," she muttered, lowering the pack to the ground on a flat area near the swollen stream, where there was a nice rock to lean against. She worked at the laces of her hiking boot, loosening them and finally pulling off the boot itself, then tugging at the heavy sock. A woodpecker called, flying overhead, and she looked up and smiled at it.

That was what she'd come for—to sink into nature and become a part of it. Her job as a physical therapist at Tyler Memorial Hospital filled her days with hard work, and it had been a long winter cooped up in her little flat in town. Now that spring was finally here, she meant to enjoy it to the max, spending every free moment outdoors.

The bird called again and her smile faded. Something inside of her responded to the melancholy note, and feelings of disappointment, of restless dissatisfaction with the way her life was turning out hit her. She had a birthday looming on the horizon, and that made the emotions especially dramatic at the moment. But it was more than that. Rosemary had been fighting these feelings all winter, and she pushed them away now, biting her lip as she dug for the pebble that had stopped her progress.

What you need, you know, is a man. Her friend Kayla's words came back to her and they stung.

She and Kayla had taken in a movie and then gone for a late snack at Marge's Diner the night before. They'd talked until after midnight, dawdling over coffee, getting sleepy and just a little punchy, and Rosemary had confided how adrift she felt. The door had opened and a young man with lazy green eyes had entered the diner and smiled at Rosemary as he passed their table.

"Hi, Rosie," he'd said casually. "You're lookin' good."

He'd gone on, not waiting for an answer, and Kayla's mouth had dropped open.

"Who is that?" she'd whispered, her gaze following the handsome man across the room.

Rosemary had gestured dismissively. "It's only Billy Joe Ocker, Carl's nephew. He works at Carl's Garage part-time and races stock cars the rest of the time. He's just a kid."

"That look he gave you was very grown-up." Kayla gazed at her speculatively. "You ought to go out with him."

"With Billy Joe?" Rosemary was too surprised to gasp. "I must be at least ten years older than he is."

"So what? I didn't say you should marry him." And that was when Kayla had given her wise pronouncement. "What you need, you know, is a man in your life. That'll get you out of this funk you've fallen into."

"A man is the last thing I need," she'd retorted. But as they got up to leave, she couldn't help but glance Billy Joe's way, and he grinned when he caught her at it.

That was yesterday, however. This was today, and Rosemary meant to enjoy her hike to the hilt. A good hike was a much more reliable intoxicant than a man could ever be.

Shaking out her boot, then her sock for good measure, she started putting them on again, anxious to continue her hike. She had only a few hours. She was due back at the hospital for a consultation at five, and the day was quickly evaporating on her.

She'd barely begun to pull on her boot when a sound from downstream caught her attention, and she rose quickly, shading her eyes to take a look. There were trees and brush in the way, but she could see that someone had fallen into the water. Gazing intently, she could make out that it was a man and that he was having trouble getting up again.

Looking around, she didn't see anyone else who'd had the sense of adventure to come out tromping in the soggy woods on this warm spring day—just the two of them.

"And only one of us has the skill required," she noted dryly. Sighing, she laced her boot quickly and shrugged into her day pack, turning back toward the helpless stranger. "Rosemary to the rescue," she muttered in mild exasperation. Was she never going to get off on this first hike of the season?

It took only a few minutes to reach the victim, and wouldn't you know it? There, floundering in the rushing waters of the spring runoff, was the man who'd examined her so insolently back at the park. He'd come out hiking in street shoes and slacks, and now he was paying for it.

She dropped her backpack and hurried forward to help him pull himself out of the water, and right away she could see that he was hurt. He was favoring his right leg, grimacing in pain when any pressure was put on it.

"Take it easy," she said, helping him find a comfortable seat on the grassy bank. "Let me have a look."

He turned his bright blue eyes toward her without gratitude, and she could see him wince with agony as he moved his leg. "It's *my* foot," he said shortly, through gritted teeth. "I'll look."

"Let's get you comfortable first," she said, speaking as she might to any stubborn patient. "Here." She went down on one knee and began to unlace his very wet Italian leather shoe.

He sat back, glaring at her, feeling like a helpless fool and trying to hide it behind a gruff exterior. "Are you an M.D.?" he challenged.

"No," she replied, glancing up at him and then back to the task at hand.

"Well, I am," he informed her, frowning as he tried to pull away from her touch. "I'll look."

Her instinct was to turn and look him full in the face, but she resisted. So he was a doctor, was he? Well, la-di-da. She worked with physicians every day and she knew how prone they were to lording it over other people. You couldn't let them get the idea you were in any way in awe of them, or you were sunk. So she ignored his claim and kept tugging at the shoe even as he tried to resist her.

"Are you an orthopedic surgeon?" she asked him crisply as she slipped the shoe off and began to peel down his wet sock.

"No," he admitted, wincing with pain again. "I'm a pediatrician."

Her silver-blue eyes met his with a measure of triumph. "Well, I'm a physical therapist. I'll handle this."

He relaxed just a little, though reluctantly. "It's my damn foot," he said again, but she could tell he was weakening. Pain often did that to people.

"That's just the trouble," she muttered as she worked off the sock. "You're too close to the situation. You need an objective analysis. Now hold still."

He held still. Her manner and deft movements gave mute evidence to her expertise, and he began to trust her. Watching, wincing when she touched a vulnerable area, he couldn't help but smile for a moment.

"You're not exactly the shy type, are you?" he noted wryly.

She shrugged. "Is that your tactful way of calling me a pushy broad?" she asked with the hint of a grin.

"Yes," he said emphatically.

"Guilty as charged." She got the sock off and frowned. The upper section of his foot was swelling badly and already turning purple. With a firm but gentle touch she examined the area, probing carefully. "Ouch. It looks like something's broken to me."

His jaw was clenched in pain, but he managed to mutter, "I could have told you that."

She nodded. "Now you have a second opinion." She probed a bit more, ignoring his grunt of agony. "I'd say you cracked a couple of metatarsals. Nothing fatal. You'll be okay. But it will take awhile to get the use of your foot back.''

He knew she was right and he swore softly, angry with himself for venturing out in inappropriate shoes, angry with fate for dealing him this wild card just when he'd set out on renewing his life. He tried to move his toes, hoping to disprove her diagnosis, but pain shot through his leg, making him gasp, and he couldn't deny her verdict.

She watched him give it a try and shook her head as he muttered in irritation at the entire situation. Stubborn man, just like most physicians she knew. Why was it so difficult for them to give control to someone else?

She started to turn away, but as she did, something about him caught her attention, and cocking her head to the side, she did a double take and studied his features. She didn't recognize the face, but there was something about his voice that kept reminding her of something or someone, though she couldn't quite place it. Rising, she looked down at his injury again. She was going to have to get him to medical care.

''Can you walk?'' she asked.

He gazed at her with indignation, hating to feel so helpless. ''My foot is broken. What do you think?''

She gazed right back. Doctors were always the worst patients. ''You'll have to use me as a crutch,'' she told him firmly.

He gave a short, mirthless laugh. ''I guess so. Unless you'd like to carry me on your back.''

She frowned down at him, remembering the way he'd looked at her back at the park. ''Listen, mister, you're very lucky I was here to help you. You'd better be nice, or I might leave you sitting on a rock and go all the way home before I call the paramedics to come rescue you.''

He bit his tongue to keep from throwing out a rejoinder. She was right and he knew it. ''Thank you very much," he told her, trying to sound sincere. But then he couldn't resist adding, "Nurse Ratched."

Rosemary ignored the jab and began to work his sock back on. "You'll have to stay off the foot as much as possible." Rising, she put his shoe in her pack and slipped the straps over her shoulders. "I think we'll do okay. I've had paramedic training. I've handled bigger boys than you."

He gazed at her speculatively. He could believe it. She had broad shoulders and a look of strength you didn't often see in a woman. She also had a no-nonsense manner that made him want to find a way to puncture her self-assurance, if just a little bit.

"Let's go," she was saying impatiently.

Paul took a deeper breath, preparing himself for what he knew was going to be an ordeal. But he'd been through ordeals before, been wounded, been left for dead. He supposed he would survive this silly cracked-foot injury, just as he had all the others. In the meantime, he was determined not to lose his sense of humor.

And so he smiled at her roguishly. "Were you ever in the army, Miss Rescue Lady? Your voice has such a familiar ring." He began to push himself up, steeling himself against the pain. "I think I heard it on a drill sergeant once," he managed to mutter as he rose.

His comment stung, but Rosemary wasn't going to let him know that and she dismissed it from her mind, helping him to his feet. His clothes, soaking wet, clung to his tall, muscular frame. He was such a good-looking man, the sort who was usually suave and debonair, not the type to fall into a stream, and suddenly the situation struck her as funny. She bit her lip trying to keep from grinning, but her eyes sparkled and he noticed.

"Amused, are you?" he grunted. "I'm glad my misfortune is good for a laugh. That's something, anyway."

"Do you always whine like this?" she murmured as she helped maneuver him into position.

But this time he didn't have an answer. She glanced up into his face and noted the white line around his lips. He was in agony, and she held her tongue. There was no point in kicking a man when he was down.

Slipping one arm around his waist, she settled him against her shoulder. He was surprisingly hard and muscular for a man with a smile like his. For some reason she hadn't expected that, and she gave him another long look. Surely she had met him before. But where?

"Where are we heading?" she asked as they took the first tentative and rather painful steps back toward the trail.

He forced himself to relax and ignore the pain. Yes, where should he go? That was a problem. He hadn't even moved into Tyler yet and already he badly needed its facilities.

"To the nearest emergency room, I guess," he said. He didn't know the town very well, though he had been negotiating with two hospitals, one in Tyler and one in nearby Belton, regarding the practice he planned to take over.

"Do you live in Tyler?" she asked, wondering if she'd dealt with him before and the memory twinges were coming from that encounter.

"No. That is, yes. I guess I do now." Despite the condition his foot was in, he gave her a shaky smile. "I was just on my way into town when I stopped at the park for lunch and thought I'd take a short hike. I used to come up here when I was a kid, but that was long ago. I'm moving to Tyler, though."

He was becoming short of breath, and she stopped and leaned him against a tree for a moment, letting him gather his resources.

Belatedly, he stuck out his hand. "I'm Paul Chambers. I'm going to be starting up a pediatric practice here."

"Rosemary Dusold," she murmured, shaking hands.

But her eyes suddenly lost focus and a bell started clanging a loud warning in her head. Paul Chambers. The name had a familiar ring, and as she searched back, she realized she had once known a man with that name, known him and resented him fiercely. But that Paul Chambers had been a young med student, with long hair that never seemed to be combed, a beard and mustache that covered his face and bright baby-blue eyes....

She gasped silently, turning so that he wouldn't see her reaction. It was him! Of course it was. He'd been that young man fifteen years ago. He'd been in medical school with her then-husband, Greg Simmons. She'd known Paul more by reputation than from much actual contact, but she'd known enough about him to wish her husband could have found a more serious friend at that crucial time in their lives.

Carefully, she turned back and gazed at him covertly. What had happened to the long hair, the beard, the scruffy exterior? His hair was trim now, and his handsome face was clean-shaven. But the eyes were the same, as bright a blue as the sky, with long dark lashes that seemed to droop at the corners and a knowing look that drove women wild.

"That man is like catnip to the ladies," her friend Charlene had said at the time. "Lots of fun in the short run, but not enough staying power for the long haul."

She and Charlene had laughed over that comment, but it had been true. And here he was. Had Paul Chambers changed? From what she'd seen so far, there wasn't much reason to think so.

"Let's try again," he was saying, leaving his tree trunk and swaying toward her.

Avoiding his eyes, she nodded and moved toward him. After all, he was basically a patient at this point, and though it meant she was going to be giving up a hike she'd looked forward to all winter, she had no second thoughts. When duty called, she answered. But deep down inside, she knew that when she got home and put her feet up and drank her hot cup of tea, she was going to realize she'd done all this for a man who had very likely helped ruin her marriage, and she was going to resent it.

They struggled along together. The path seemed endless, and he got heavier and harder to maneuver as they went. She had to admit his humor was awfully good for a man in the sort of pain she could see he was in. The set of his mouth with its white line gave mute testimony to that, as did his breathing, which tended to catch and then become strained for a moment or two. Still, he cracked jokes and commented on the landscape, and she could see it took a major effort.

"Just hush and concentrate on staying off that foot," she said at last.

She felt him draw in his breath sharply and she knew he'd taken another false step. But his voice was strong when he replied. "Can't do that, dear old Nurse Ratched. Gotta laugh. If I don't..."

"You'll cry, yes I know." She shook her head, trying not to smile. "Go ahead and cry. I told you, I'm a physical therapist. I've seen six-foot-five musclemen sob like babies. I'm used to it."

"Well, I'm not." He gave her a baleful look. "I do my crying alone, thanks just the same." And he started off again.

She sighed and set off after him.

In another few moments, they reached the clearing that led to the park. People gasped and came running to help, and soon Rosemary was relieved of her burden. Giving a few crisp orders and looking into Paul's face to check how he was handling the pain, she went quickly to the telephone and called the paramedics.

"I don't think it's serious," she told Maxie, the dispatcher who answered. "But it's quite painful. He'll need an X ray. I could drive him in."

"The boys have been hanging around here," Maxie told her. "The park isn't far at all. I'll send them out with the van to get him. You sit tight."

That was fine with her, actually. Rosemary went back to the picnic table where the helpful people had placed Paul, only to find him surrounded by bright young women, each vying to be the one to nurse him back to health. Funny how all the flattery seemed to have lifted his spirits and dampened the pain. She had to smile, watching him. No matter how outrageous he got, he was always likable. That was another thing she remembered about him.

The paramedics came with sirens blaring and caused even more excitement. Paul didn't seem to mind all the attention, and she barely got another word with him before they carted him away.

"Hey, Nurse Ratched," he called out, craning his neck to get a last look at her. "Thanks a million. I couldn't have done it without you."

"No problem," she said, smiling a bit wryly. "No problem at all."

They lifted him into the back of the van. She glanced at her watch, thinking she might be able to hike for a couple of miles or so if she hurried. At the same time, the part of her mind that was still paying attention heard Paul's answer when the paramedic asked him his address in order to fill out a form. The doors on the ambulance were closing as he replied, "Uh, let's see. Oh yes. It's 153 Morgan Avenue."

The ambulance began to drive away, and her head snapped around as that address registered. "Wait a minute!" she cried, taking a step after the vehicle. But it was too late, and it sped away.

Stunned, she stared after them. That was her address—153 Morgan Avenue. That was her address. What the heck was going on here? She sighed, her shoulders sagging. More hiking was definitely out of the question. She would have to go on home and see if she could find out why Paul Chambers thought he lived in her building, a lovely old Victorian subdivided into four apartments. Whatever the reason turned out to be, she had a feeling she wasn't going to like it.

CHAPTER TWO

THE SPRAWLING OLD HOUSE on Morgan Avenue had a faded elegance that Rosemary had fallen in love with from the first. Two stories high with a wraparound porch and forest-green shutters on the beveled windows, it presided over the street like a proper aunt who served tea in porcelain cups and encouraged good table manners. Lace curtains graced the bay window. A creaky swing hung at one end of the porch. Whenever Rosemary stopped to look at it, she seemed to feel the pull of another century, of ice cream socials and bands playing in the park.

Best of all, it was home. She'd lived here since she arrived in Tyler five years before. At first she'd resisted the temptation, thinking she really wanted a house where she could spread out and maintain her privacy. But she'd fallen under the spell of the place and moved in temporarily, only to find that the other tenants were just as independent as she was. She rarely saw them, barely heard them and had little more than a nodding acquaintance with any of them. They didn't get in her way any more than she would get in theirs. And so she'd stayed, and now this lovely house was a home.

She took the wooden steps two at a time, her mind on the puzzle she'd been mulling over since she'd left the park. Could Paul have some relationship with one of the other tenants?

Strains of Chopin coming from the upper right apartment told her Harriet Ambers, the piano teacher, was in.

Rosemary hesitated in the hallway, wondering. Could Paul be planning to stay with Harriet?

The thought brought a smile to her face as she pictured the woman at the keyboard, her hair cut short and sensibly, her horn-rimmed glasses slipping down her high-bridged nose, her lips pursed in concentration. The Paul she'd known years ago would have been attracted to a jazzier woman than Harriet had ever been. No, a connection between the two of them just didn't seem reasonable.

How about the Coopers, the young couple across the hall from Harriet? Gina Cooper was taking courses at Sugar Creek Community College and working part-time as an operator at the phone company, and her husband, Ned, was night manager at the supermarket. Rosemary couldn't imagine how Paul could fit into that scenario.

The door directly across from hers opened and a small woman with bright brown eyes that shifted quickly, like those of a bird, looked out at her. "What is it, dear?" she asked anxiously. "Did you lose something?"

Rosemary gave her a slight smile. "No, Mrs. Tibbs. I was just wondering..." She hesitated. But after all, why not? "Are you expecting a visitor, by any chance?" she asked her neighbor.

Mrs. Tibbs looked startled. Her eyes blinked rapidly and she shook her head. "Who told you?" she asked, her face tragic. "No one was to know until it was over."

Rosemary opened her mouth to reply, but the woman had already slammed her door. Hearing her footsteps retreat through the apartment, Rosemary frowned. Mrs. Tibbs and Paul Chambers? Well, what if she were his aunt, or a friend of his mother's, or... Who knew? And yet it seemed very strange.

Taking out her key, Rosemary let herself into her own apartment, sighing as she dropped her backpack on the floor. The hiking season had not gotten off to a very promising start, that was for sure. She flexed her shoulders, looking around her living room. The place was charming, if she did say so herself. It had come furnished with antiques and decorated with historical pieces that created a comforting atmosphere. Often the ambience seemed to envelop her, making her feel part of the past and important in the present like nothing she'd ever known before.

But today she couldn't relax and enjoy it. The encounter with Paul Chambers nagged at her. What had he meant when he gave her address to the paramedic? It just didn't make sense.

She paced the shiny hardwood floor restlessly and thought about taking a long, hot shower, but shrugged that idea away. She had to find out. Bolting out the doorway impulsively, she ran up the stairs to Harriet's apartment and knocked.

Harriet opened her door, blinking from behind her thick glasses. "Oh, hello," she said rather absently. "How are you, Rosemary?"

"Fine. Maybe." Rosemary gave her a perfunctory smile and got straight to the point. "Harriet, do you know a man named Paul Chambers?"

"Paul Chambers?" Harriet frowned and put a finger to her chin. "Isn't that the new owner?"

Rosemary's world was suddenly quivering in the balance. "New owner?" she repeated hoarsely, swaying a bit where she stood. "What are you talking about?"

Harriet raised an eyebrow and adjusted her glasses. "Didn't you get the letter? I got the announcement a few weeks ago, and I know the Coopers got one, too." She frowned thoughtfully, making Rosemary twitch with impatience.

"I'm not sure about Mrs. Tibbs," Harriet continued slowly. "She's so secretive you just can't talk to the woman. But you should have received one as well." She shrugged and smiled, finally getting to the point. "It seems old Mrs. Chambers has died and left the building to her grandson, Paul.''

Rosemary stared at her, hardly able to digest this news. ''Do you mean to tell me I've been living all these years in a house owned by Paul Chambers's grandmother?'' she said tragically, hardly able to believe it. ''Why didn't I know this?''

''Perhaps you don't pay attention, my dear,'' Harriet scolded lightly. ''You're always in such a rush, what with all your commitments, I never feel we have time to talk.''

''Paul Chambers owns the building I live in,'' Rosemary said, trancelike. ''I can't believe it.''

Harriet's eyes narrowed. ''Do you know this Paul Chambers?'' she asked curiously.

But Rosemary didn't hear her. Her eyes were on a distant time and her mind was racing. Absently, she thanked Harriet and started back down the stairs to her own place. The letter had come two weeks ago, Harriet had said. Rosemary had been on a trip to Chicago, giving a guest lecture in musculoskeletal pathokinesiology at Loyola University. And when she'd returned, she remembered, she'd found a huge stack of mail waiting for her. Everything that looked boring she'd stuck in a drawer in the kitchen.

Striding into that room, she pulled open the drawer, and sure enough, there was the mail she'd forgotten all about. Riffling through the envelopes, she came up with the pertinent one and ripped it open. Signed by the rental agency that handled the house, it informed the tenants of the change in ownership and warned them to be prepared— that other changes were in the wind.

''No,'' Rosemary whispered fiercely, looking around at her spacious kitchen with its huge, plant-filled greenhouse window that let in shimmering rays of sunshine at just the right time in the afternoon. ''No changes, thank you very much. I like it just the way it is.''

She'd lived a vagabond life before coming to Tyler. An army brat, she'd grown up moving every two years, never putting down roots. Then she'd married Greg, and it had been a wild ride from one university with a teaching hospital to another, Rosemary often working two jobs to foot the bills, Greg working hard on his education and expecting a full-time wife to pick up the slack. The tension between what they each wanted out of their relationship and what was actually realistic was just too much for them to endure the added problems Paul Chambers threw in their path, and by the time Greg had finished his residency, the marriage was over.

The divorce had sent Rosemary into a tailspin for a couple of years, and then she'd gone back to school, become certified in physical therapy and launched her career, moving from city to city in search of the perfect job situation.

Finally she'd settled in Tyler. This was it, as far as she was concerned. And this house was the center of her life.

"No, don't change a thing," she repeated, examining her living room and walking toward the bedroom, looking at everything afresh—the drop-leaf table, the antique Singer sewing machine, the beveled glass in the corner window. "This is mine."

But she had that five o'clock consultation at the hospital to think about. Sighing, she began shedding clothes as she headed for the shower. Paul Chambers and the problems he might possibly bring into her life were forgotten for the moment.

It was almost time for her to leave for the hospital when she heard a car pull up in front and she went to the window to see who it was. Ernie Glickman's yellow cab stood at her front curb, and Ernie was busy helping Paul Chambers out, new cast, crutches and all. He was wearing jeans now, and they had been slit open in the right leg to allow for the bulk of his cast. Ernie opened the trunk of the car and pulled out a duffel bag and a sports bag. It seemed Paul had come to stay.

Her heart skipped a beat. "The enemy is at hand," she muttered, withdrawing from the window and taking a deep breath. She was going to be pleasant. She was going to be reasonable. But she was also going to find out what the heck was going on.

PAUL PAUSED on the sidewalk, looking up at his grandmother's house with satisfaction. It looked very much as he remembered it from his childhood—the turrets, the shingles, the swing on the porch. This was heartland America, and he'd been away too long.

The memories hidden in every nook and cranny of this house were happy ones. In fact, they were about the only good ones from his childhood. He could see his grandmother coming to the door and calling him in to dinner; see his grandfather open up the big old Bible they kept on a stand in the living room, so that he could read a verse or two before they ate; see the steam coming from the creamed vegetables; hear the radio playing soft tunes. With a rush, his childhood came back to him in vivid pictures. He'd found it again.

Yes, he was going to like it here.

"Need any help?" Ernie asked solicitously.

"What?" Paul stirred himself from his reverie to smile at the short, dark cabbie. "Oh, no thanks. I'll only be here for about ten minutes. I can manage."

"Tell you what," Ernie said, chomping down on the cigar he never lit. "I need to fill up old Bessie, and there's a gas station just a few blocks from here. I'll go on over and get that done and be back to pick you up."

"Fine," Paul responded, still looking at the house and savoring the moment. "Take your time."

Ernie drove off and Paul started up the steps, suddenly finding the going more difficult than he'd expected. He'd only had the cast for half an hour and he wasn't used to the crutches yet. They seemed to hinder more than they helped, cutting in under his arms in a painful way, and by the time he reached the top of the stairs, he was swearing softly and breathing hard.

"And you call yourself a pediatrician? Mothers, cover your babies' ears."

His head, lowered so that he could see what his feet were doing, snapped up and he found himself looking into Rosemary Dusold's wary face. She was standing in the doorway, and for just a moment he blinked and stared at her, afraid his recent trauma might be causing him to hallucinate.

"You?" he asked, squinting against the sun and the shadows.

"Yes, it's me," she responded crisply, hands on her hips. "When we met before, I didn't realize you were my landlord." She frowned, reverting to her caregiver instincts. He did look exhausted by the effort of coming up the steps. "Come on in and sit down. You look like you need a rest. I'll get your bags," she added, picking them up from where Ernie had left them near the door.

"I'm perfectly fine," he protested, but he followed her through the entryway into her apartment and sat on the couch where she led him.

"Damn foot," he muttered as he lowered himself. "This is a real nuisance." He shoved the crutches out of the way. "You know, I think I'll try walking without them, once the swelling goes down. It will probably be easier."

"I'm sure the orthopedic surgeon would advise against doing that," Rosemary told him sensibly, perching on the arm of the couch opposite and looking him over with a half smile.

She couldn't help it. There was something rather satisfying in seeing him helpless and vulnerable. It was certainly a change from the man she'd known in Chicago all those years ago. In those days, he'd seemed to have the world on a string and she'd been the one fighting to keep her head above water in a stormy sea.

He surveyed her just as frankly as she did him. She'd changed her denim shorts and tank top for the white uniform of a medical professional and swept her hair back in a twist, but she still had that vibrant look he'd admired in the park. He'd never seen a woman who looked healthier. Just gazing at her made him feel more alive.

He smiled at her and the spark of humor was back in his intensely blue eyes. "Hey, I went to medical school," he reminded her. "I can make my own diagnosis."

She cocked an eyebrow. "'Physician, heal thyself.' Don't they call that having a fool for a patient?" she reminded him.

"No, that's lawyers and their clients," he corrected with a chuckle. "You're mixing professions."

"Ah yes. Of course. How silly of me."

He grinned at her. She was a strange woman. For some reason he had the feeling she was standing back, watching him and what he did in a judgmental way he wasn't used to. He was an attractive guy and women usually responded in kind. When a woman remained aloof this way, it only made him more determined to charm her.

"You've certainly kept the place beautifully," he noted, glancing around the room. He recognized a piece of furniture here and there. "How long have you been living here?"

"Five years," she told him. "I love it."

He nodded as though that were a matter of course. "Did you ever meet my grandmother?"

"No. Actually, the only person I ever had contact with was someone from the rental agency."

He nodded again. "She used to love this house, but about ten years ago, she became too frail to keep it going and she had to go into a nursing home in Milwaukee."

Rosemary winced. That was so often the nightmare many of her patients dreaded. "Oh no. Couldn't you have taken care of her? Or at the very least couldn't she have gone to Worthington House here in Tyler? It's a lovely place."

He flashed a brief smile in response to her note of horror at the thought. There was no point in going into his own whereabouts for the past ten years. His grandmother wouldn't have come along, even if he had been able to invite her. The thought of her trudging behind him through some of the jungles he'd endured, or camping in the Bedouin desert, brought a chuckle that he had to fight to hold back. "Don't worry about my grandmother," he said reassuringly. "She went to Milwaukee because her sister was there, already ensconced in the best nursing home available. It was like living in the Waldorf Astoria, with nurses instead of bell hops. Grandma's last years were very comfortable."

Rosemary regarded him narrowly. *Oh, yeah?* she couldn't help but think to herself. *What would you know of it? You weren't the one who had to go through it.* Still, it sounded as though his grandmother had made the best of a bad situation. Well, more power to her.

"I'm sorry you lost her," she said aloud.

He nodded, his eyes suddenly serious. For just a moment he saw her standing in this very room, a lovely and gracious woman. Time went too quickly, and the loss was too complete. "So am I."

Rosemary looked away. There had been a note of real emotion in his voice when he'd said that, and she resented it. The last thing she wanted was to feel sorry for Paul Chambers. There were many things she'd felt toward him in the past, but pity was never one of them, and she wasn't going to start now.

"Why are you here?" she asked abruptly, trying to get the conversation back on track. "Checking up on your holdings?"

He nodded slowly, his gaze traveling around the room again. "You might say that. But there's more to it." He glanced at her. "I'm moving to Tyler. Didn't I tell you that in the woods? I'm buying out old Dr. Darlington's practice."

"Dr. Darlington?" That meant Paul Chambers really was sticking around. Too bad. She groaned silently, but kept a stiff upper lip. "Is he still alive?"

"Very much so. I'm taking over his pediatric practice."

She frowned, trying to remember what she'd heard. "I thought he'd been semiretired for years. Wouldn't you have done better to start something up wherever it is you've been practicing up until now?"

He gave a short laugh. That was what happened when you spent your life abroad and didn't establish a base of capital for these things. He'd had to take what he could afford.

"I'll admit the man doesn't have much of a practice left. But there's enough for me to get a foothold in the community."

That had an ominous sound, and the corner of her mouth twitched in reaction. "Well, you're not planning to live here in one of these apartments, are you?" she said quickly. "I mean, that would be difficult. You see, we're filled up, and all of us have been here for years. We're established here. There is no place, really, for most of these people to go."

He waved a hand in the air, dismissing her protest. "I'm told Tyler has an abundance of new apartment buildings out by the highway. I don't think that will be a problem."

"Oh. Good." She smiled with relief. It seemed as though her apartment was secure, after all.

Her smile widened warmly as she gazed at him. After all, if he wasn't a threat, maybe she could stand having him in the same town. She would probably never see him, anyway. "Have you looked for a place yet? I mean, with your cast and all..."

"No problem. I was going to stay in that little room in the basement until I got things squared away."

"Oh no," she said quickly. She knew what room he meant. There was a bed behind a door just off the laundry room, but the place wasn't fit for human habitation. "No, you can't stay there. It's not fixed up properly."

He shrugged. "Well, luckily that won't be an issue, because a nurse at the hospital took pity on me and invited me to stay at her place."

Oh brother. Rosemary had no doubt nurses were falling all over themselves with invitations, not to mention desk clerks and even female physicians. Typical. It just went to show that he hadn't changed.

"Nurse?" She looked at him curiously. "What nurse?"

He scrunched up his face, trying to remember the name. "Uh, Sally Rogetti, in Pediatrics," he said finally, in a relieved tone.

"Oh. Of course." Rosemary had to resist rolling her eyes. Nurse Rogetti would be right down his alley. A tiny, vivacious redhead, she had a roving eye and a wild reputation. Rosemary was sure he would enjoy his stay at her place. What man wouldn't? Oh well, better there than here.

She glanced at her watch. She still had a couple of minutes before she had to take off. "Would you like something to drink?" she asked him, feeling hospitable.

"No thanks. Actually, I ought to be getting along." He began fussing with his crutches, gearing up for the major effort of rising to his feet again. "I was planning to take a look at all the apartments," he said as he struggled to stand, with Rosemary helping him. "But Ernie, the cabdriver, is picking me up in a moment. He's going to take me over to Sally's apartment."

"Ah yes. Mustn't keep Nurse Sally waiting. I'm sure she has things planned."

He laughed, shaking his head. "Actually, I feel like I haven't slept in three days. I hope she'll let me go right to bed."

Rosemary looked at him in surprise and actually believed him for a moment. But then she remembered the Paul Chambers of the old days and knew she would have to be dreaming to expect sensible behavior from the party boy. He was kidding, of course.

But he was also fighting awkwardly with the crutches, and she took his arm and let him lean on her. She could feel the hard, taut muscles beneath his shirt and something—a shot of adrenaline?—burst through her, throwing her off balance for a moment. But she got herself straightened out quickly and silently scolded herself for being such a ninny. After all, she put her hands on men of all kinds every day. There was nothing new here.

Meanwhile, Paul hadn't noticed a thing, and he was going on about his problem with the crutches.

"I'm really not adept enough at this broken-foot stuff yet," he said, looking up toward the second-floor apartments, "to maneuver my way around the place, especially up and down stairs." He turned and looked at her. "I'll have to leave it for tomorrow. I hope that will be convenient."

"Any time." She wanted to give him a little push, hurry him along. She was ready for him to be gone. "I'll be glad to introduce you to the other tenants."

"Thanks. I appreciate it. Say, do you mind if I leave my bags here for now? Maybe in the basement..."

"No problem," she said quickly, glancing down at them. They could go in her entryway closet just fine. He hobbled out through the door and she followed him. The cab was waiting at the curb, and as Paul started awkwardly down the stairs, Ernie jumped out and came to help him.

Rosemary watched rather impatiently. It was growing late. She had to get to the hospital herself. She was about to say her final goodbye when Paul turned back at the bottom of the stairs.

"Listen, how soon are you going to be able to move out?" he asked her.

She gazed at him blankly. Surely she'd heard him wrong. "What do you mean?" she asked, bewildered. Maybe he wanted to paint the place. Maybe he had exterminators coming. If it was something like that . . .

"I'm going to want to get started with renovations right away." Turning, he pointed at Mrs. Tibbs's door. "I thought I would use that as the entry to the clinic, but your living room is perfect for a waiting room, so I'm revising plans as we speak. Say, do you know a good contractor?"

She stared at him. "What do you mean?" she repeated breathlessly.

He looked at her brightly. "The pediatric clinic," he said. "I'm having the place remodeled for my practice. I thought you knew. I asked the rental agency to have you all out by the end of the month at the latest, but if you could find a new place to live sooner, I'd appreciate it."

"But—but you said you were going to live in one of those apartments out by the highway."

"No." He shook his head firmly. "I'm afraid you misunderstood. I said there were plenty of apartments out there. I meant for you and the others. Why would I live in an apartment on the highway when I have a perfectly good house right here?"

Why indeed? He continued toward the cab and Ernie helped him into it, but Rosemary didn't say a word. She was in shock. It wasn't until he was driving away that she called out after him.

"Wait!" she called. "You can't do this. You can't!"

But he was disappearing down the tree-lined street and it was quite evident that he thought he could.

CHAPTER THREE

THREE HOURS LATER, Rosemary was back from her consultation at the hospital and still seething with indignation. She'd finally made a perfect nest for herself, and now it seemed someone wanted to tear it apart. She couldn't let that happen. Paul Chambers had been instrumental in ruining her life once before and she was damned if she was going to let him do it again.

Hunting through her papers, she found the emergency number for the rental agency and dialed it, producing a rather disgruntled woman who seemed to be in charge, but was less than happy to be called on a Sunday evening.

"Paul Chambers is the new owner, dear," Miss Giverston said sharply. "He wants all tenants out by the end of next month and is prepared to pay a nice bonus for those who leave quickly and quietly. He plans to renovate and convert the building into a pediatric clinic. Letters to that effect went into the mail yesterday. You should have yours in hand tomorrow."

"What?" Rosemary was sputtering in anger. "There is no way I'm going to move out of a perfect apartment so Paul Chambers can use it as a waiting room for five-year-olds."

"Sorry, dear. I'm afraid there's not a thing you can do about it."

This was a nightmare. She shook her head in disbelief. "But don't we have leases?"

"Let's see...." There was a rustling of paper. "You signed a lease five years ago. It ran for twelve months. At the end of that period, your rental contract converted to a month-by-month basis. Bottom line is, at the end of next month your rights pretty much expire."

This was incredible. How could it all happen so suddenly, with no warning? "But I can hang on, can't I?" she asked the woman, anger mixing with desperation. "I mean, you always hear about how hard it is to evict people. Don't I have to be given notice and things?"

Miss Giverston sighed. "Yes, of course. If you like things done the ugly way, you can fight it in court if you want to. If you can afford to. But I wouldn't advise it. Mr. Chambers will win in the end."

"Will he?"

"Yes, he will."

The agent sounded very definite, and that put Rosemary's back up. It was obviously time for community action. What did most tenants do when they had grievances? Didn't they band together and picket and sign petitions? That was it. She and the others could put together a petition.

She glanced at the clock. It was growing late, but this was important. If she was going to rally the troops, she would have to get the word out. Leaving her own apartment, she ran up the steps to knock on Harriet's door.

She'd never been inside Harriet's apartment before. Light and airy with windows on every side, it was decorated in blue and white, with cherrywood chairs, a sleek buffet and exquisite white carpeting.

Harriet was friendly enough, but before Rosemary could launch into her warning and her idea, she noticed that cardboard boxes were set all along the edge of the room, and that some of them were full of books and knick-knacks.

"Are you packing things away for storage?" she asked hopefully.

Harriet sighed and kicked a pillow out of the way. "Actually, that's exactly what I'm doing. You see, I've been offered a position at the Chicago Twelve Trees Music Conservatory."

Rosemary stared at her. "You're moving?" she said, her voice quavery, her frown puzzled. "You're leaving this apartment?"

Harriet nodded. "It's something I've dreamed of for years. The chance of a lifetime. But it does mean I'll be giving up this place." She pushed her glasses higher. "It's time, I think. And now with the new landlord, there will probably be changes. I decided it was the perfect time to make a change of my own."

She beamed, and Rosemary groaned inwardly, then explained her mission to Harriet, who sympathized.

"I'm sorry to leave you in the lurch like this," she said. "Why not go next door and talk to the Coopers? I know how much they love their place. Maybe they will want to join in some sort of protest with you."

"I guess I'll do that." Rosemary tried to smile. She'd been counting on Harriet. But now the young couple next door would have to do.

Her enthusiasm wasn't quite as high as she trudged over to the Coopers, but when Gina opened the door to let her in, Rosemary started off with as much fire as she could muster, explaining what was about to happen to their happy home and building up to a pep talk for action. She was doing fine until she noticed the drawing of a floor plan spread out on the kitchen table. It didn't seem to be a plan of their apartment, and she paused and looked questioningly at Ned. He nodded, looking sheepish.

"We're moving," he told her simply. "Gina's going to have a baby."

Rosemary whirled and looked at the younger woman, who was laughing and holding her tummy with cupped hands. Sure enough, the signs were clear.

"Oh, I'm—I'm so happy for you," Rosemary said, and halfway meant it. But her spirits sank. What now? She and Mrs. Tibbs on the picket line? Somehow that picture wouldn't quite come into focus.

"So of course we need more room," Gina was saying. "And we're buying a house. A lot of places have opened up since the fire."

"Oh," Rosemary said. "I suppose that would happen, wouldn't it?"

The main industry in town, Ingalls Farm and Machinery, had burned down in a horrible fire a few months before. There was some question as to whether the owner, Judson Ingalls, would rebuild. A lot of people had been out of work for a long time now, and many had left town, seeking jobs elsewhere. Naturally, that meant the real-estate market was probably down as well, which was a boon to those looking for a bargain in a house for sale.

"We're trying to decide between that new housing development on Briar Road or the old Norton house on Elm."

"Modern construction and a nearby elementary school," said Ned with a laugh, "or history and charm and a lot of leaky plumbing. Which will it be?"

"I'm sorry, Rosemary," Gina said, realizing this didn't help her neighbor. "We won't be here long enough to make a difference."

Rosemary's smile was forced. "I guess that leaves me with Mrs. Tibbs," she said.

"Oh." Gina bit her lip and looked tragic. "I'm afraid you won't have her, either. You see, she asked Ned to come down and help her program her VCR yesterday, and while he was at it, she told him she was getting married."

Rosemary's eyes widened. "Mrs. Tibbs?"

Gina and Ned both nodded, standing side by side.

"Yes," Ned said. "It seems someone from her past has reappeared and is sweeping her off her feet. She was a bit secretive about the details, but she was definitely planning to leave her apartment." He gave her a pitying look. "Sorry, Rosemary."

She went back down to her own apartment, feeling abandoned. All her neighbors were leaving, and that probably meant she was about to lose her home. Common sense told her that fighting this on her own just wasn't going to fly.

So what were her options? Slim and none. She sat on her couch, clutched a plump pillow to her chest and stared into the gathering shadows.

"But I can't leave," she whispered, feeling as close to tears as she ever got. "This is my home."

It was painful to face the fact that this was so important to her because she didn't have anything else in her life. Her family had never been very close, and now that her parents had died, she seldom heard from her older sister and brother. Her marriage had fallen apart before it had really taken off. Her career was successful, and that was nice, but hardly enough to satisfy that place inside that longed for a connection, a center, a focus of the heart.

Her apartment had supplied that. The loving details she'd made in her decorating, the care she took in maintaining the antiques, the way she put a piece of herself into everything she did here, all helped give her soul space and expression. And now she was in danger of losing all that.

There had to be something she could do about it. But she went slowly and sadly to bed without thinking of one good idea.

PAUL SIGHED with satisfaction and leaned back in the comfortable chair, shifting his plaster-encased leg just enough to relieve the tension. Nurse Sally Rogetti was keeping her promise to take very good care of him. She'd pampered him and fixed him a great dinner—filet mignon and roasted onions—and now she was chattering away in the kitchen while he relaxed with a glass of wine in her plushest chair.

The woman did tend to babble, but that was all right. As long as he grunted now and then to let her know he hadn't fallen asleep, she seemed happy enough with him as a listener. She seldom demanded an answer of any consequence, and so he was free to let his mind wander. The situation was fraught with danger, though. He was so tired, he was bound to nod off at any moment.

He was glad he'd taken her up on her offer of a place to stay. Sally's sofa was bound to be more comfortable than that old bed in the basement at his grandmother's, especially now with this damn broken foot. And it sure didn't hurt to have someone feed him and fuss over him. In fact, it felt darn good.

She was a pretty little thing. Right now, she was filling him in on the fire at the Ingalls F and M. It seemed to have been the biggest thing to happen in Tyler for years, the way she was going on about it.

"You should have seen that column of fire," she said enthusiastically. "It looked like it was going straight up into the sky, like a comet. And smoke...you've never seen such smoke. The sirens were wailing and the bells were ringing. And Henry—the fellow I was dating at the time—he went up to help fight it. He got burned a bit and Judson Ingalls made sure his medical bills got paid right away. He's a really nice man, that Judson Ingalls. His ancestors started this town, you know. Just a few years ago, he got charged with murder. Did you hear about that? But it turned out it wasn't him at all...."

Paul tuned out her voice. The woman did talk too much. Instead of listening, he gazed at her over the rim of his glass, watching the way the kitchen light put flashes of fire

in her bright red hair, and suddenly he thought of the
woman who had rescued him from the wilderness and he
frowned. Talk about opposites. Where Sally was a colorful little hummingbird, Rosemary was a cougar, sleek and
elegant and strong.

"And damn bossy, too," he muttered to himself, emp-
tying his glass. Somehow he couldn't picture her pamper-
ing a man like this.

"What was that?" Sally asked, untying her apron and
coming out to join him in her living room, her head cocked
to the side and a look of anticipation on her pretty face.

He smiled at her. "Just thinking out loud," he said.
"Thanks for that great meal. I haven't eaten anything that
good in weeks."

"Well, you know what Mama always says," Sally said
brightly, leaning over to adjust the pillows behind his back.
She'd changed out of her nurse's uniform into a frilly, low-
cut top and tight velour stretch pants and was as feminine
as any man could want. "The way to a man's heart is
through his stomach."

He laughed along with her, but not quite as convincingly. He had to admit he was getting a little uncomfortable with the pointed looks she was giving him and the
vaguely suggestive quips she kept throwing out. After all,
he didn't want to lose his focus here. He'd come to Tyler
with a plan in mind. He was looking for a lifelong mate.
Sally Rogetti was looking for something very different, and
she was obviously not going to be in the running to fit in
with his plans.

However, she sure did put on a nice dinner, and she
knew all about making a man feel at home, so he stretched
back and sighed happily, feeling sleep coming on like a
velvet fog. "This is the life," he told her, his eyelids
drooping. "I could get used to this."

"Don't get too comfortable," she warned, perching on
the arm of his chair. She leaned over him and draped an

arm around his shoulders while brushing his hair off his forehead with the other hand. "I've got plenty more planned for our evening together."

"You do?" He could have sworn his voice broke when he said it, and he tried to smile and at the same time pull away from her embrace. "Hey, hey. You're dealing with a disabled man here."

"Mmm, don't you worry," she crooned with a wicked smile. "I'm sure you still have lots of parts that work just fine."

Paul avoided her and tried to smile, wondering why he was feeling so awkward with all this. It wasn't as though a woman had never come on to him before. He'd run into women like Sally all over the world, from Milwaukee to Milan to Malaysia, and he'd never been known as a shy guy. Did this mean he just didn't feel like a player any longer?

He studied her. She was awfully pretty, especially with that come-hither look in her eyes. So what was wrong with him, anyway? He'd always managed friendly relations with the opposite sex smoothly in the past.

But this was different. Those days were over.

So, with a sigh and a bittersweet smile, he shook his head at his lovely temptress and said, "Sally, sit down. We need to talk."

IT WAS THE SOUND of a car door slamming that woke her. Rosemary lay still in the darkness of midnight and listened, hearing a clumping on the stairs, a sharper sound, as though someone had stumbled, and then a muffled curse in a masculine voice. Ned Cooper was the only male in the building and this didn't sound like him.

She rose slowly, her eyes wide, her heart thumping, and for the first time in her life, she wondered impatiently why she'd never looked into purchasing a gun. Slipping on her robe, she hurried out into the living room and went to her front door, staring out the peephole.

It was a man all right, and though it was dark, she could see that he was trying to open the door to the basement. As she watched, something he'd been leaning on crashed to the ground and he swore again, and she realized with a start that it was a crutch. This had to be Paul.

She pulled back the bolts quickly and swung open the door. "What are you doing out there?" she called out in a loud whisper.

He turned and looked at her, his face a stormy reflection of his mood. "Trying to find a place to sleep. What would any sane person be doing at this time of night? The key won't work and..."

She threw up her hands and marched out into the entryway, her heavy terry-cloth robe flapping against her bare knees.

"I thought you were a burglar. I almost called the police."

"I wish you had called them. Maybe they would let me sleep in a cell." He tried again to force the key into the lock.

"How did you get here?" she asked, still confused.

"Ernie drove me over. He's offered to be my personal cabbie any time I'm in need. He's a great guy." He turned and stared at her. "Hey, I'll bet you have a key, don't you?"

She nodded, thinking fast. So many conflicting feelings were rattling around inside her. She hated him for the past, she felt responsible for him and his broken foot, she wanted to fight him because of the house, she wanted him out of her life, she wanted to keep him close so that perhaps she could talk him out of his plans. In less time than it took to tell about it, she resolved everything in favor of control.

"Come on into my place," she ordered, leaning down to pick up the crutch and handing it to him with a stern look. "I'll fix you a place to sleep."

"No," he said stubbornly, jabbing the key into the lock again and twisting impatiently. "I'll sleep in the basement."

She hesitated. The basement was a mess.

"We'll talk about that later," she promised, tugging on his arm. "But if we stand out here arguing, we're going to wake up everyone in the house. Come on in and have a cup of coffee and we'll see what would be best to do."

He was still frowning, but he let her lead him into her apartment, then sat on the straight-backed chair she indicated at her kitchen table while she went around turning on lights and putting on the gas under the teakettle.

Little by little, he began to relax. What a day! All he wanted was a place to lay his head—a place where he wouldn't have to fight off women. Fighting off bugs in the basement was preferable at this point.

Maybe he should stay here at Rosemary's. He grinned to himself. At least he wouldn't have to worry about her intentions. She'd made it obvious from the first that she rather despised him. Watching her, he wondered if she was that way with all the men she met.

He couldn't help but note again the contrast she made to Sally Rogetti. Sally had been all smooth and polished and dainty. Rosemary wore a plain cotton shift for a nightgown. He could see it peeking out at the neck of her robe, which was simple and tied at the waist with a belt. She wore warm, fluffy bedroom slippers that looked as if she'd attached Persian cats to her feet—rather worn-out, disreputable Persian cats.

But her hair—ah, her hair. This was the first time he'd seen it loose, and it fell around her face and draped about her shoulders like a cloud of spun gold. He had an irresistible urge to reach out and plunge his hands into it, and he pulled back, groaning. The straight and narrow path was full of more potholes and detours than he had ever imagined.

It had been a strange night, and if he didn't watch out, it would just get stranger. This was hardly the way he'd pictured beginning his life in Tyler. He had to get back on track or lose this entire opportunity for a new life. "Buck up," he ordered himself under his breath.

"Are you in pain?" Rosemary asked him, staring down with concern, thinking about his broken foot.

He blinked at her and then realized why she'd asked. "Uh . . . no, not really." His smile was just a bit sheepish. "I was just . . . thinking."

She looked at him suspiciously, then sank into the chair opposite the one he sat in. "Coffee will be ready in a minute," she told him, folding her hands on the table and studying him. She was finally shaking off the cobwebs of sleep, and the more awake she became, the more puzzling his behavior seemed. What on earth was he doing here?

He shook his head and gave a gigantic yawn. "Actually, I appreciate it, Rosemary, but coffee is the last thing I need. Sleep is the first."

"Don't worry. It's decaf." She gazed at him, eyes narrowed. She had a bone to pick with him and a case to present. But that could wait. First, she had to know why he'd come waltzing in during the middle of the night.

"Are you going to give me an explanation," she asked carefully, "or do I get to make up my own?"

He hesitated. "Explanation for what?" he asked, all wide-eyed innocence.

The twist at the corner of her mouth told him she wasn't buying it. "For why you're not at Sally Rogetti's right now."

"Oh. That." His smile was guileless. "Well, it turned out there wasn't as much room at Sally's as I thought. I just didn't fit in."

Rosemary nodded wisely. "What did she do, kick you out?"

He took a deep breath. "No...not exactly." He looked at the stove, grimacing. "Say, how about that cup of coffee you were offering?"

She rose to get it, but she knew he was avoiding the question. She looked at him closely as she returned with the pot and a cup for him, suddenly dying to know. Just what had happened at Sally's?

But that wasn't important, and there were other things that were. She poured him a cup of decaf and sat down again, watching him sip the hot liquid.

"I need to ask you a question," she said, her soft voice belying the anger simmering below the surface. "Just where do you get off throwing tenants who've lived in this house for years out in the street?"

He turned to look at her, startled. "I told the rental agency to offer each of you a bonus. Didn't they tell you?"

"A bonus!" She tossed her head and glared at him. "You think money will make up for destroying a home?"

His dark brows drew together quizzically. "But this is just an apartment. There are apartments all over the place."

"Not like this one. Can't you see that I've made this place my own?"

He looked about at the gleaming counters, the plants in every corner, the collection of porcelain teacups on a shelf.

"You've done a very nice job," he said politely, though it was clear these individual touches didn't mean a thing to him. "I'm sure you can recreate it all in some other nice apartment."

She resisted the urge to yell, biting her lip and keeping the lid on. "Haven't you ever had a home that you loved?" she said at last, her voice slightly shaky. "A place that was the center of your life?"

He thought for a second and yawned again. "No, not really."

She gripped the arms of her chair until her knuckles turned white. This was going to be harder than she'd thought. If he had no conception of what she was talking about, how was she going to convince him of how important this was to her?

"If it will help, I'll see if I can make the bonus larger," he offered, his eyelids drooping.

She stared at him, speechless. He really didn't get it. Swallowing hard, she rose and carried her cup to the sink.

"Never mind," she told him quickly. She would have to think this over, find an angle of attack that had a better chance of working. She could see this wasn't going to get her anywhere.

"Never mind," she said again, moving briskly. "And you can sleep on the couch. I'll get you some bedding."

"Here?" He turned to look into her living room, remembering that he hadn't wanted to do this. Leaving Sally's on the run, he'd vowed never again to stay with a woman until he'd married her. But he was just too sleepy to resist a resting place. "What a great idea," he murmured, following her lead.

The couch was more comfortable than it looked, and he sank into the pillows with relief. It had been a long day. He needed sleep, and he got it. In less than a minute he was fast asleep.

Returning with an armload of bedding, Rosemary hesitated, reluctant to put herself in the position of caretaker. But that was basically what she was, whether she liked it or not, and she finally relented, leaning down to spread a blanket over him and pretty much tuck him in. Then she stood looking down at him for a few minutes.

There was no denying Paul Chambers was an attractive man, even with those beautiful blue eyes closed. The hard angles in his face softened as he slept, and his long dark lashes rested on his cheeks, making him look even younger than he did awake. She could see why women fell for him in droves.

It was a good thing she herself was immune to the disease. With a shrug, she turned away from him and switched off the light.

CHAPTER FOUR

HE WASN'T SURE what woke him, and for just a moment, he wasn't sure where he was. He thought he'd opened his eyes, but instead of darkness, he saw a firefight in the sky, with shells bursting overhead, and the baby was crying. He had to get to the baby. She was hurt. He'd been carrying her just before the first round hit and now he didn't know what had happened, where she was. But he knew she was hurt. He could hear it in her voice. He had to help her, save her. He was struggling with something, trying to get to her, and then another shell burst, and suddenly the silence was deafening.

"No!" he cried out. "No, oh no!"

And then he really was awake, staring out the window at a tree whose branches were swaying in a light breeze, brushing against the windowpane with an eerie sound. There were no planes overhead. There was no bombing, no shelling. And no baby lying silent in the mud.

Taking a deep breath, he forced himself to relax, waited while his heartbeat returned to normal.

"I can't keep doing this," he muttered to himself, shifting position and wondering how long it was going to take before he would be able to get to sleep again. "I can't keep reliving it."

But he would.

He had been for more than a year. The nightmares were a part of what was motivating him to change his life, go for the normalcy that should have been his birthright. If he could meet the right woman, marry, have children, he was sure the dreams would fade. He couldn't have said what made him so certain. It was a feeling, something deep inside. But it lived in him and he couldn't get rid of it until something changed.

"Either the world has to declare peace in our time," he told himself mockingly, "or I have to find my way out of this trap on my own."

It seemed the latter path was the one he was bound to follow. Settling down under the covers, he tried to think about the woman he wanted to marry. The picture had been developing in his mind over the years, coming clearer every time he found himself involved in the violence the world had to offer. He'd spent hours once, lying on a grass mat in a bamboo hut, unable to sleep. Instead of counting sheep, he'd tried filling in the details of the vague dream he had.

His ideal wife. She would be a sort of cross between Donna Reed and Loretta Young, all sympathy and smiles and pink dresses with full skirts. He knew she was out there somewhere. All he had to do was start looking.

And that was why he'd come to Tyler. What better place to find the woman—and the life—of his dreams?

ROSEMARY GOT UP at the crack of dawn and went jogging on the sleepy morning streets. It wasn't so much the exercise she wanted, it was the space to think. What she needed was a strategy. She had to look at this like a war, with Paul as the enemy. She had to anticipate his moves and figure out countermeasures of her own. Her mind worked quickly as her legs pounded the sidewalk, and by the time she was back, she thought she had a plan.

Running up the wooden steps, she burst in through her own front door like a brisk spring breeze and glanced toward the couch. It was empty.

Whirling, she looked into the kitchen. There was a note on the counter.

Thanks for the bed, Rosemary. Ernie came by to take me to meet some contractor friend of his for breakfast. I'll probably see you later on today.

                               Thanks again, Paul.

"Back to the drawing board," she muttered, crumpling the paper in her hand. "The battle is postponed."

But not canceled. She showered and dressed for work, still thinking about arguments and maneuvers she might use on him. Whatever it took, she had to keep him from ruining her home.

She spent the morning at the hospital seeing patients who had been referred to her by physicians, then spent an hour in the therapy center working with a group of three people recovering from recent strokes. One, Jim Hassler, had a breakthrough of sorts. While she was encouraging him in the whirlpool, he finally was able to bend his left leg twice in a row. Everyone in the room cheered for him, and Rosemary left the session with a glow she hadn't felt in days.

It was great to feel needed, as though you'd made a difference. She didn't seem to get that feeling often these days. That vague sense of dissatisfaction was always in the way.

The sound of a low wolf whistle turned her head and she found her friend Pam Casals Kelsey coming down the escalator toward her floor.

"Hey, kiddo," she called back, laughing. "Don't get my hopes up that way."

"What hopes?" Pam teased back as she stepped off the escalator. Her shiny brown hair fell around her animated face like a soft frame and her coat fell open to reveal a tummy as round as a basketball.

"From what I hear, you've sworn off men," she said to Rosemary, grinning at her friend. "Wasn't it after the Kurt Korning incident? Didn't you tell me never again?"

"A major overreaction on my part," Rosemary replied, waving her hand airily. "Just because the guy took his shoes off to drive and wanted to know if I would be interested in sharing a houseboat with him and a motorcycle gang in crocodile country, there was really no reason to let that turn me off men altogether."

Pam laughed, tossing back her hair. "Maybe it was what happened before that with that man Arnold Grimes, when he tried to convince you he could save money by living with you and eating only every other day."

Rosemary remembered and shuddered. "A wise man, I thought at the time," she noted with a touch of sarcasm. "How could I know he would turn out to have three grown kids he wanted to bring along?"

Pam grinned. "You have dated a few doozies, haven't you?" She patted her friend's arm. "Just don't give up. The right man will come along and you'll have stars in your eyes."

Rosemary shook her head and made a face. She'd given up on that dream. After all, she'd thought she was in love when she'd married Greg, and look what had happened. She'd had her turn and maybe wouldn't get another chance. At any rate, she wasn't going to hold her breath.

"Have you had lunch?" she asked Pam. "Come on back to my office with me and share my sandwich. We haven't talked in ages and I want to tell you about my latest dilemma."

"A man?" Pam asked hopefully, striding with her down the hall.

Rosemary hesitated, then laughed. "You might say that. A man named Paul Chambers, who is bent on ruining my life."

Pam raised an eyebrow, and Rosemary unlocked her door and ushered her in, still talking as she opened her little refrigerator and took out a sandwich, a container of yogurt and two cans of ice tea, laying out a picnic on her desk.

"I know this man," she explained earnestly to Pam after she'd described his plans for his vintage Victorian. "He's never stuck to one thing in his life. He'll have a great time renovating the building and then tire of it all and move on to something else. Meanwhile, I'll be living in a sterile apartment out on the highway and hating every minute of it."

Pam pursed her lips and took a sip of tea. "Well, he must be able to stick to some things if he got through medical school."

"Oh, that." Rosemary rolled her eyes. "I don't know how he made it. I swear he was the biggest party animal in town at the time. While everyone else was studying until their eyes stung, he was dancing the night away with some new babe."

Pam's faint smile was perceptive. "And what did he do to you?" she asked softly, studying her friend's face.

Rosemary gave her an indignant stare. "Me? I hardly knew him." She looked away and bit her lip for a moment before adding, "But he and Greg were good friends for a while. I always thought..."

Her breath caught in her throat and she forced a smile as she met Pam's gaze again. "Actually, I sort of blamed what happened to Greg on Paul. I mean, Greg was working so hard and Paul seemed to be having all the fun, and I know Greg envied him. So when Paul began inviting him along on his little capers... well, Greg just couldn't resist."

Pam nodded in sympathy. "Other women?" she guessed softly.

Rosemary nodded, then shook herself and smiled again, though her eyes couldn't shake their sadness. "But that was all years ago. That was then and this is now." She hesitated, frowning. "Still, I know this man. He's not serious. And while he's playing around, he'll be ruining something else I dearly love. I'm not going to let him do that again."

Pam empathized but didn't have any great ideas up her sleeve, and their talk soon turned to her own condition.

"How is that coming along?" Rosemary asked, nodding toward her stomach, gazing at it obliquely as though she were somewhat spooked by it.

Pam patted the rounded bulge comfortably. "Being pregnant when you've got MS is no picnic, but if I take it easy and get checkups regularly, they say I ought to be okay. So far so good."

Rosemary finished off her half of the sandwich and began to straighten up her desk, crumpling the wrapper in her hand and closing the yogurt carton. She remembered when Pam had first come to Tyler and stayed with her at the Victorian. Pam had been hired as the football coach at the high school, a situation that had infuriated Patrick Kelsey, son of one of the founding families of the town and local athletic hero. As a teacher and coach at the high school himself, he'd thought he was in line for the job. When Pam, an ex-Olympic runner and coach at other schools, had been brought in instead, his nose had been put out of joint. But that had changed rapidly, and the two of them had fallen in love and married, both of them now coaching, teaching and sharing a happy life as well.

"I know Patrick must be excited about the baby coming," Rosemary murmured casually.

Pam's mouth twisted. "You think so?"

Rosemary stared at her, her hand poised over the trash can. "What is that tone for?"

"Oh, nothing." She gave a crooked grin and shook her head. "I'm just being a whiner. It's probably the hormones or something." Her grin faded and her eyes dimmed. She hesitated, then decided to go on. "But he's gone so much lately, I hardly feel like we do more than wave as we pass in the night."

Rosemary frowned, disposing of the trash and turning back to look at her friend. "Is he still coaching and teaching at the high school? That takes a lot of time."

Pam nodded. "Sure. And he has to do twice as much since I haven't been working these past few weeks. You know he got the director of athletics position?"

"Yes, I heard. Congratulations."

"That makes him just that much busier." She pressed her lips together and looked at her old pal with a glint in her eye, then added softly, "And then, of course, there's Hayley."

Rosemary raised her eyebrows, recognizing understatement when she heard it. "Hayley? Who's Hayley?"

Pam sighed and her shoulders drooped. "Patrick's girlfriend from his teenage years," she said heavily.

Suddenly the picture was clearing. "Oh," Rosemary said, as though that explained everything.

Pam smiled brightly, pretending to brush crumbs off the desk. "Yes. His first love. She's back in town and he got her a job as swim coach at the high school."

"Oh." The vibes were bristling in the air. "How nice of him."

"Yes." Pam looked up and met Rosemary's gaze, but her smile was strained. "She's very nice. We've had her over for dinner. Three times."

"Oh."

Their eyes met and suddenly they both burst into laughter. Rosemary reached out and took her friend's hand. "Now come on, Pam," she chided gently. "You can't be jealous. That man is so crazy about you...."

"Oh, I know that." Pam shook her head, still laughing at herself and at her own silliness. "And I'm not really jealous at all. It's just that, well . . ." She looked at Rosemary earnestly. "I'm not used to staying home alone all day and I miss him."

Rosemary nodded wisely. "And you're pregnant. Doesn't that make you sort of weepy or something?"

Pam gaped at her friend. "Do I look weepy?" she demanded, and Rosemary laughed.

"No, of course not. I guess I've been listening to the propaganda and stereotyping again, haven't I?"

"Darn right. Being pregnant doesn't turn me into a different person."

"But will you be able to say the same once the little one is here?" Rosemary shook her head in candid wonder. She knew Pam was about five years younger than she was, but that still made her about thirty-three. "I can't tell you how brave I think you are to do this. It's going to change your life." She winced, remembering how her own mother had complained about how children had ruined *her* life. Roseanne Dusold had been a beauty and had put off having children for as long as she could, then had been saddled with three of them, one right after another. She never let any one of them forget how they had destroyed her figure and changed the tenor of her days. Rosemary had vowed from the time she was a little girl that she wouldn't end up like her mother, a bitter, complaining woman. She knew she would have more in her life than looks, and she'd worked hard to get where she was today. But even now, the distortion her mother had drummed into her echoed. Children changed your life, and not for the better.

It wasn't going to be that way with Pam. Rosemary was sure of it. Still, old thought patterns died hard. "But you . . . you've seen the road ahead and decided to go for it." She shook her head again. "You're a better woman than I am." She looked into Pam's eyes, hoping she hadn't offended her.

But Pam was smiling. "You know, I used to feel exactly like that. Even a few months ago, I was terrified. But things have changed radically. I don't know what it is. Maybe hormones do take over. But I've never felt so happy about a decision, so at peace. Once I felt her move inside me..." Her face brightened with a new thought. "Hey, have you ever felt a baby move?"

Rosemary's sudden alarm revealed itself on her face. "No. And no thanks. I believe you. I don't need empirical evidence." She nodded toward Pam's rounded belly, her expression wary. "There's a baby in there. No doubt about it."

Pam grinned, sensing a vulnerable area in her usually strong-minded friend's makeup. "Are you telling me you've never felt a baby kick?" she demanded.

Rosemary looked worried. "I don't think so."

Pam's laugh was filled with pure anticipation. "Well, here's your chance."

"No." Rosemary shook her head quickly. "No, that won't be necessary, thanks just the same."

"Oh, come on," chided Pam, laughing. "It's just a tummy, and just a baby. There's nothing scary here." Reaching out, she grabbed Rosemary's hand and tugged on it. "Come on."

Rosemary blanched, resisting. "Pam..."

"You're a medical professional, for Pete's sake. I thought you would have felt just about everything."

Rosemary shook her head, eyeing the rounded belly as though it were a snake. "I don't deal with pregnant women very often and it would be a bit awkward going up to a stranger in the supermarket to ask if I can feel her stomach."

Pam laughed but brushed aside her remarks. "Well, you have to deal with me. Come on. Put your hand right here."

She guided Rosemary's hand to a position on her rounded belly and waited as though listening for a sound in the distance.

Rosemary waited too, though her heart was pounding. She wasn't sure why this was so disquieting, but it was. And nothing was happening, so what was the big deal, anyway?

"There's nothing," she said and tried to pull away.

But Pam held her there. "Wait," she said softly, her eyes luminous. "Just wait."

Something moved. Rosemary drew in her breath. Something moved again, stirring just under her palm—pushed out strongly, then withdrew. Her eyes widened. "Whoa. What was that?" She looked up at Pam, her gaze filled with astonishment.

Pam grinned at her. "Isn't it wonderful?" she whispered. "Don't you love it?"

She didn't have to urge her friend to leave her hand where it was. Nothing could drag Rosemary away now. She stayed where she was, her hand pressed to the place where she'd felt that little arm or leg, and held her breath, waiting to feel it again. There. Something real, something alive. She laughed and moved her hand, forgetting all about Pam and her belly and searching for that sensation again.

A baby. A real, live baby. This was the first time she'd ever felt she understood a bit of the miracle. This was really neat.

And she especially appreciated it because she knew she would never have that feeling herself. It had been a long time since she'd even contemplated having babies in her life. Now she was quite sure her time had passed. Even if she fell in love, even if she married, it was too late to go that route. But she could watch Pam and cheer from the sidelines. That was okay. She might as well enjoy it.

AFTER PAM LEFT, Rosemary saw a few patients, did some paperwork and closed up shop for the day. On her way out she passed Sally Rogetti in the hall, but she could read nothing from the casual greeting the woman gave her and she pushed all speculation aside. She didn't want to get sidetracked. Her focus had to be on her fight to keep her home.

As she drove up to the old Victorian, she saw Paul standing on the curb, leaning on his crutches, waving goodbye to a moving van, which was just pulling away.

"What was that?" she asked, emerging from her car and looking anxiously down the street. Someone had already moved away. It was too soon. She was beginning to feel utterly abandoned.

But Paul didn't notice her distress. He gave her a friendly salute, his blue eyes looking her up and down in a way that would have seemed insolent if any other man had done it, but seemed perfectly natural with him.

"It's your neighbor, Harriet. What a nice lady. We had a long talk about you." He raised an eyebrow in a teasing way. "She's already moving on. Isn't that great?" He grinned at Rosemary happily and waved a metallic measuring tape at her. "Listen, I'm drawing up plans. Come on. You can help me."

Turning, he started up the stairs. He was getting pretty handy with the crutches and they didn't seem to hold him back at all any longer.

Rosemary watched him, frowning. After another exasperated glance down the street, she followed reluctantly, stopping on the porch when he did.

"Perhaps I haven't been completely clear with you," she said, her eyes flashing in annoyance at his casual joy in the disintegration of her house and home. "I hate you doing this. I hate you renovating the place I call home. I—I hate it all."

He looked at her as though she just didn't understand. "Oh no," he said cheerfully. "You're going to love it when it's done. Just look at these drawings. You'll get the picture."

He pointed out sketches he'd strewn across the porch, artist's renditions of how he wanted his restored Victorian to look when this was all finished, lovely drawings of an idealized dream.

She glanced down at them and then looked back at him, glaring. His good nature was really annoying. He was purposely ignoring her meaning.

"I've already got a contractor," he said before she had a chance to express her views. "Ernie recommended him and I think he's going to be perfect."

"Contractor?" There was a sound very much like the strike of a hammer and she jumped, then looked around suspiciously. "Who did you hire?"

"Hi there, Rosemary," came a voice from above.

Shading her eyes, she looked up at a figure climbing on the roof. It was Joe Santori, a man she knew well.

"Hi, Joe," she called back weakly.

"My contractor," Paul said with a flourish. "So you know him already? Good."

Rosemary waved at Joe, then looked at Paul, hope sinking in her chest. The contractor was already on the job. She was beginning to feel as though the whole town were conspiring against her. If Joe was in on this travesty, she was in for the fight of her life and she knew it.

It was pretty much now or never for her plan—time to put it in motion. She stood silently as Paul pointed out items on his blueprints, hardly listening while he went over the renovations he planned to make. Finally, he paused, looking at her for reaction, and she tried to smile.

"You've been thinking about this for a long time, haven't you?" she said.

He looked surprised, as though he hadn't realized it himself. "I guess I have," he said, rubbing his hand on the back of his neck. "I guess I've been wanting a change for longer than I thought."

She wasn't sure what he meant by that, but she had other things on her mind. Time for Operation Mind Change—aimed right at Paul. "Listen, do you have a minute?" she asked him. "I have something I'd like to show *you*."

His blue eyes softened, as though he took this as a gesture of friendship and he appreciated it. "Sure," he told her. "What is it?"

Smile at him, she told herself. *Don't let on how you really feel.* She had to be subtle and use feminine wiles, never a strong point in her repertoire. She tended to go at things headfirst, barging in the front door rather than sliding in through the side entrance. Instinct told her that wasn't going to work with Paul, and that she had to adjust her tactics.

So she smiled, though her smile was secretive. "Come with me," she said, turning toward her car. "I'll have to drive you there."

He came along, chatting cheerfully, but she hardly heard a word. She was nervous, wondering how best to present this in a light he would be swayed by. She drove quickly through town and out toward the hospital, turning just a block before the usual street and pulling up in front of a brand-new five-story building on Briggs. The edifice shone in the sun, all slick concrete and dark glass, looking very modern and trendy. The landscaping was new and crisp, all molded bushes and beds of bright red tulips, their heads bobbing.

"Nice, isn't it?" she commented, getting out to open the car door for him and help him out.

"It's beautiful," he agreed, handing her his crutches. "What is it?"

She smiled and led him to the front door, and then in through the lobby. A brand-new pharmacy had just opened on the ground level, but they walked past it to the elevator and she pushed the button for the fifth floor.

"The second floor has a medical library," she commented. "And an orthopedic surgeon and an allergist. The third has a suite of dental offices, and the fourth is an internal-medicine clinic."

The elevator doors opened on a lobby gleaming with new paint and carpeting, but empty and echoing. "The fifth floor has three offices available," she noted, leading him out onto the plush carpet. "Come take a look."

She glanced at him out of the corner of her eye, trying to judge what he was thinking. He looked bemused, but not skeptical. That was encouraging, and she smiled happily.

"Look at the size of this office. Look at this waiting room. You could set up a play area in the corner. In fact—" she turned and looked at him earnestly "—you could do all the things you're planning to do but put them right here in this brand-new office with its wonderful access and its position right near the hospital. Look at the parking available to your patients. Think of the feeling of confidence this sort of setting would give them."

He laughed softly, leaning on his crutches and looking at her. "You're really something, Rosemary," he said softly. "Yes, you take the cake."

She couldn't tell if that reaction was good or bad.

"Come." She drew him farther into the office, showing him around as proudly as though she'd set the place up herself. "Look at this. Look at the scale of things, look at the windows."

He nodded. "Really nice," he murmured, then went to the far end of the room and looked out the huge floor-to-ceiling windows. "Wow, what a view."

She joined him. "Yes, isn't it lovely? I thought you'd like it." She glanced at him, noting his genuine interest, and felt encouraged. "Couldn't you just see yourself gazing out at this view every afternoon?"

He nodded. "It's great. You can see half of Tyler from here, spread out like a giant map. There's the high school, and there's the town square, and—" His gaze sharpened and he stared down at something a few blocks away. "Say, isn't that . . . oh my God!"

He grabbed her hand, gripping it tightly. "Look at that," he said, barely holding back his excitement.

"What?" She had no idea what he'd seen and she wasn't sure she liked it. After all, she didn't want his attention diluted. "What are you looking at?"

Turning, he grinned at her, his blue eyes sparkling. "Come on," he said, pulling her along with him, hobbling but hardly noticing his crutches any longer. "Come on. I've got to show *you* something."

She was torn. She wanted him to stay, to look at the rest of the place. And yet, if he was so excited by something he could see from the window... Was that good? Was it bad? What could she do but go with him and find out?

CHAPTER FIVE

WHATEVER IT WAS necessitated the use of the car again. It was too far to walk. Paul directed Rosemary, though he pointed her down two blind alleys before they found their way to his destination. She parked where he told her to, in front of the old duck pond at the corner of Beech and Haywood. She frowned, looking around. The place was unkempt and overgrown with weeds and untrimmed brush. The caretaker's house had been neglected and looked more like a shack than a building anyone could live in.

"Is this it?" she asked, incredulous.

"This is it," he told her happily, opening the car door and beginning the effort to get himself out without her. The crutches were beginning to be almost as much a hindrance as a blessing, and he tossed one of them back into the car and made do with the other.

"This was Old Man Brentwood's duck pond years ago," he told her, bending down to look back at where she still sat in the car. "I used to come here when I was a kid."

Nostalgia. So that was what they were here for. Sighing, she got out and followed him into the jungle, pushing aside branches as they made their way to the pond.

The water was brimming with life. Ducks and geese paddled happily, making a racket, while smaller birds flew off in a cloud of alarm as the two humans approached. Paul reached the edge of the mossy pond and stood taking it all in, feeling a warm tightening in his chest.

"It's just like it was," he murmured, talking to himself rather than to her. "I loved this place."

Seeing it now, he didn't know how he could have forgotten it for all these years. There was something real about it, basic and good. Something of earth and water and the animals that passed through. Something still touched by love that brought his past in line with his present. He could see himself as a boy, holding his grandfather's hand as they came through the same bushes and found the oasis hidden here. Finding the pond again tied him to his background the way nothing else had in a long time, not even the house.

Rosemary had to smile. There were times when the man seemed so genuine, she had to remind herself of what a jerk he'd been in the past. "I've always known this pond existed," she told him, looking around and shaking her head, "but I've never actually been here before."

She had to admit it had a certain rustic charm. In some ways, elements of nature she hiked for hours to find were concentrated right here in town, blocks away from where she lived.

"It's exactly the same," Paul said again. "I feel like I just stepped back in time. I could close my eyes and be a kid again. Look at them—wood ducks, ring-necked ducks, mallards." He shook his head, delighted. "I used to bring bread for the Canada geese, and then they had feeding corn that you could buy...."

He looked around. "There used to be a dispenser over here...." Pushing aside a spray of serviceberry, covered in white blossoms, he exclaimed in delight, "There still is! See?" He dug into his pocket and pulled out a nickel. Cranking it into the dispenser, he caught the handful of feed corn that came plummeting down the chute. "We can feed them."

He poured half his bounty into Rosemary's hand and grinned at her, and she laughed. She couldn't help it. She'd never seen a man so completely abandon himself to happiness like this. He smiled back at her and somehow that made her a part of it all—the joy, the memories. She shook her head as he turned away. He was irresistible. And, she had to remind herself, that was exactly what made him so dangerous.

The mallards seemed to know immediately that food was at hand, and they came scrambling, tumbling over one another to get closer to the source. Rosemary threw all her corn out to them, and feathers flew. Paul turned back to the dispenser and retrieved another handful, which he tossed, bit by bit, into the water. The flock followed the sinking kernels, and he laughed along with Rosemary.

Suddenly, a voice called out from the shabby building near the pond, "Hey there, sonny, mind yourself with those ducks."

They both turned and watched as an elderly man came shuffling down the steps of the building toward them. His face was leathery despite his wild white beard and his clothes hung on him loosely, but the cloth was good-quality wool and his hunting cap was new and dapper.

"Don't you hurt them ducks, now," he cautioned as he approached. "We want them to feel welcome here." He nodded, gesturing with his walking stick. "Some of those ducks have come a long way and they need to rest."

"Old Man Brentwood," Paul muttered, his mouth open in astonishment. The man hardly looked different from the picture in his memory. "It is you, isn't it?"

The old fellow peered at him with watery eyes that had seen a lot of years. "Who's that?" he demanded.

Paul smiled at him. "You won't remember me. I used to come here with my grandfather when I was a boy."

The man stopped before them and waved a hand in the air. "Oh, sure. Lots of people used to bring the children to see the ducks. Still do. The kids like to feed them." He looked pointedly at where the animals were hunting around for the last remnants of corn. "Not so many come nowadays. Too busy playing those damn computer games, I guess. Poor kids don't know what they're missing, do they?"

Paul nodded, watching the old man with a sparkle in his eyes. "You're right. It was great. Every summer I came here as often as I could. And I remember you being here."

He turned to Rosemary and said under his voice, "He was an old man then. He must be a hundred if he's a day."

But Mr. Brentwood was not to be dismissed so lightly. "What's your name, boy?" he demanded, jabbing his stick in the air toward Paul.

Paul grinned. It had been quite a few years since anyone had called him "boy." "Paul. Paul Chambers. This is Rosemary Dusold. And my grandfather's name was—"

The man frowned fiercely, his whiskers trembling. "You don't mean old Doc Chambers, do you?" he cried.

"Yes." Paul turned fully toward him. "That's him. Do you remember him?"

"Remember him?" The old man harrumped. "Why, he still owes me ten bucks." His watery eyes narrowed and he looked at Paul accusingly. "I guess that's why I haven't seen him around lately."

"Lately. Yes, I guess you could say that." Paul smiled, shaking his head, feeling a twinge of regret for the absence of his grandfather. He would have enjoyed bringing him here again. "He passed on a good fifteen years ago."

Mr. Brentwood grunted. "Some folks will do anything to keep from paying up," he said philosophically.

Paul's gaze met Rosemary's and he grinned. "What did he owe you ten bucks for?" he asked quickly.

"We had a bet." Mr. Brentwood frowned as though trying to remember. "He had a kid here with him. Grandson, I think it was," added the old man with a sudden twinkle in his eye. "He bragged about that kid all the time. Said he could do just about anything. I said, bet he couldn't catch one of my ducks with his bare hands. Old Doc said, why, yes he could, too. So I bet him the ten bucks on it.'' He chuckled, looking back through his mind's eye.

Paul was frowning, trying hard to remember. He could recall catching frogs, watching a raccoon wash its food in the water. But catching ducks...?

"We were tagging them that summer," the man went on. "The ducks, I mean. Some wildlife expert was here and all. They were having trouble catching those ducks, and they were using nets. But this boy, he gave it his best." He laughed aloud, slapping his knee as he recalled the scene. "He tried and he tried. Finally, he got up on top of that there bridge and jumped down on a duck. Nearly squashed it flat."

Paul's face lit up. "I remember that," he said. "That was me. Yes, I remember."

"Only trouble was," Mr. Brentwood said, as though Paul hadn't spoken, "it weren't no duck. It was a big old domestic goose got in with them that day. And that goose didn't take kindly to being squashed."

He cackled, remembering. "He went after that boy, pecked at him like crazy, yanked out some of his hair. They were racing around the pond and old Doc and I were rolling on the ground, laughing so hard I nearly lost my teeth."

Paul was nodding, smiling at his memories. "I remember," he said softly, almost to himself, and unconsciously his hand went to his head where the tuft of hair had been snatched away.

Mr. Brentwood nodded as though satisfied, his eyes sparkling with laughter. "See, I thought you would. Well, your grandfather, Old Doc, he never did pay up."

"Hey, no problem," Paul told the man, digging into his pocket. "I'll pay it for him."

The man lifted both of his hands, shaking his head, his mouth turned down. "Oh no you don't. I'm waitin' on Doc."

Paul shrugged, a bit nonplussed, his wallet in his hand. "But he's dead."

Mr. Brentwood looked disdainful. "I know that. I'm going to be dead one of these days, too. Hell, we all are. I figure I'll wait my turn. Someday..." He waved a forefinger warningly. "Someday, I'll catch up with him."

Paul turned and met Rosemary's gaze and they smiled at each other. Mr. Brentwood went on relating tales from long ago that had nothing to do with Paul and his grandfather, and more recent stories about the murder at the lodge and the fire at Ingalls F and M. Paul and Rosemary listened and smiled and nodded at the right places.

When they finally tore themselves away, Paul put a hand between her shoulder blades to help guide her through the thicket back to the car. Despite his awkwardness with the crutch, the gesture was a natural one. He didn't even think about it before he did it. But he could feel her stiffen, as though she didn't at all like what he'd done, and he let his hand slide away. He didn't want to do anything that made her uncomfortable.

And uncomfortable was exactly what she was suddenly. His hand felt hot, burning through the cotton fabric of her shirt, and she was very glad when he took it away. Still, she didn't know why it would make her uneasy. He was just being polite. Maybe Kayla was right—maybe it had been too long since she'd had a man of her own.

Still, he didn't seem to notice her displeasure. As they emerged from the brush, he chuckled, shaking his head, still thinking about the old man at the pond.

"What a character. I can't believe he remembers me so well. I can't believe I remember *him* so well. After all these years, and all the places I've been and the experiences I've had, trying to catch a duck in a muddy pond in Wisconsin looms a lot larger than you would think.''

"You're getting old," she said, half teasing as she opened the car door for him.

He gave her a wry look. "I like to call it maturing," he countered, then his face sobered. "But you're right. I'm getting older. That's exactly the point. That's why I'm here."

She looked at him curiously, but he settled into the car, moving more and more deftly despite his cast and crutch. She closed the door and went around, refocusing as she went. The main thing was to get his mind on the office space again.

"Would you like to go back and finish checking out the place I was showing you?" she asked hopefully as she started the engine. "There are still things you haven't seen. It's such a good building, such a good setting...."

He glanced at his watch. "No. Actually, I want to get back to the house and settle some things with Joe before he leaves for the night." Looking at her face, he read the disappointment there and hesitated.

"Listen, Rosemary. I appreciate what you're trying to do. I understand. But it's not going to make any difference. I'm renovating my house."

Her jaw tightened. *His* house. Well, he had a right to say it.

"I wish you'd look at the Briggs place a little more." She glanced over at him as she stopped at the light. "Or there are others. There are a lot of alternatives to gutting the Victorian and changing everything around."

Her emotions finally spilled out into her last sentence, drawing his surprised gaze toward her again. "Of course there are alternatives," he said carefully, frowning. "But this is what I want to do. I've been thinking about it for a long time. My mind is made up." Reaching out, he touched her arm. "Rosemary, bottom line here is it's my house."

To her shock, she felt tears prickling her eyelids. She never cried. What was the matter with her? She would die before she'd let him see that sort of weakness in her.

"Use anger," she told herself silently. "It's the only way." Her jaw hardened again. "So my five years of blood, sweat and tears, of everything I've put into it, mean nothing," she said evenly.

He heard the anger in her voice and tried to counter it with humor. "I wouldn't say that. You've had a nice place to live for five years. Hey, come on." He smiled tentatively. "You've been lucky."

Glancing over, she caught the smile, caught the look in his beautiful blue eyes, and something lurched inside her. She turned her head quickly, taking a shallow breath that was close to a gasp, and tried to pretend nothing had happened. But her pulse was beating like a hummingbird's heart and she couldn't make herself hear what he was saying.

"Hey, you missed the turnoff," he mentioned calmly.

"What?" She forced herself to concentrate. "Oh. The turnoff. Uh . . . the next one is better at this time of day."

It was a lie, pure and simple, but she couldn't help it. She had to lie, especially to herself. The truth would be too frightening to confront.

CHAPTER SIX

THEY MADE IT BACK, and Paul went in to discuss things with Joe Santori. Rosemary let herself into her apartment—or rather, her ex-apartment—and wandered from room to room, prepared to go into mourning over what she was going to lose. But a funny thing happened. She couldn't really concentrate on how sad and angry she was; Paul's face kept getting in the way. That smile...

"Stop it!" she ordered herself, taking a deep breath.

This wouldn't do. She couldn't let herself fall into this trap. She knew she'd reacted to him on a purely physical level and she hated herself for it. But she had to admit there was a reason this man was so attractive to women.

And guess what? She was a woman. It even worked on her.

"Even knowing all I do about him," she mused.

A memory surfaced from fifteen years before. She and Greg had been in downtown Chicago, trying to find a place that would reupholster their worn-out sofa without putting them into bankruptcy. Funds had been tight. They were mostly living on her paltry salary at the time.

They'd been feeling their poverty that day, and as they strolled unhappily down the street, past stores they couldn't afford to buy anything in, they'd stopped in front of the Trattoria, a trendy new restaurant everyone was talking about. Standing side by side, they'd read out loud from the menu, mouths watering. But they knew they couldn't afford the place.

They had started to turn away, but Rosemary had an idea. "Let's get one meal to go, take it home and share it," she suggested.

Greg had hesitated, but the temptation to have at least a taste of luxury was too strong and he'd finally agreed. She'd gone in to order the meal while he waited for her in the lobby. She remembered the happy feeling she'd had after she'd ordered the angel-hair pasta with shrimps and scallops. This was going to be a treat after all their tuna casserole dinners. She could hardly wait to get it home.

Coming out into the lobby, she'd found that Greg was no longer waiting alone. With him, chatting happily, were Paul and two very pretty girls. Both women were hanging on Paul's arms, but flirting madly with Greg at the same time. Rosemary had stopped, startled by the way the group was interrelating. She'd never seen her husband look so entranced before.

She didn't really know Paul at the time, though she knew all about him. He was the talk of the wives of most of the young residents at the hospital, the bane of their existence. The stories about him and his amorous exploits were legendary. No one could understand how such a playboy could be doing so well at medicine. It didn't seem fair.

"Ah, come on," Paul was coaxing, looking very devil-may-care in a fashionable suit with a scarf hanging carelessly about the shoulders. "I need your help, Greg. I can't handle both of these lovely ladies on my own. Don't let me down."

Greg was laughing, looking into the eyes of the redhead and saying something amusing, when he caught sight of Rosemary standing in the doorway. His expression changed and he backed away from the threesome, shaking his head and making excuses. Paul and the girls went on into the restaurant. Greg stayed with Rosemary.

But everything in him wished he could go with Paul. She'd sensed it then, and she knew it now. And that same bubble of dismay and resentment rose in her again, just as it had that night.

No, Paul Chambers was a playboy who had never had any respect for marriage or anything that went with it. In those days, there'd been nothing to indicate that he had any concept of hard work or moral standards, and that was something to keep in mind. He might be fun and charming now, but deep inside, he was the same old Paul, and she would forget that at her peril.

"Back to the trenches," she whispered as she watched him saying goodbye to Joe. She didn't want to get tangled up in old memories. There was still a fight to be waged here. She knew things looked bad for her side, but she couldn't give up.

"Are you going to be staying on my couch again to-night?" she asked him briskly from her doorway as he turned back onto the porch.

He looked up at her, startled. "Do you mind?" he queried. "I took a look at that bed in the basement and you were right. The place is a mess. I'd rather camp out on the lawn."

"Of course I don't mind," she forced herself to say, smiling brightly. "My house is your house." She added with a twist of irony, "Quite literally."

He laughed. "Well, thank you. Tomorrow I'll get a cot or something set up in the vacant apartment upstairs and then I won't have to bother you any longer."

"No bother," she insisted, leaving her door open as she went back into her place. "I'll just fix us some dinner. I have to eat too, you know."

He went on measuring and working with his plans while she went through her supplies in the kitchen. She wished she knew what Sally had fixed him for dinner the night before. She didn't want to duplicate it.

So what did he like? Was he a New Age trendy? Did he need goat cheese with his arugula? Was he a meat-and-potatoes man? Was he allergic to seafood? There was no way to guess, so she compromised on lasagna. Everyone loved Italian food.

She did it up right, throwing a red-and-white-checked tablecloth on the table, breaking open a bottle of red wine, tossing a green salad and toasting some crusty garlic bread. She used her good china, her best silver and the tallest wineglasses she could find. She hesitated over candles.

"Maybe this is overkill," she muttered, looking at the silver tapers she'd been saving for something special. But she decided to use them anyway. She was going for broke tonight.

"I wonder what he would do if I were to beg him on my hands and knees and soak his shirt with my tears?" she asked herself sarcastically. "That just might work."

Too bad it wasn't her style. In fact, it wasn't even a style she could fake. No, she was going to have to go for straightforward argument. In the meantime, she wanted to make things as inviting as she could.

All this took time, but he didn't seem to be any more anxious to hurry to the table than she was. She could hear him, still working with the designs and drawings, moving around on the porch, and occasionally up in Harriet's old place. It was rather convenient that his cast made such a commotion everywhere he went. That way Rosemary could keep tabs on him and know what he was up to. But that also reminded her that she had to hurry. After all, the longer he worked, the more he would have invested in this, and the slimmer the chances she would have of his changing his mind.

Still, it was long after dark when she finally called to tell him everything was ready.

He came down the stairs and stood in the doorway. She looked up and saw him there, dressed in jeans and an open shirt, his hair mussed and his blue eyes dark in the shadows, and her breath caught in her throat. Why did he have to look so romantic? For a moment she wondered if he did it on purpose, but then she dismissed the idea. No, the man was just attractive. There was no getting around it. He'd been born like that. All she could do was fight the natural reaction she had to him.

He was still standing there, looking from the table to her and back to the candles. Everything glittered and sparkled, giving off a luxurious sheen. His gaze met hers again, narrowing slightly. "You're not planning on trying to seduce me, are you?" he asked, his tone more wary than amused.

"What? Hardly!" She burst out laughing, trying to ignore the nervous note in her voice. "Are you finding that a problem lately?" she asked, forcing a smile as she stood awkwardly at the table, waiting for him to come in and take a seat. "I would have thought such things would be right down your alley."

His gaze was slow and deliberate and his head tilted to the side as he regarded her. "Now what would make you think a thing like that?" he asked her softly.

She was about to say "experience," but she quickly realized that would be revealing too much. He still didn't seem to remember her from the old days, and that was the way she liked it. But it did make her wonder again what had happened the night before with Sally Rogetti.

"Why don't we sit down and eat?" she said instead, offering him a chair. "And I'll take an oath that the only designs I have are on this lasagna."

He smiled and sat and let her serve him. She seemed slightly awkward at it, as though she weren't used to having company. Or maybe, he thought with sudden insight, it was just that she wasn't used to having male company.

He hadn't seen any hint of a lover around. And it was a damn shame, too, because she was a good-looking woman.

He glanced over the rim of his wineglass, watching her serve the salad. She had taken her hair down again, letting it flow around her shoulders, and he liked it that way. As she sat down across the table from him, the candlelight caught the golden sheen and made her look like a queen in a fairy tale.

Yes, a queen, not a princess. There was nothing waiflike about Rosemary. She was a solid, strong woman. He'd liked her in the tight shorts on the weekend, but all he'd seen her wear since were nurse's slacks and shirts, which didn't reveal her feminine side the way they might have.

"Do you always wear pants?" he asked between bites of the delicious meal.

"Inevitably," she said brightly, waving her fork in the air. "I'm not much of a nudist."

"No, I meant..." His own laughter choked off his words.

"In any relationship, as in 'who wears the pants in the family?'" She gave him an impish smile. "Yes, there too. I guess that's one reason why no one is breaking down my door suggesting marriage."

Reaching out, he grabbed her hand and held it, his eyes dancing with laughter. "Will you let me finish? What I meant was, I've never seen you in a dress. Don't you wear them?"

She wanted to pull her hand away, but he was holding it tightly. "I don't go to places where you wear dresses," she told him, avoiding his gaze. "It's not that I'm opposed to them. The situation just doesn't come up."

That wasn't entirely true. She hated wearing dresses and avoided it whenever possible. In her mind, dresses were for a certain sort of woman, a woman who needed men around. She'd never worked hard to attract male attention and she wasn't about to start now. It was take it or leave it, as far as she was concerned. She was herself and friends accepted that.

"I'm out there in a man's world," she continued, finally tugging her hand free of his and lifting her chin. "I've beat out a lot of men in my day. And I don't need feminine wiles to do it."

"I'll just bet you have," he murmured, looking her over appreciatively. "Beaten out a lot of men, I mean. You're certainly a . . . well, I mean you're quite a woman."

He could see by the look on her face that his statement, meant in all honesty as a compliment, had hit a nerve, and he wished he could take it back. But trying to repair it now would only make matters worse, so he turned away instead and helped himself to another piece of garlic bread.

She thought she knew exactly what he meant and she flushed. She'd never been delicate. At five foot eight, she seemed even taller with her broad shoulders and athletic bearing. As a child she'd been embarrassed by her size. Always the tallest in every class, she'd been teased by boys and shunned by dainty little girls, and the taunting had hurt a lot.

But as she reached adulthood, she began to see her strength as a source of great pride. So she was different— that only made her unique, not abnormal. She stood tall these days, proud of herself. But she knew her statuesque, muscular frame was not the ideal of many men, and she accepted that. She'd never been an object of male adoration and never expected to be.

But sometimes it hurt. Sometimes she wished, in her secret heart of hearts, that just once she could be small and cute and adorable. And right now, she had a tiny, traitorous urge to see something in Paul's baby-blue eyes that she hadn't really seen—something close to your basic, downhome, sexual attraction.

But that was crazy. No, what was she thinking? She didn't want that at all. If she did see it in his eyes, she would have to kick him out, wouldn't she? And then where would she be? She pushed that thought away and changed the subject back to where it belonged.

"Let's talk about the house," she said, clearing her plate away to make room for discussion and folding her hands on the table. "Let's talk about alternatives to destroying this wonderful place."

He put down his fork and wiped his mouth with a napkin. "Hey," he said casually, his eyes hooded as he met her determined gaze. "Destruction is not part of the strategy."

"Yes it is." She lifted her head and gave him a defiant look. "You're going to destroy everything I've built and loved for five years. And I'm trying to find a way to keep that from happening."

He leaned toward her, his blue eyes dark in the candlelight, his gaze searching her face. "I'm sorry," was all he said.

She stared at him. "Sorry isn't good enough," she told him softly. "There has to be a way...." Her voice trailed off and she shrugged, helpless but still determined.

He stared back for a long moment, then sighed and straightened. "Okay, Rosie," he said, shaking his head. "Listen up. I want to give you the big picture here."

Resentment flashed through her. "My name is Rosemary."

Her tone was icy, and he noticed, but he merely drew his eyebrows together and gave her a pained look. "Whatever. Now, I didn't come here to Tyler just because I inherited a house and decided to play around with it. I came with a very specific purpose. I have a plan."

"You too?" she murmured ironically, taking a long sip of wine.

He looked surprised. "Why, do you have one?"

Hadn't he noticed? "I don't think it has anything to do with what yours is," she assured him.

"Well, okay. Here's mine." He gave her that smile again, the one where his teeth flashed white against his skin, the one where his blue eyes sparkled with some special knowledge that she was dying to know, the one that sent a current right through her soul. And then he went on as though he had no idea of how much power he seemed to be gaining over her emotions.

"I'm getting married," he told her with a sheepish grin.

She gripped the arms of her chair without realizing what she was doing. Shock reverberated through her again. Her voice was forced when she finally managed to reply, "Oh? Who's the lucky bride?"

He shrugged, casual about this as he was about everything. "I don't know that yet. I don't think I've met her."

Her smile flickered and she looked away while she gathered her senses together. It was absurd to let him throw her. She had more backbone than this, surely.

"That makes it a little difficult, doesn't it?" she said quietly, pleased with the control she heard in her own voice.

"Not really." He took a sip of wine and glanced at her with a slow, lazy look. "I know what she looks like. I'll know her when I see her."

"Oh brother," she said, exasperated with him all at once.

How did he dare throw her for a loop with such a statement and then back off so rapidly? She felt as though she'd wandered onto a roller coaster by mistake and it was heading into a tunnel. She wanted very badly to get off.

She glared at him, but he didn't notice. His head was tilted back and he obviously was musing over his requirements for his ideal woman.

"In fact, I can pretty much see her now," he said dreamily. "The face is a little hazy, but she's pretty, of course. The figure is light and graceful. The hair is between brown and honey gold and swings in loose ringlets around her face. She wears soft dresses that swish when she walks and—"

"And she was last seen serving her kids milk and cookies in a sitcom in 1960," Rosemary noted crisply. "Really, Paul. You're impossible."

He raised his head and looked at her, his eyes tragic. "You don't think she exists any longer?" he asked quite seriously.

Rosemary stared at him, and then, despite everything, she had to laugh. "No, Paul. That sort of woman went extinct about the time you hit high school. Face it, you're going to have to learn to deal with modern women."

"So I'm in trouble?"

"You're in big trouble."

He heaved a sigh and looked at her, his shoulders sagging, his huge blue eyes melancholy. "Well, how about you, then?" he asked, gazing into her eyes. "Would you like to marry me?"

Her own eyes flashed. "I would sooner eat a bug."

He laughed aloud, throwing back his head and enjoying the moment. "I should have seen that coming. You haven't exactly been a fan." He frowned, looking at her. "In fact, you've acted like you had something against me right from the beginning, even before you knew I owned this house." His frown deepened. "Now why was that?"

She shrugged and looked away. "Some personalities just clash," she said evasively. "So tell me, once you find this perfect woman, what are you planning to do with her?"

"Make babies," he said promptly. "That's the whole point." He glanced at her. "Don't you ever want to make babies?"

She shook her head, a slight smile on her lips but none in her eyes. "Not me. It's too late for me."

His eyebrows rose. "Why do you say that?"

She looked at him and then she laughed. "I'm not that gullible," she told him. "Babies are for young women whose systems are chockfull of hormones. I've gone way beyond that.''

"No babies for you," he said softly. "Won't you miss them?"

"Not a bit." She said it with conviction because it was absolutely true. "But we were talking about the house," she reminded him.

"Ah, yes. So we were." But he was still staring at her, puzzling over that slight hint of familiarity he caught every now and then. He'd seen her somewhere before; that belief was beginning to grow in him. If only he could remember...

"You were giving me the big picture," she prodded.

He nodded, coming back to the present. "Yes, I was. I want to explain to you some of the reasons behind my move here. Maybe then you'll see why your arguments are not going to sway me."

"They're not?"

"No." He shook his head firmly.

She sighed, though she'd known it from the first. "Would tears make a difference?" she asked caustically.

He looked interested. "I don't know. Tears would take us to a whole other level." He tipped his head to the side, considering. "I mean, there would have to be the comforting, and kissing away the teardrops, and—"

"Forget it," she said, pressing her lips together. "I've never cried in front of a man before and I'm not about to start now."

He grimaced. "That's a pity. Consoling you might have been nice."

She glared at him, but it took an effort and she couldn't keep a spark of amusement from showing in her eyes. "About the big picture," she reminded him.

"Okay." He settled back and refocused. "You see, most of my life has been pretty directionless. I've sort of drifted with the currents. Living where the weather suits my wardrobe."

She frowned and drummed her fingers on the tabletop. "That's very close to plagiarism," she told him warningly. "Too clever by half."

He smiled. "But it gets the point across."

Her severe look was meant to put him in his place, but she knew it wouldn't work and she wondered why she bothered. He was adorable; there were no two ways about it. She just had to remember that the adorableness was there for everyone and not aimed specifically at her. It was nothing personal at all.

"If you're trying to imply that you're a superficial chaser after excitement and diversion," she said evenly, "that you've never had a serious thought in your head and never plan to, it came across beautifully."

He looked a bit dumbfounded. "Well, that wasn't quite it. But I guess it will have to do."

She nodded, waiting.

He shook his head, looking at her. It was such a change to come up against a woman who wasn't easily swayed by his charm that he found her intriguing. "Are you this tough on all the guys?" he asked, his mouth twisting. When she didn't answer, he shrugged and went on.

"The fact is, I'm not getting any younger. One of my patients called me a moldy-oldy the other day. And—" he flashed his riveting smile "—this may seem odd, but I didn't go into pediatrics because I wanted to avoid surgery. I really do like kids. And I realized, if I didn't get a move on, I might end up without any of my own. So here I am. I guess you could say I want to hear the patter of little feet and know that they are smaller versions of mine."

She stared at him again, not sure whether to take him seriously. "First you want to get married, now you want children," she said a bit breathlessly. "What next? A kingdom of your own?"

His grin was crooked. "Does normal life really seem so outlandish to you?"

She nodded. "Yes. But please go on."

He nodded as well, and a different look came over his face as memories began to surface. "My parents were divorced when I was seven. My father was a surgeon, a heart specialist, and that was when they were first having success with heart transplants and all that. He was gone most of the time, traveling all over the world, wherever there was something new to learn about it or someone to practice on. I hardly ever saw him. And at the same time, my mother was a cellist. Once the divorce came through, she packed me off to boarding school and took off with an international orchestra. I didn't see her at Christmas, because there were always holiday concerts to perform, and I rarely saw her during the summer, because she would go on loan to European orchestras. The only time I ever had the feeling of family was when I came here to stay with my grandparents. Those were the times I loved most of all."

Rosemary swallowed, wishing she dared to swear out loud. It was happening; he was getting to her. She'd sworn he wouldn't touch her, but he had. Now what? Was she supposed to cry and tell him it didn't matter? That because he'd been a sad little boy, he was allowed to tear her home apart now?

No. It didn't compute.

"Did I know you then?" he asked suddenly.

Jumping, she turned her startled eyes to meet his. "When?"

"I don't know. Teenage years maybe. Did you ever go to the swimming pool at the rec center? Hang out at the diner?"

She shook her head. "I'm not originally from Tyler. I only moved here five years ago."

"Ah." But he was still frowning as he looked at her, studying her face and wondering.

She rose and began collecting the dishes, as much to get away from his scrutiny as anything else.

He watched her for a moment, and then gave a huge sigh. "Okay," he said, throwing his napkin down. "You win."

Whirling, she stared at him. "What do you mean, I win? Win what?"

He smiled at her, shrugging. "I give up. You can stay."

"I can stay?" She sank back into her chair, hardly daring to believe it. In fact, there was something just too good to be true about it, and she gazed at him suspiciously.

He nodded. "Yes, you can stay. But not here." He thumped his hand on the table. "Not in this apartment."

She stared at him blankly. "I don't get it."

"I'm still going through with the renovations." He pointed toward the ceiling. "I always planned to keep the upstairs divided into two apartments. You can stay in the one directly above. I'll take the other one."

"But..."

"I know how attached you are to this place, but I just can't let you stay down here. I'm going to need it for medical offices and a waiting room. There is no way around that. But the place upstairs is basically just like this one. You can make it over the way you've done here and you'll hardly notice the difference."

Conflicting emotions swam through her system. She wanted to thank him, but she wasn't quite sure if she should. She wasn't going to keep her current apartment, but she would get a fair facsimile. The hitch was she had to live next door to him. Was that a good exchange? She had her doubts. But at least she wasn't going to have to go live in one of those new, anonymous boxes out on the highway.

"Thank you," she said softly. "I think."

He grinned. "Have you ever lived in a house under renovation?" he asked her.

She shook her head.

His expression was pure John Wayne. "Let me warn you, it's going to be rough. It's going to be tough. It's going to be low-down and dirty."

She couldn't help it; she had to smile at him. "I can take it if you can," she said stoutly.

"Good." He held a hand out to her. "Shall we shake on it?"

Rosemary should have seen the trap coming, but she was too confused by all the quick changes he'd already made to see this one in her future. Blindly, she held out her hand to take his and shake, but before she knew what was happening, he'd pulled her toward him across the table, and his lips touched hers.

They touched lightly. A bare minimum of a kiss. More of a salute, really—gentle and quick and not at all threatening.

"Great," he said, drawing back. Dropping her hand, he rose from his chair, grabbed hold of his crutch and headed back outside. "I've got some things to pick up out here. I'll be back in a minute. And then, if you don't mind, I'm going to get some sleep. It's been a long day."

And he left her behind, shaken and gasping. Because his kiss had brought up other memories—ones she hadn't dealt with yet.

Paul Chambers had kissed her before. Obviously, he didn't remember it, but she did. Oh yes, she did.

CHAPTER SEVEN

THE NEXT FEW DAYS flew by. Things were changing rapidly. In the evening, when Rosemary got home from work, she spent most of her time packing away nonessentials in boxes and moving things she was going to need upstairs. The Coopers moved out of their apartment and into their new house on Willow, leaving with much waving and regretting, as though they were very good friends indeed.

Rosemary wondered why that so often happened. While they had lived side by side, they'd barely noticed each other. But now that they were leaving, they suddenly became bosom buddies. Life was strange.

Paul was still sleeping on her couch. They had never made a decision that he should. Not really. But he never again offered to go somewhere else, and she didn't ask him to.

She told herself it was because she felt indebted. After all, he didn't have to let her stay in the house. He could have forced her out easily. And since he was the last person she would want to feel indebted to, she could make up some of it this way, by offering him a place to stay.

Still, it was uncomfortable with him there. She never really felt as though she could relax. Having a stranger in the house made her nervous. And having a man around who was this friendly, and this oblivious to her sense of reserve, made for awkward confrontations now and then.

"Why are you letting me stay?" she asked him one evening when they'd had a run-in.

He turned and looked at her with half-closed eyes. He'd been asking himself that question every now and then. Especially when she acted like a scalded cat every time he came near her.

"Maybe I like the company." And there was some truth in that. It would be damn lonely without her here. At least until he had a woman of his own to fill the emptiness.

But she was shaking her head. "You don't really like me very much. We don't seem to get along very well."

For some reason, her words shocked him. "Is that the way you see it?"

She shrugged. "How do you see it?"

He gazed at her for a long moment before he said, "I think we can be friends."

"Friends." She rolled the word around in her mouth. Could she be friends with Paul Chambers? Did she have any choice?

But there were to be no more casual kisses. She was making sure of that, staying as far away from him as possible at all times, moving away when he came too near. She didn't want to be too obvious about it, but intended to make sure nothing happened.

He noticed, of course, and teased her about it, but at one point told her quite seriously how he felt. "You don't have to be wary of me, Rosemary," he said. "I'm not in the market for easy sex. I know what I want and I'm going after it."

She had taken a deep breath and forced a smile. "Your perfect fifties wife?"

He'd nodded. "That's pretty close. No ulterior motives," he'd promised. "Honest."

She believed him. Though she knew his background, he had been the perfect gentleman around the house. What could she say? Maybe he *had* changed.

But this situation wouldn't last forever. Soon Joe and his men would have the upstairs completed. The renovations were minor in that part of the house—mostly modernizing plumbing and electrical wiring and putting in new shelving and a large bay window in each flat. "Someday, when I'm married and have kids, I'm going to turn the entire second floor into my own home," he told her sunnily. "But for now, it will be two apartments and we'll be neighbors."

That prospect wasn't as daunting as it might once have been. She was actually looking forward to it. She just hoped she would end up with most of the lovely antiques that helped make her place so special. When the house was originally divided into apartments, most of Paul's grandmother's things had been placed in the one where Rosemary now lived. Hers was the only flat rented out as furnished, and she'd always felt lucky to have it. There were pieces she'd grown devoted to, things she would offer to buy if it came to that. She could only wonder if Paul was as attached to the antiques as she was.

The rooms upstairs were practically identical in layout to her own, but the Coopers had painted pastel colors throughout and Rosemary ached to return to her favorite antique white, the perfect backdrop for her decorating style.

"We'll have the painter do all the walls," Paul told her airily. "Keep things in boxes so you'll be mobile. We're going to live like gypsies for the next few weeks."

Living like gypsies would have been an improvement over what they were going through at the moment. At least gypsies were wild and free. Rosemary felt as though she were in some sort of prison.

Not only did she have to put up with dust and noise and splinters and things never being where she was sure she'd left them, she also had to endure strange men walking through at all hours, peering in windows, asking where they could plug in their electrical equipment.

And once she'd gotten used to that, the children started arriving.

The first patient Paul saw at the house was a very sick little girl who showed up in her mother's arms in the middle of the night. A light rain was falling, and the wet and bedraggled mother and child looked like something out of some legend that included no room at the inn. Rosemary's heart went out to them both immediately, and she ushered them in.

"Chicken pox," was Paul's quick diagnosis of little Jennifer. "Is she in preschool? If so, you'd better inform them right away."

Daphne Sullivan, Jennifer's mother, looked to Rosemary to be in a state of barely controlled panic. "I—I don't know what I'm going to do," she said. "I have to work, and I always take her to TylerTots. She loves it there. But I don't have anyone to leave her with if she's sick."

Paul and Rosemary exchanged glances. Another single mom coming up against the wall of indifference in a cold, busy world. Rosemary often was impatient with women who thought they could raise a child by themselves without any sort of family support, but in this case, when she came face-to-face with it, she felt nothing but compassion.

"I have a friend," she told the woman quickly, searching a drawer for a paper and pencil to write down information. "Her name is Kayla Cannon. She has a sister who is in college and works weekends at the conventions at Timberlake Lodge. I know for a fact that her sister is having trouble making ends meet, what with paying for her tuition and books. She's on the lookout for odd jobs. I know she'd be happy to make some baby-sitting money. Why don't you give her a call? Let me give you her number."

Daphne's gratitude was quick and heartfelt, but fleeting. She had a sick child to care for and she wrapped her carefully in a blanket before taking her out into the rain again.

Paul smiled at Rosemary once she'd left. "Quick thinking," he commented. "You're a problem solver, aren't you?"

"Sometimes," she admitted. But at the same time, she began to wonder just how much of this sort of thing they were going to be having.

Paul had arranged to have temporary office facilities at the hospital medical building, so that he could begin seeing patients, and he spent a few hours there every day. But once he began to be known, people started coming to the house as well, showing up at all hours, with all sorts of ailments. It seemed there was always some sort of emergency, from a three-year-old putting a bean up his nose to broken bones and punctured feet.

And where did these poor wretches end up? In Rosemary's living room, of course.

There was no other place to go. Joe and his crew of construction workers had gutted the upstairs by now, tearing down walls and refitting pipes. Mrs. Tibbs was still holed up in her apartment, and Rosemary's place was the only habitable space left.

The doorbell would ring and Rosemary would open the door, and there would be some distracted mother holding a child, her eyes tearful and frantic. Paul would come up and let them in, as though Rosemary had no say in the matter at all. Brothers and sisters of the injured or sick child would run rampant through her home while she attempted to help Paul with his patient. Though Rosemary felt guilty about her feelings, she did resent it.

It wasn't that she didn't like children—not at all. It was just that she'd never been around them much and never expected to be. Her therapy practice had been devoted almost exclusively to adults and the few younger patients she'd treated, up to this point, had all been teenagers. Now that children were showing up in her life, she didn't know quite how to handle them.

Her first inclination was to treat a child as a small adult, and she spoke coolly and politely to the little boys and girls littering her living room. But that didn't seem to work very well. The little girls would stare at her, openmouthed, and the little boys would invariably try to sneak around her to play with the autographed baseball she kept on her shelf. It was all she had left from her father and she definitely didn't want six-year-olds tossing it through her beveled windows.

One set of twins tortured her for fifteen minutes one evening. Paul had asked her to keep an eye on them while he talked privately with their mother out on the porch. Rosemary had been sure from the start they had the eyes of fiends, and it turned out she was right. Little Ricky Pulver would grab some item off a shelf and run with it, and while Rosemary was chasing him, his brother Randy would grab something else and run in the opposite direction, forcing her to come after him in turn. When she'd finally put all the ceramic bowls and porcelain figurines in a pile on a shelf too high for them to reach, they took turns jumping out at her and yelling "Boo!"

Her frustration was rising quickly, along with her voice, when the mother came in and just in time saved her children from being tied to chairs and gagged.

Rosemary realized she'd let them get the better of her, but she didn't know how to make sure that didn't happen again. So she resorted to treating children like household pets, speaking in loud, short sentences and ordering them about, then checking every few minutes to make sure they were still sitting where she'd told them to.

As a result, the children were terrified of her. Paul finally had to speak to her about it.

"They shouldn't bring their children here," she'd responded fretfully. "It's too dangerous with the renovations going on. And look at all the dust they breathe in."

He gazed at her coolly, wondering what she thought a pediatrician was meant for. "What do you want me to do, turn a sick child away at the door?"

That sounded cold and hard and she didn't want to be those things. "Make arrangements to meet them at the hospital," she suggested.

"Not in the evening, for simple emergencies." He looked at her in frustration for a moment, then grabbed her hand and held it. "You're going to have to lighten up," he told her bluntly. "They're not monsters. They're just kids."

"They may be benign to you," she retorted, pulling her hand away. "But to me, they are aliens with sticky fingers you've let sit on the chairs of my living room. I'm not the one who opted to spend my life with children; you are. And I'm not too happy to be drafted into the movement."

They were sitting over a cup of coffee and she was just about to dash off for work. He studied her for a moment, weighing what she'd said.

"Why no children in your life, Rosemary?" he asked softly at last, his blue eyes searching hers. "What are you afraid of?"

She wanted to snap at him, say something devastating, but she bit her tongue and counted silently to ten. "Tell me this, oh wise one," she said calmly at last. "Why have you reached this late stage in your life without a wife? Or even a dog to call your own?" She smiled in triumph as his head shot up.

"You see, two can play that game," she told him, gathering her things and rising, about to head out the door. "And I won't even insult you by asking you what *you're* afraid of."

She was on the verge of turning away, but he caught hold of her wrist and stopped her, forcing her to look down into his eyes as he spoke to her.

"I'll tell you what I've been afraid of," he said quietly, his eyes luminous. "I've been afraid of real life. I've been running from it since I was young myself. It's only been in the past year that I've realized what I was doing and made some effort to turn things around." He shook his head slowly. He'd spent so much time moving from one place to another, it had taken him years to realize he was running away from something rather than toward it. Now that he had a better perspective on life, he was determined to build something instead of running.

"You ought to look in the mirror yourself, Rosemary. Life really isn't as scary as you think."

She gazed down at him, appalled. Who was he to speak to her this way? What did he know about her and her life?

"I'm not afraid of much," she insisted, yanking her wrist out of his grasp. "I can take care of myself."

"So you can," he assured her, his eyes suddenly warm, almost laughing. "I'm sorry if I spoke out of turn." His casual shrug completed the apology, and she hesitated, not certain what to say next.

She was angry, and yet she knew he had a point. She was going to have to relax around kids if she were going to stay in this house. She knew a big part of her problem with them stemmed from her mother—from the way she'd railed against children all the time Rosemary was growing up. And on a logical, rational level, she knew that was ridiculous. But emotionally, she still had to settle it. It was probably about time she did so.

"I—I'll try to be better with the children," she said, avoiding his gaze. And then she disappeared out the door.

Paul listened to her car leave and then he sat playing with his coffee cup, turning it round and round. He was finding it harder and harder every day to avoid thinking about Rosemary after she left in the morning. One picture in particular kept filling his mind—Rosemary in those great, tight shorts. Why did she insist on wearing the baggy pantsuits she lived in? She seemed to want to hide her beautiful body the same way she wanted to hide from life. What he really wanted was to see her in a dress, something soft and off the shoulders, something he could take up in his hand and . . .

Hell. Suddenly he threw back his head and laughed aloud. Damn! So that was what was eating away at him. His libido was aching to take the plunge. But what the hell, just because he was lusting after her bod didn't mean he wanted to marry her. After all, that sort of thing hadn't been in the cards for him before. The only thing that had changed was the finale. Now he wanted to end up with a wife and kids.

Which meant he'd better keep his hands off of Rosemary.

"But I don't really think that will be a problem," he said aloud as he rose to rinse out his cup in the sink. "I think Rosemary will handle that side of things quite well on her own. She's not going to let me get anywhere near her."

And he laughed again. He had to admit, the lady had a certain style.

ROSEMARY ATTACKED her work with a vengeance, but she couldn't get Paul's words out of her head: *Life isn't scary, Rosemary. Look in the mirror.*

What a jerk! Who was he to tell her what life was all about? He should keep his two-bit philosophizing to himself.

But she went from anger to anguish in an amazingly short time. In just under an hour her resentment for him saying such a thing to her turned into speculation about whether he was right.

Was she afraid to face up to real life? Was she?

By lunchtime, her attitude had switched again, and now she was scoffing at every word he'd said. Real life? What the heck did that mean? Life was life. You couldn't avoid living it. It happened to you whether you wanted it to or not.

"I can't let him get to me like this," she told herself fiercely as she stared blankly at her computer screen, unable to remember what she'd been writing. "If I let things go too far..."

And he was a man to take them too far. At least, he used to be.

Closing her eyes, she remembered events she'd tried to block out for years. She recalled when Greg started lying to her about having to work late, having to meet his study group, having to do some research in the library. She had accepted his excuses at face value, only to find out later they were all untrue.

At first, she'd been puzzled and had accepted his lame explanations. She'd accepted them because she'd had very little choice. If she didn't, she was going to have to admit that her marriage was in trouble, and at the time, that was unthinkable to her.

She'd been proud of Greg when she married him, happy to think she was finally going to have the stable family life she'd always wanted. The years of moving from state to state, country to country, were over. She'd married a man who was going to be a doctor. How much more secure could you get?

But when the lies started, the firm foundation she thought she'd built crumbled and she found herself on very precarious footing indeed.

At last there had been a night when he didn't come home. At three in the morning, she'd gone to the hospital and asked where he was. A young medical student she'd met before recognized her and laughed.

"They're all at a party at Paul Chambers's place," she'd told her. "Didn't you know? He's having some blowout of a celebration because he's been offered a fellowship at Homeret Medical Research Center. You don't get much more prestigious than that."

Numb, Rosemary had followed directions to Paul's place, afraid of what she was going to find, but even more afraid of not confronting it.

The apartment was full of people. The music wasn't loud enough to rouse the wrath of the neighbors, but it was a constant, pulsing background to the scene that met her. Rosemary had hunted through the rooms, looking for her husband among the couples swaying to the music, laughing over a keg of beer or making out in the corners.

She didn't see him, but somehow she knew he was there. She turned down a hallway and found another set of rooms to explore. She'd twisted the knob on the first door she came to and found a darkened room, but before she could turn back, a hand shot out from the gloom and grabbed her arm, pulling her into the darkness.

"Caught you at last," said a slurred voice, and then she was in someone's arms and his mouth was on hers, crushing her with a kiss that tasted of beer and cigarettes and masculine desire.

Shock paralyzed her for one long moment, and the kiss seemed to suspend time, sending heat cascading through her bloodstream. Greg's kisses had never been like this, nor had his hand ever gone quite so quickly to her breast, to begin a brazen caress. She was stunned.

But not for long. Outraged, she had thrust the man away with a cry of anger, wiping her mouth with the back of her hand.

"Lisa," the slurred voice said. "Hey, it's only a game...."

The light came on and she was staring at Paul. A very drunk Paul. He swayed where he stood before her, gazing at her blearily.

"Hey," he said, staring hard as though she were difficult to see. "You're not Lisa."

"Where is my husband?" she demanded, fury and fear mixing with confusion.

He frowned as though he couldn't quite grasp what she was saying. "Lisa's not married," he told her wisely. "I know that. I asked her."

Still shaken, she wiped her mouth again and looked about the empty room. "I want to find my husband," she insisted.

"Okay, okay." He put up a hand as though to calm her, swayed again, but then regained his balance. "I'll find your husband. Honest I will. But tell me this. Who the hell is he?"

She clutched her arms, feeling cold and resentful. "Greg Simmons."

Impatient with his intoxicated reaction time, she started toward a door she saw at the other side of the room. "He's married to me and I want to see him, now," she said over her shoulder as she headed toward her goal.

He looked alarmed and actually seemed to sober a bit. Stepping forward, he grabbed her arm again and turned her back to face him. "He's not here now," he said quickly, draping an arm around her shoulders and trying to lead her away from the area. "Listen, I'm sorry about this. If I ever knew Greg was married, I guess I'd forgotten. I will definitely get word to him and have him go home pronto."

"Will you get your hands off me?" she demanded, trying to pull away.

"Listen," he said, not releasing her and forcing her to come along with him out into the hallway. "Don't be scared of me. I'm going to make sure you get home okay and I'm going to make sure Greg gets home soon. That's it. I'll take care of everything."

She'd begun to tremble. She wasn't sure, now that she remembered the sensation, whether she'd been trembling with fear of what she might find out or anger at what she already knew.

"Hey." Stopping with her at the entrance to his kitchen, he'd pulled her into his arms and stroked her hair, and for some reason, she'd let him. "Don't do that," he murmured, trying clumsily to comfort her. "It's going to be okay. Come on."

Of course, it wasn't okay at all. Not by a long shot. But she let Paul lead her out into the living room, and she let him get a friend who hadn't been drinking to take her home. And when Greg finally showed up, she was packed and ready to leave him and their marriage in the dust....

The knock sounding on the door to her office jerked her back to the present, and looking up, she saw Paul standing in the doorway. For just a moment she stared at him, not sure if he was a manifestation of her memory or the real thing.

"Hi," he said, clearing that up with a grin. "I dropped by to see how you were doing."

Because of their argument in the morning? Maybe.

She stared at him a moment longer before she answered, wondering if this could really be the same man who had kissed her in the dark all those years ago. He seemed so different, and yet the similarities were striking. No, she couldn't risk thinking he'd changed all that much. He was still the man whose life-style had tempted her husband into throwing their marriage away. She mustn't forget that.

"Are you okay?" he asked, beginning to look concerned.

She smiled quickly. "I'm fine, Paul. How about you?"

"Me?" He looked surprised. "There's nothing wrong with me that getting back a working foot wouldn't cure."

From down the hallway, a female voice told a joke Rosemary couldn't quite make out and Paul turned, laughing. An office a few doors away erupted in feminine laughter in return. Paul glanced in at Rosemary and shrugged.

"I've got to go. My fans are calling," he said with a grin.

"Mustn't disappoint your public," she agreed, shaking her head as he disappeared.

That was another thing about Paul. You always seemed to be sharing him with someone else. She pitied the woman who ever tried to compete with the multitudes.

But even thinking that made Rosemary smile. She couldn't help but like him. Who could?

Now that was odd. Why would remembering what a jerk he'd been in the past, and thinking about what a trial he was in the present, make her feel friendlier to him now? It didn't make any sense and she knew she ought to squelch the impulse.

"Okay," she whispered as she began to pull her things together for a quick escape. "Consider the subject of Paul a dead issue. As of now."

ROSEMARY WAS LOOKING forward to the weekend. She had a long hike planned, a day in the wilderness where she would forget all her problems and just let herself go with nature. Communing with the great outdoors had always been her favorite way to relax.

But Saturday dawned with a cloudy gloom, and by afternoon, the rain had begun. She ended up staying in with Paul and playing Scrabble with him in front of a roaring fire.

It started out as a friendly game, but soon the two of them were playing in a cutthroat manner, as though winning really mattered. Paul spent his time coming up with strange words that Rosemary challenged every time, usually winning when the words couldn't be found in the dictionary.

But they'd been playing all evening, and now they were getting a little punchy.

"Okay, here we go," Paul said with satisfaction as he put his letters down on a triple word score that was going to put him way out in front if it passed muster. He was sitting on the couch while she was sitting cross-legged on the floor. The Scrabble board was set up on the coffee table between them.

Rosemary frowned at the word suspiciously. "Hickey?" she said, her finger playing in her hair. "Is that a real word?"

"Sure it is." He sat back and smiled triumphantly. "A hickey is the country version of a hippie."

She groaned, shaking her head. "No way." She looked toward the dictionary, but hesitated. The way they were playing, if she found a real definition listed, she had to pay him ten points. If there wasn't one, he owed her the same amount.

Paul coughed delicately. "Of course, there is another definition," he said smoothly, his eyes barely concealing his smile. "Surely you remember hickeys from high school."

She stared at him for a moment, then grabbed the dictionary, just as he lunged for it at the same time. She won, gave him a superior look and flipped the pages, hunting for the word.

"Hickey," she muttered scathingly as she searched. "Oh brother."

"It's a perfectly good word," he assured her, his face radiating innocence. "I use it all the time."

"I'll just bet you do." She found it and jabbed with her forefinger to hold the spot. Reading the entry quickly, she looked up at him with a smirk. "The only *hickey* listed isn't a real word. It says here it's short for *doohickey*, which is an unnamed object being pointed out, as in 'Get me that doohickey.'"

He threw out his hands, a grin starting to form. "Well, then, it's a word."

She snapped the book shut and gazed up at him in mock defiance. "No, it's not."

"Hey." His suspicions aroused again, he leaned toward her. "Let me see that dictionary."

"No." She held the book out of his reach. "No need," she told him, her eyes sparkling. "I took care of it."

"Oh no you don't." His face took on a disbelieving look, though there was barely concealed amusement kindling in his eyes. "Do you think I can trust you?"

"Of course you can."

"Not for a moment, lady. I want to see it."

"No," she said, inching away from him and beginning to laugh. "You're just a bad loser, aren't you?"

"Me, a loser? I hardly think so." He held out his hand commandingly. "Let me take a look at that book."

She made a face at him. "No."

He began to gather himself to rise from his seat. "I'm warning you."

"Ooh, I'm so scared. You're so tough." Her eyes were dancing with taunting laughter.

He gazed at her speculatively for a moment. This was new. She'd never teased him this way before and he wondered if she realized what she was doing. Maybe it was the rain on the roof. Maybe it was being cooped up here for so long on a Saturday. Or maybe it was just a logical step in their relationship. But teasing like this often led to the sort of intimacy she'd been resisting like crazy ever since he'd first seen her in the woods. And he wasn't sure it was wise to risk it.

"Rosemary," he began warningly.

"Can't take it, can you?" she mocked softly.

He hesitated, then he grinned. "Okay, Rosemary. You asked for this," he said, diving at her.

She waited until the last moment, then rolled out of his way, eluding him again, laughing as she sprang to her feet and began to race across the room, clutching the dictionary to her chest.

He followed, hindered only a little by the cast on his foot, cutting her off in the hallway. She took a detour into her bedroom, and he caught her around the knees, toppling both of them onto her bed in a flailing mass of arms and legs and laughter.

"Give me that book," he demanded, pinning her down and rising above her.

"What book?" she said, biting her lip and trying to keep it hidden beneath her shoulder, where it had landed.

"You know what book. The dictionary..."

His voice trailed off as he looked down into her eyes, and his mind began to fuzz over the details of why this had happened. That didn't seem to matter any longer. What mattered was the feel of her beneath him, the rounded curve of her breast revealed where her shirt had pulled open, the tangle of her blond hair against the spread, her face as she looked up at him, the sudden change he saw in her eyes.

He didn't think. What was there to think about? There were certain things that just came naturally, and when a man and a woman were in this position, a simple kiss was the least of what might be expected. And so he kissed her.

To his surprise, her mouth was soft and yielding. He hadn't expected that, and he quickly took advantage of it, taking possession, taking control. She seemed to melt to his touch, until a hot liquid shot through him, turning the kiss harder, deeper, making his body move against hers.... Then he realized her hands were against his chest, pushing him, and instead of responding as she had at first, she was trying to escape the demands of his mouth.

He pulled back, looking down at her with eyes that were glazed with desire, and she blinked quickly, hardly able to meet his gaze, gasping for breath.

"No," she managed to blurt out, shaking her head so that her hair swung about her face. "No, Paul. Get off me."

He hesitated. He didn't want to stop. But he could see the look in her face, the determination in her eyes, and he knew it was over. Over before it had really begun. He lifted himself away, propping himself up on one elbow. "What is it?" he asked her. "What's the matter?"

She stared at him, slowly getting her equilibrium back. What could she say? "You can't do that, Paul."

The laughter was gone from his eyes and a certain hardness had taken its place. "It was just a friendly kiss."

She shook her head, finally getting her breath back. "You can't do that. We can't have friendly kisses."

His face was like granite. "Tell me why not."

"Because we can't, that's all." She rolled away from him, leaving the dictionary behind and rising from the bed. She didn't dare look back at him. Instead, she headed for the door, going back to the living room where it was safer. "We just can't," she said again as she left.

Well, she'd wondered what it would be like to see sexual attraction in his eyes, and now she knew. It made her shiver. And it had also ruined the mood they'd built between them, the fun they were having.

But she couldn't claim it was his fault. She'd wanted to flirt, wanted that kiss. And now she had to stop this before it went too far.

And he wanted to know why they couldn't have a friendly kiss between them. How could she explain to him something she didn't have words for? All she had were feelings, feelings that it wasn't right, that it couldn't happen. The two of them had to stay away from that sort of thing.

And now she knew how dangerous it really was. She had to face the fact that she was as much to blame as he was. Temptation was there, rising in her like the coming of the sun, bold and bright and irresistible. To turn away from it was painful. To turn away from him was darn hard.

Walking on into the kitchen to start boiling water for tea, she blamed it on a lot of things, but not really on Paul himself. After all, he was just a man, the only man around at the moment. It meant nothing that he'd felt a momentary attraction. It meant even less that she had.

There were other factors involved. It had been a long time since a man had touched her, touched her heart, touched her body. And she had a feeling it was going to be a long, long time before it happened again. And when it did happen, it wasn't going to be Paul.

How could it be? Paul was the one who had betrayed her, though he probably didn't even know it. He'd ruined her marriage, ruined her life.

But wait a minute. She stopped herself, her eyes squinting against the kitchen light. She'd been holding on to this mantra for so long, she hadn't updated it lately. Ruined her life? What was she talking about? Her life wasn't ruined; she was fine now. If she were honest, she would have to admit she was glad things had turned out the way they had. She wasn't happy her marriage had evaporated on her, but she'd made her peace with that and gone on. And she had built a new life, a life she was pretty happy with.

And yet the resentment lingered. Paul Chambers had dangled temptation in front of her husband like a barker at a carnival, and poor Greg had fallen for the hype. A rather quiet, introverted type, he hadn't dated much until he'd met Rosemary. In fact, she was pretty sure he'd never kissed another girl before their marriage. She'd loved him. He'd seemed levelheaded and ambitious and hardworking—and just a little innocent. That had attracted her as well. For a few years, they had done quite well together.

And then along had come Paul with his devil-may-care attitude and his exotic life-style, and his women—and Greg had been mesmerized.

"The Pied Piper," Rosemary murmured. "That was what he was."

The Pied Piper played a tune and off Greg had gone. He couldn't resist.

Sitting with her cup of tea, she wondered if she was going to be any stronger.

THE NEXT MORNING was just as cool and rainy, and Rosemary called Pam and invited herself to church with her and Patrick. Afterward there was Sunday dinner at the Kelsey Boardinghouse, where most of the Kelsey clan gathered on a Sunday afternoon. Rosemary enjoyed the day with that rambunctious crowd, and from what she could see, Pam and Patrick were doing just fine. Pam was happily pregnant and Patrick seemed completely enchanted with the whole thing, the perfect and very attentive husband and father-to-be.

It was only later in the evening that a strain began to show. Pam had planned for Rosemary to come home with them and have some time to talk, but Patrick wanted to go by the high school to get some things done, and his leaving put a damper on Pam's peace of mind. She wouldn't talk about it, but Rosemary could feel the tension grow. She tried to lift her friend's spirits, but not much seemed to work.

Still, all in all, she had a wonderful time and didn't return home until late in the evening. Walking in, she found Paul sitting on the couch with the television turned down low, leafing through a magazine.

Seeing him there all alone, she immediately felt guilty for not having invited him along. Still, they weren't exactly joined at the hip. He had his life, she had her own life.

"Did you have a nice time?" he asked.

"Wonderful," she said, shrugging out of her raincoat. "Have you been here all day on your own?"

"No, not at all." He put down his magazine and gave her half a smile. "Ernie came by and took me to see his kid in a basketball game. Then we all went to eat at a fried-chicken place. We had a great time."

"Oh. Good." She flopped down beside him on the couch. Right now, she figured the best thing to do was be his friend. Being friends might give them strength to hold off anything more serious. "Did you meet any women?" she asked brightly.

He gave her a wary look, not sure just where she was going with this one. "Sure. Tons of them."

Wasn't that good? Why was he frowning? "Any good prospects for your marriage search?"

The look he gave her now was exasperated. "Not really."

"Oh come on," she said encouragingly. "You're a good-looking guy. There must be tons of women dying to get married in this town. You ought to be able to find one."

His frown deepened. Coming from her, for some reason the cheerleading tactics were very annoying. "Listen, this is not just a business proposition. I've got to fall in love."

She looked at him skeptically. "Have you ever fallen in love before?"

"Sure," he responded defensively. "Plenty of times."

"But not deeply enough to marry, is that it?" she noted perceptively. "Or didn't it last long enough to make it to the altar?"

He stared at her for a moment, then looked away. "I had a different mind-set in those days."

She nodded. She knew that from personal experience. "So now you're ready to fall in love and you've got to do it on a timetable."

"Damn right," he muttered. "Time is fleeting."

She smiled. "Lots of luck, mister."

He nodded slowly, but the look in his eyes was defiant. "I'll need it. But I'm an optimist. I think I can do it. She'll come along."

Rosemary sighed. She'd had her own hopes in the past. "Just like in a fairy tale. And you'll live happily ever after."

He searched her face, sensing vulnerabilities she might be bringing to the table. "That's the plan. That's my dream." His gaze sharpened. "What's your dream?"

She hesitated, then gave him a tight-lipped smile. "I don't have a dream."

"You must have some plans for the future."

"Nope." Not any she would share with him, at any rate.

"That's criminal. You can't live that way." He threw out his arms, exasperated with her. "You've got to have a dream."

"Oh please, Paul." She gave him a look of pure exasperation. The next thing she knew, he would be breaking into songs from *South Pacific*. "Don't be corny."

"No, wait a minute." Reaching out, he cupped her chin in his hand and gazed at her narrowly. He shouldn't take everything she said at face value, should he?

"I'm falling for a snow job here, aren't I?" he said accusingly. "You've got dreams, all right. You've got plenty of dreams. You just won't tell me what they are. Am I correct?"

For some reason, a lump rose in her throat at his words. She stared back at him, completely incapable of answering, and suddenly realized that if she didn't get out of there, she might start growing teary. Quickly, she pulled away from his touch and got to her feet.

"Good night, Paul," she said firmly, striding toward her room with a no-nonsense step. "I'll see you in the morning."

He stared after her, watching her go and swearing softly at himself for having botched it again. Somehow they couldn't seem to connect, and tonight had been worse than ever. Why had he found her so annoying? She'd tried to be friendly. And the more she tried to be a friend, the more he felt like snarling. Funny.

"Yeah," he muttered to himself, rising to his feet and hobbling off to the bathroom, on the leg that stiffened now every time he sat too long. "About as funny as a broken crutch."

CHAPTER EIGHT

"ARE THERE an unusually large number of twins in Tyler?" Paul asked over breakfast the next morning.

Rosemary looked up from the toast she was buttering. Relations between the two of them were settling back to normal. They could be friends; she was sure of it. All it would take was a little extra effort.

"Twins? What are you talking about?"

"I don't know what it is, but everywhere I go, I'm seeing two of everyone." He looked downright worried. "You don't suppose my eyes went when my foot broke, do you?"

"Oh, twins!" She laughed as her mind cleared. "That's right. There's a twins convention in town."

"A twins convention?" He mused over that as he took a long sip of coffee.

"Yes. The new manager at Timberlake Lodge, Sheila Lawson, set up all these conventions. It's really been a help to the local economy. So many people have been out of work since the fire at the F and M, and bringing tourists in has helped a lot. And she has so many great ideas. As I remember, next weekend is a national twins convention. There will be twins from all over."

He shook his head, putting down his coffee mug and rising to help clear the table. "Just what do you do at a twins convention?" he wondered.

"Oh, I don't know. Get together. Share experiences. Maybe play twin games."

He gave her a quizzical look as he passed where she still sat at the table. "Twin games?"

"Sure." She rose, patting her mouth with a napkin and getting ready to dash for work. "Sheila will think of something good." She glanced at him, thinking for the thousandth time how handsome he was and wishing she didn't notice so regularly.

"Did you ever wish you were a twin?" he asked her, staring out through the greenhouse window.

"Sure. When I was a kid. In fact..." She smiled, remembering. "When I was very little, I had an imaginary twin. It used to drive my mother crazy."

"So you have a long history of it," he said softly as she passed him.

She turned and looked up into his eyes. "A long history of what?" she asked innocently.

Reaching out, he touched her hair. "Of driving people crazy," he murmured. But when she looked, startled, into his eyes, they were filled with laughter, and she turned away, feeling as though he were teasing her.

ROSEMARY LEFT WORK early that afternoon. Even so, she didn't beat Paul home. He was wandering around her living room on one crutch, making chalk markings on the walls, when she arrived.

She watched him for a moment before she made her presence known. She had to admit she did enjoy watching him move. The shame of it all was that he was so gorgeous. It was the human condition to be attracted to beautiful things. So her attraction to him was perfectly natural, wasn't it? And hardly unusual. But it did get in the way.

"Friends," she told herself stoutly. "We can do it."

"Oh, there you are," he said as he noticed her in the doorway. "These walls are going in a few days."

Looking around, she winced. She didn't want to talk about it.

"Where is the construction crew?" she asked as she came on into the room, dropping her sweater on the couch and her briefcase on the floor. "I don't hear any hammering or sawing. The silence around here is deafening."

"They've gone to buy lumber or something," he said absently, writing down a figure on his notepad. Looking up, he pocketed the pencil and gazed at her speculatively. "Listen, I really need to take a shower."

Spinning to stare at him, she shook her head firmly. "No way," she said with a finality that should have ended the matter.

He blinked at her, puzzled by her vehemence. "No way, what?"

She drew herself up. "I will not help you take a shower. I draw the line right about there."

A slow grin spread across his face. "Why, what a delightful idea. I hadn't thought of that before."

She hesitated, not sure if he were teasing her again, then turned to go through her mail which he'd left on her dining-room table. "You can quit thinking about it now, too, because it's not going to happen," she said, slitting open a bill, looking busy.

He groaned, following her. "I have to take a real shower, Rosemary. These alternate measures are just not making it." He came closer, standing right beside her. "Actually, I wasn't asking for company. What I need is a plastic bag and a heavy-duty rubber band."

She looked at him warily, suspecting a plot of some kind. She wouldn't put it past him. "What?"

His smile was sunny. "I just want to cover my cast. To keep it from getting wet while I take a shower."

She frowned, turning to look at him, then glancing down at his cast. "You're not supposed to do that."

"Hey," he said with a casual shrug. "Who's the doctor here?"

"Sometimes I wonder."

"I'm not going to hurt it. I'll make sure it doesn't get wet. But I can't stand these sponge baths any longer. I've got to have a real shower." He gave her a wink. "You want me clean, don't you?"

I don't want you at all. She didn't say it aloud, but it was on the tip of her tongue. And at the same time, she knew it was a lie.

So she shook her head as though she were exasperated with him, then turned and went to the kitchen. She pulled a big plastic bag out of one drawer and dug into another for a rubber band, then turned to hand them to him. "Will these do?"

"Perfect." He gave her his charming smile as he took the objects from her. "And there's just one more thing. I'm going to need help getting it on."

She frowned, not sure at first what he meant, then realized and rolled her eyes, shaking her head. "Here you go again."

He laughed. "Not really. I just need some help. You can close your eyes...."

"Never." She turned on her heel and began to stride away.

He caught up with her before she disappeared into her bedroom, blocking her doorway and forcing her to look into his face. "Okay, I admit, I am going to have to take my clothes off—"

"Paul!"

"But I'll wear a towel. Honest."

A towel. As if that could stand between her and unwelcome fantasies. She complained bitterly, arguing and protesting and even calling him names. But in the end, she agreed to help him. After all, there was no other way he was going to be able to do this.

He went off to prepare and she pretended to wipe down the counter, just to give her hands something to do and her mind something to think about. She couldn't believe she had let him talk her into it. This was crazy. This was insane. This was going to severely test her composure. But when she thought about it, a smile seemed to curl her lips and she almost laughed aloud.

At last his voice came from the bathroom. "I'm ready."

Taking a deep breath, she turned to join him. He was standing just outside the shower enclosure with a thick white towel wrapped around his hips.

She'd thought she was prepared, but her stomach fell away anyway, and she had to breathe quickly to catch her rhythm back. The sight of him was too much. She'd known he was muscular, but she hadn't expected him to look like something carved in a Greek courtyard. She walked forward, almost stumbling on the rug, and avoided meeting his gaze as though to meet it would be to turn to stone herself.

She fumbled with the plastic sack, her heart beating like a wild thing in her chest. She knew she was blushing, but she couldn't help it. There was no way to stop it, so she would have to ignore it. He was saying something, making a joke, probably, but there was a buzzing in her ears and she couldn't hear a thing.

The sack came up over the cast easily enough, but getting the rubber band up over it, and then into position with enough of the sack opening caught to make sure no water seeped in was a problem. Rosemary went down on one knee, struggling with it and trying to get it into place. As soon as she got one side fixed, the other side pulled free.

She looked up into his face, feeling desperate, and she saw a strange thing. His usual sense of humor seemed to have evaporated. His eyes were deep blue and his full lips were pressed together as though he were holding something in. While she looked up at him, he reached out and buried his hand in her hair, and something in him seemed to feel more pain than pleasure.

She wasn't sure how long she sat looking up at him, but suddenly there was a noise in the apartment, and before she could react, Joe was coming in the door of the bathroom with a keyhole saw in his hand.

"Whoa, excuse me." Shocked to find them there—Rosemary on one knee in front of Paul, who was wearing nothing but a towel—he jumped backward and turned to make a run for it.

But this was her only chance to escape.

"No!" Rosemary called, scrambling to her feet. "Joe, come back, quick! You can help."

He stopped and glanced back, looking confused.

"You do it," she told him, gesturing back toward the bathroom. "Please?"

"Me?"

"Yes, you. He just needs the rubber band adjusted on his cast." She shook her head quickly. "I've got to go to the store," she said, making up an excuse on the spot. "I'll be back soon." And she was gone.

Joe shrugged and went back into the bathroom cautiously, saluting Paul, who was beginning to look disgruntled.

"I just want to take a damn shower," Paul grumbled. "I need a little help."

Joe got the picture and grinned. "Here we go, buddy," he told him. "I'll get you squared away in no time." He reached down and tugged at the sack, holding it with one hand while he adjusted the rubber band with the other.

"Thanks, Joe," Paul told him lightly. "You're a lifesaver. I guess Rosemary couldn't handle all this bare skin at one time."

Joe grunted as he worked with the rubber band. "Oh, she could handle you, all right." He looked up at his friend and grinned. "It's her own nature she's having trouble with."

Paul raised one quizzical eyebrow. "You think so?"

Joe nodded. "Women. You know how they are."

Paul frowned and gazed into space. "Actually, I'm not certain I do. I used to think so. But now I'm not so sure."

"Aw, just wait until you get married. Then you'll be an expert."

"That's exactly what I'm aiming at, getting married. Getting married and having some kids." Paul sighed, leaning back. "Only I don't seem to be making much headway."

Joe looked pensive as he finished up with the cast and sat back on his heels. "Listen, have you thought about Rosemary?"

"Rosemary?" Paul was startled. Had the man been hallucinating? "Rosemary is not in the market. She lets me know that every day."

But Joe waved that away. "Sure, Rosemary. I mean, look at her. She's perfect. She may be beyond her girlish years, but she would still have time to get a couple of kids in for you before the deadline."

"The deadline?"

Joe grimaced. "Well, women don't last forever, you know."

"Oh, that." Paul grinned. "Neither do men."

Joe looked around to find where he'd left his saw. "Yeah, but we guys can still carry on the species."

"Be serious," Paul chided cheerfully. "They bottle what we've got to offer the reproductive cycle these days. Once they get a big enough supply, we may all be toast."

Joe laughed. "You think about Rosemary," he advised. "And yell if you get stuck in that shower. I'll be out here sawing a hole in your floor." He left the room, closing the door behind him.

Paul turned on the water and adjusted the spray. "Rosemary, huh?" he murmured, shaking his head ruefully. "When pigs fly."

PAUL GLANCED AROUND his sterile office with a sense of wonder. He just couldn't get used to it. Everything was so clean, so available. He wasn't accustomed to practicing medicine in such an ideal environment. For the past few years, he'd operated in mud and monsoons, or heat and dust storms, or dodging bullets and running out of antibiotics. This was pure luxury.

He only spent a few hours a day here, usually seeing two or three patients and getting caught up on paperwork. It was different seeing kids here in a peaceful place like Tyler. What he got these days were colds and the flu and kids with splinters in their fingers. How nice and normal it all seemed. A splinter was a lot easier to handle than a shrapnel wound.

But there were cases with a little more complexity. That morning he'd seen a boy with a strange rash on his stomach. He'd prescribed an ointment he thought would take care of it, but he wanted to do some research, just to make sure. He was just taking down a medical book on dermatology when a knock sounded on his door.

"Come on in," he called, and a bright face appeared around the door frame.

"Hi there," Pam Kelsey said with a smile. "Are you Dr. Chambers?"

"Guilty as charged."

"Good. Do you have a moment? I'd like to talk to you about you being my daughter's pediatrician."

The young woman had a vibrant look. Her brown hair was short and casual, her body athletic, her abdomen very pregnant. Paul liked the look of her from the start. He rose and escorted her into the office, pulling out a chair across the desk for her.

"Is this the young lady we're talking about?" he asked, eyeing Pam's rounded tummy as she lowered herself carefully into the chair.

Pam patted her baby proudly. "The very one. She's due to arrive on the scene in June."

Paul nodded approvingly. "You're looking great. You've got that having-a-baby bloom."

"Do I? Do I really? I sure hope so."

She seemed a little too eager to hear that and he looked at her curiously, wondering what was causing those shadows he noted in the depths of her eyes.

"I really am happy," she said, twisting the strap of her purse in her fingers. "And I really want this to be the happiest time of my life. The best time."

He smiled at her, but something in her voice sounded a bit too tense, and in his experience, that deserved attention. She was an older first-time mother, probably in her late thirties, and he knew older mothers tended to be a bit more anxious about things. That was likely all there was to it, but he made a mental note to keep her anxiety in mind in the future. He liked to have as much information as possible about his little patients' entire family.

"Dr. Darlington was the pediatrician for my husband when he was a child, and all his relatives going back to the Jurassic Age. But I hear you've taken over his practice."

Paul nodded. "That I have."

"And you come highly recommended."

He raised one eyebrow. "Do I?"

"Yes. I'm a good friend of Rosemary's"

Both eyebrows shot up. "And she recommended me?"

Pam nodded, holding back her smile. "Why does that surprise you?"

He hesitated, picking up a pencil and playing with it. "Rosemary and I have had our differences," he said evenly.

Pam smiled. "The house?"

"The house. And other things." He gazed at her for a moment, trying to judge just how good a friend of his housemate's she might be. "Rosemary and I get along great most of the time," he continued carefully. "But every now and then..." He shrugged and stared into space. "Well, things are not always calm."

Pam smiled again, watching the play of light on his handsome face. "You're not what I expected."

He looked at her sharply. It was obvious where she would have obtained her expectations. "What did Rosemary say about me?"

"I can't repeat that," she said with a laugh. "But I did expect someone a little more—" she narrowed her eyes and studied him "—a little more dangerous looking."

"Dangerous looking?" He frowned, perplexed, and threw down the pencil. "Why would Rosemary describe me that way?"

Pam hesitated. This was really none of her business. Rosemary hadn't been completely open about how she felt about this man. Pam had sensed a lot of conflicting emotions in her friend. But, darn it, Rosemary needed a man and this one seemed perfect, despite all the bad things she'd hinted at. Perhaps she just needed a push. Maybe Pam herself could help. Maybe. In the end, she just couldn't resist.

Leaning forward, she said softly, "Because she's scared to death of you. Can't you tell?"

Paul looked at her as though she were spouting Greek all of a sudden. "No she's not," he contradicted pointedly, wondering where this woman would get such notions.

But Pam nodded, eyes sparkling. "Yes, she is. She came to see me last night and all she could talk about was how annoyed she was with you."

He threw up his hands. "You see?" He sighed deeply and his blue eyes took on a look of sadness. "I know why.

Did she tell you about the shower and the towel?'' he asked distractedly, running a hand through his thick dark hair.

Pam's eyes widened. "Noooo, not exactly. She didn't go into any details.'' And she waited.

But he didn't notice her interest or take the hint. Sighing again, he shook his head. "I know it embarrassed her.'' His sad eyes met Pam's. "She's sort of sensitive about...well, the man-woman thing, isn't she?''

Pam blinked. "Rosemary?'' she asked in a squeaky voice.

"Yes.'' He frowned. "Every time I come near her, she jumps away as though...''

A look of satisfaction came over Pam's face and she nodded. "As though you're dangerous,'' she said helpfully.

He gave her a quizzical look. "I guess so,'' he admitted reluctantly. "But I'm not, you know. I'm a teddy bear. Why on earth would she think...'' His voice trailed off and he remembered how familiar she seemed so often. Was there something he was forgetting, something he just wasn't thinking of?

Pam watched him worry for a moment, then launched into questions she had prepared to ask him, questions concerning his philosophy on medical care and child rearing, his experience with children, his devotion to his chosen field. She liked his answers, and finally she smiled and held out her hand, taking his and shaking it. "I like you, Dr. Chambers. I hope you'll agree to be my baby's pediatrician.''

He came back to earth and gave her a warm smile. "I'd be happy to do exactly that. And let's hope this starts a long and happy relationship. We'll see if we can go as long as Dr. Darlington did with your in-laws.''

"Let's.''

She rose to go and he followed her toward the door. Suddenly a noise came from the hall, a crash, followed by a sharp sound that seemed to slice the air.

Paul didn't stop to think. He reacted with the instincts he'd developed in war zones around the globe. Grabbing Pam, he pressed her up against the wall and leaned against her, shielding her with his body.

Pam gasped, then cried out. "Doctor! What are you doing?"

He held the position for only a heartbeat longer, then drew back quickly, his face white, his breath coming fast. "I'm sorry," he said, drawing her back into the light from the window. "Are you all right? Did I hurt you? Oh God, what a jerk I am. I can't believe I did that to you."

"I—I'm fine." Shaken but unhurt, she gazed at him in confusion.

"I can't believe I did that. You're pregnant and I slammed you up against the wall. Are you sure you're okay?"

"Yes, I'm sure. You didn't 'slam' me at all. I'm not hurt. Don't think twice." She was staring up at him, searching his face. "What did you think that was?" By now it was quite clear that a cart of supplies had overturned in the hallway. Voices could be heard, the sounds of a cleanup underway. "Gunshots?" she asked.

"I . . ." He shook his head. "Oh, God, I'm sorry. I've spent too many years overseas. Old habits die hard. I'm not fit for civilized society any longer." He looked down at her belly. "Are you sure I didn't hurt you? Maybe we'd better get one of the gynecologists to check you out."

She grabbed his hand with both of hers and held it. "I'm fine. Really." She searched his face again. "But I'm worried about you."

His smile was crooked. "Don't be. I'm not the one who's pregnant."

"No. But you're the one who's slightly shell-shocked." She bit her lip, studying him. Something in the shadows of his eyes reminded her of someone else in town, someone else who'd seen too much ugliness in the world. "Where have you been? What have you been doing?"

Paul smiled at her. She was nice, sympathetic, understanding. He felt like an idiot for having shoved her up against the wall that way, but instead of attacking him, she was willing to understand why it had happened. He owed her some sort of explanation.

"Actually, I've spent a good part of the past fifteen years in some pretty ragged areas. Bosnia. Ethiopia. Chechnya. Lebanon. I was with Doctors without Boundaries for a number of years, and also an outfit called Doctors to the World."

Pam gaped at him. This was hardly the playboy Rosemary had described. "Do you mean to tell me you were out fixing children in war zones when you could have been handing out suckers to the pampered offspring of yuppies?"

He grinned. Yes, he was liking her more and more. "That's one way of putting it."

She shook her head, amazed and impressed. "Does Rosemary know about this?"

He thought for a moment. He and Rosemary always seemed to have too many things between them to talk about the past. That was too bad, really. Maybe it was time to get some things out in the open. Maybe then he would find out what sort of tie they had, where they'd known each other.

"No, I don't think I've said anything to her about it. Why?"

"No reason." She shook her head, but her eyes were hooded, as if she were deep in thought. "What a great guy you are," she said with a slight smile.

"Oh no." He shook his head. "Not at all. You mean for spending my life out chasing disasters?" He laughed shortly. "There was nothing altruistic about it. Actually, I couldn't have spent a lot of time in a plush job those first years after becoming a pediatrician. I had too much on my mind, too much to work through. I needed the rough side of things just to..." Suddenly he realized he was revealing his innermost thoughts to a complete stranger. A complete stranger who knew Rosemary. What was he, nuts?

He gave Pam a weak smile and backed away. "Anyway, that's all over," he said jovially. "I'm here in Tyler to have a normal life, to get married and have a houseful of kids." His smile got steadier. "If you happen to know a nice lady interested in doing those things, too, send her my way. I'm taking applications."

"Are you?" She laughed. "I'll keep that in mind." She turned to leave once again, then looked back. "You know, there is a local man you ought to meet—Cliff Forrester. He's had his problems overseas. Mostly Vietnam, I think. He's living with a few ghosts. You and he might have a lot in common."

Paul smiled politely, but filed that away in the Rolodex of his mind. "Maybe we'll get together some day," he agreed, just to make her feel good. But he already knew that wasn't going to happen. After all, there was nothing really wrong with him, nothing that needed to be fixed by therapeutic counseling with Vietnam vets, for Pete's sake.

He said goodbye to Pam and turned back to his desk.

Shell-shocked, she'd called him. He frowned, rubbing the back of his neck with his large hand. Was that what he was? He didn't think so. There was nothing wrong with him that a good meal couldn't cure. Giving the cab company a quick call, he turned his attention to putting his papers away, then grabbed his coat and threw it over his shoulder, took up his crutch, locked up and headed for home.

Home. That had a nice sound to it. He began to whistle as he hobbled out to meet Ernie.

CHAPTER NINE

ROSEMARY COULDN'T believe it—her walls were gone. She'd come home from the office, tired and ready for a soothing cup of tea, and when she'd walked into her apartment, she found her walls were gone.

It was a good thing she'd finished taking down all the pictures and knickknacks and things off the shelves and had packed them away. She had been prepared. Still, it was disconcerting to come home and find she no longer had a wall between her bedroom and the living room.

"Hi," Joe told her, walking in as she turned slowly, examining the destruction and silently mourning inside. "Hey, we're really making progress now. Sorry the apartment upstairs isn't ready for you yet. We've run into a snag. Gotta put in an elevator we weren't planning on at first. Plus the painters are late. Marv Griff is the guy we use. He's an artist and he's laid up right now. Got the chicken pox, if you can believe that. A grown man. But we'll get you in as soon as we can. Meanwhile, I'm going to have to tape up this corner with plastic so the elements don't come in. You see this? Daylight." He was pointing out an area of ceiling that was no longer there. "We'll get it sealed off for you before we leave tonight."

"Great," she said faintly. "That—that would be great." She looked around at the tiny area that was left to live in. "But how are two grown people going to exist in a place like this?"

Joe grinned at her. "It'll be cozy, that's for sure. Good thing you two are friends."

She glanced at him coolly, wondering what exactly he thought of Paul and of their cohabitation. Joe was invariably cheerful. It wasn't easy to read what was going on behind that smile.

"What makes you think we're friends?" she asked.

He shrugged, careless and unperturbed. He was going through his tool case, looking for something. "Would enemies get along like you two do?"

She gave him a mock glare. "A lot you know about it."

She took a swipe at the top of her dining-room table and came up with a fingerful of heavy dust. She gazed at it sadly and shrugged. "It just so happens that we fight all the time."

Joe grinned, looking up from his toolbox. "Yeah, right. I've seen some of those fights." He located the wrench he'd been looking for and waved it at her. "Hey, that Paul Chambers is one great guy, don't you think? I took him down to meet a bunch of people at Marge's Diner. Everybody really likes him. He's a regular guy, you know?" His smile was full of pride, as though he'd brought the man into their circle of friends himself. "Everyone who meets him wants to help him settle into the community. Lots of people are pulling for him."

Rosemary stared at Joe, feeling a little overwhelmed. "What are you talking about?"

"He's one of us. Everybody's planning to start taking their kids to him. The women are all working on matching him up with somebody nice—the usual when people in this town like someone."

She gripped the edge of the table. She knew things about Paul no one else did. For the first time she had a discomforting thought. Should she tell people? Should they know about his past? It wasn't as though he'd been convicted of a crime, of course. But he had been so—so...

What was the word she was looking for? If she couldn't even articulate it to herself, how was she going to explain it to others? And was his background as a womanizer, a playboy, a careless dilettante really relevant to his present ability to provide medical care?

"People shouldn't be too hasty," she warned, not ready to decide just yet. This was something she was going to have to think through.

"Why not?" Joe said, blithely unconcerned. "He deserves support."

She folded her arms and looked at him severely. "How do you know? He's just barely arrived and you're ready to hand him the keys to the city. How does anyone know this man?"

"All you have to do is look into those baby blues of his," Joe said with a grin. "You can tell a lot about a man by the look in his eyes." He nodded happily, putting the wrench into his tool belt. "He's some guy."

"He's some charmer all right," Rosemary conceded. "And those are the kind you should watch out for."

Joe looked at her, obviously puzzled by the way she was resisting this charm she admitted Paul had. "Hey, a gal like you could use a man like that."

That did it. Her outrage knew no bounds. "What? Joe Santori, I am not looking for a man right now. And if I were—"

But Joe was in attack mode. "Oh yeah? What's this I hear about you and Billy Joe Ocker? Hmm?"

"What?" she said weakly, stunned by this turn in their conversation and unprepared for a good defense.

He nodded as though he'd caught her out. "I heard you two were making eyes at each other. Is there anything to it?"

"You heard what?" Oh! That was small towns for you. You couldn't cough in the wrong place without somebody noticing and telling everyone they knew. "No," she said coldly. "There is nothing to it at all. We've barely met."

"Good." He looked at her wisely. "Then there's still time for me to warn you."

"Oh? Warn me about what?" Her face took on a rebellious look. Small-town people might know everything you'd done, but they could hardly dictate what you would do next.

Joe gazed at her for a moment, his face serious at last. "Stay away from him, Rosemary," he said quietly. "He's not your type at all. He's young. He's crazy."

She hesitated. She could see how sincere Joe was in his opinion and she respected him. Her impulse was to agree to follow his advice. But that streak of rebellion raised its head again. After all, what did Joe really know about this? He thought Paul was wonderful.

"I don't know, Joe," she said lightly, lifting her chin. "Maybe I need a little young and crazy in my life."

He scowled, shaking his head. "No, you need a good solid man like Paul Chambers." He waved a warning finger at her. "Believe me, I've been around and seen a lot of relationships come and go. Paul is the guy for you."

She glared at him. "Paul Chambers is the last thing I need in my life."

"You'll come around. I'll get to say 'I told you so' before too long. Want to bet?"

She sighed with exasperation. She didn't want to fight with him. He was a good friend and he was doing a good job on these renovations, annoying as they were. So she softened her statement with a smile and added, "Joe Santori, since you married Susannah, you've been trying to match up everybody in town."

"Why not?" He flashed his wide, warm smile. "I want everybody to be as happy as I am."

Her own smile faded and a tiny frown appeared between her brows. "Can't people be happy without pairing up with someone of the opposite sex?'' She really needed an answer to that question all of a sudden, and she turned, wanting to see his eyes when he told her the truth.

But Joe didn't notice; his mind was on getting back to work. He shrugged, turning to go outside and begin taping the gaping holes. ''Sure. It can happen,'' he said carelessly. ''It's just easier to achieve when you've got someone snuggling up against you in bed on a cold night.''

With a wave, he was out the door.

Rosemary stood where she was and considered his words. *Snuggling up against you in bed on a cold night.* The image rolled around in her head, then seemed to flame through her bloodstream like a shot of hot brandy. What would Paul be like to snuggle with? The way he had looked the day before swam into her mind's eye, all hard, rounded muscles and golden skin, and she gasped aloud and put a hand out to steady herself.

''Wow,'' she murmured, shocked at her own response. This was going too far. She would move out of her beloved house before she would let herself fall for a man like Paul Chambers.

ROSEMARY WENT OUT to do some errands and when she returned, Paul was home. He turned and gave her a welcoming smile, but she refused to smile back. She had to stiffen her defenses against his blue eyes and warmth. The heck with this friends business. She had to find a reason to dislike him intensely. That was the only way she was going to get through the next few weeks without succumbing. She could feel the weakness in herself as she looked at him, feel the warm tendrils of excitement start to spread when their eyes met. She couldn't let that happen. She had to be strong.

''There's not much left of the place, is there?'' he said, gesturing toward the missing walls. ''Sorry. This must be hard for you.''

She glared at him. How dare he offer her sympathy? "Not at all," she said crisply. "I know it's just temporary."

He nodded, examining her with new eyes, wondering about what Pam had said. Was Rosemary really scared of him? Was that why she seemed so jumpy around him?

He watched her push back the plastic and make her way into the kitchen, calling back to him about how they were going to have to subsist on take-out food. He called out an answer, something simple, but his mind was on the way she looked. She wore a blue sweater over her white pantsuit. Extra padding. He wanted to see more of her, to see her legs, to see the outline of her breasts, her hips. This was driving him crazy. What was she trying to hide?

He had helped her pack away the clothes from her closet that morning before she'd left for work, and he'd commented on the fact that there wasn't a single dress in her wardrobe.

"Sure there is," she'd said, searching through the garments. "Look at this."

She'd pulled out a straight, dark blue number with epaulets on the shoulders that would have done an admiral proud.

"And this." She pulled out another item, this one beige and dowdy, with a high neckline and a baggy waistline. "I used to wear this all the time," she said defiantly, looking into his eyes as though that really proved her point.

He'd eyed what she was wearing to work that day and said, "Okay, you win." But his fantasy life had been reinforced. He couldn't help but try to imagine what she would look like in feminine garb.

She came out of the kitchen, still discussing the cramped quarters they were going to have to put up with, and he watched the way her lips moved, the long, graceful line of her neck, the way wisps of hair had pulled free from the twist she'd put it in and were flying playfully around her pretty face.

There was no getting around the issue. He wanted her and the desire was burning in his gut. Turning so she couldn't see it in his eyes, he swore softly and took a deep breath.

"Hey," he said brightly, pushing away his thoughts. "I got a call this afternoon. Something has happened next door."

Rosemary turned to look at him. "At Mrs. Tibbs's? What happened?"

He shrugged. "I'm not sure. Let's go exploring."

With a twinkle in his eyes, he grabbed her hand and forced her to follow him. Marching conspiratorially across the porch to Mrs. Tibbs's place, he produced a key.

"What are you doing?" she asked him, aghast. "You can't just barge in on her, even if you are the landlord."

"Just watch me," he challenged, turning the key in the lock.

Rosemary gave a small cry of horror and he grinned. He wasn't sure why it was so much fun to shock women you liked, but there really was something exhilarating about it. He glanced at her, remembering what Pam had said. "Dangerous," was he? Hah.

The door opened, and the cry died in Rosemary's throat. The front room was empty. They craned their necks, peeking inside, then Paul looked down at her questioningly. She ignored him and slowly entered.

"Look at this," Paul said, leading the way into the dining area. "It's empty as a tomb in here."

His words echoed from the stark wall. Lace curtains hung limply at the windows and the hardwood floors creaked beneath their feet. There was no one here.

"Where do you suppose Mrs. Tibbs went?" Rosemary wondered, feeling just a little spooky.

Paul turned, as if searching the corners of the room for clues. "Left as mysteriously as she came," he whispered, leaning close and arching a brow.

Rosemary withheld the giggle that was trying to escape. "How do you know she came mysteriously?" she asked him, not moving away as quickly as she normally did.

"Just guessing." But he looked very sure of himself, leaning one hand against the wall and bending closer. "They say she got married over the weekend."

Rosemary turned and stared up at him. "So what the Coopers said was true! But I never saw anyone come or go—not once! Wow! Mrs. Tibbs *married . . ."*

Paul gazed at her wisely. "That's what they say."

It was a fascinating notion, but for a moment, she lost sight of it. She'd noticed something she'd never paid attention to before. As she stared up into his face, she saw for the first time that his eyes had stars in them—stars that burst out in silver rays, stars that looked like snowflakes. Why hadn't she ever noticed that before? She felt as though she could sink into them, take a plunge, like diving into cool blue water.

The moment lasted much too long and she had to shake herself to get back to the conversation. What had he been saying? Something about Mrs. Tibbs getting married? Yes, that was it.

"Who are 'they'?" she asked, forcing herself to stay with the program.

"The rental agency."

He'd noticed her hesitation, noticed that she'd been captivated by something she saw in him, and that a spark had been lit. He wanted to touch her. He wanted to kiss that beautiful mouth. If she kept watching him like that, he wasn't going to be able to ignore the way he was beginning to feel about her.

He turned his gaze away and frowned. "I called the rental agency to find out what was going on. It seems she left in the dead of night or something. She'd been taking things out, piece by piece, for weeks. And they said she was married."

Rosemary took one last look at the stars in his eyes, then shook her head wonderingly, ducking under his arm and wandering through the rooms again.

"You know, I have a hard time believing that. She never saw anyone. She never had any visitors." She threw out her arms. "Where did she meet this elusive lover?"

Paul gave her a superior look. "On the Internet, of course."

Rosemary gasped and her hand went to her mouth. "Do you think . . . ?"

"Sure. Why not?" He pointed out an electrical outlet that had been converted to be compatible with heavy computer use. "Everybody's doing it."

Mrs. Tibbs on the Internet. It boggled the mind. Rosemary looked up at Paul, her eyes laughing. "I guess I'm just behind the times."

"I guess maybe you are."

Their gazes met and held and something happened. The moment seemed to stretch out forever and hold them both, like a shaft of sunlight abruptly darting through a window, like a silver lining appearing under a dark cloud.

She knew she ought to look away, but she didn't want to. She seemed to be drifting closer to him, as though pulled by a force she couldn't deny. Those stars in his eyes were hypnotizing her, drawing her to him.

"Rosemary?" he said softly, and he reached out to caress her cheek with the back of his hand.

His touch seemed to break the spell, and she lurched back, eyes wide with horror. "Don't," she said quickly, reaching up to put her own hand where his had been, to erase the sense of him. "Don't do that."

"Rosemary, I—"

"No," she said firmly, staring at him. "We're not going to do anything like that."

His face was bewildered. "Like what? Rosemary, I'm not trying to do anything. I just wanted to—"

"No," she said, turning away and walking toward the window. "Let's just pretend that never happened."

He stared after her, confused and vaguely angry. There was no need to pretend. Nothing *had* happened. At least, nothing very noticeable.

He started to say something, then stopped and swore under his breath, turning away himself. Maybe Pam Kelsey was right. Maybe Rosemary was scared of him. But why, he couldn't imagine, and it made him angry to think about it. He had never done anything to hurt her, and he never would. So why the revulsion?

He strode through the apartment, shaking the thoughts away, throwing open a pair of closet doors and standing back to look inside. "I guess maybe the elevator should go in here," he suggested stiffly, trying to get their attention on something else, anything else.

It took a moment for her to catch her breath, but once she dared, she came quickly to where he was standing. She couldn't let him think that moment—whatever it was—had changed anything.

"Joe mentioned an elevator," she said, forcing her voice to stay calm. "What on earth do you need an elevator for? There are stairs."

Paul didn't turn to look at her as he normally would do. Instead, he stared at the nook in the room he was referring to, as though he couldn't look away. "It's compulsory in Tyler for a two-story medical building. It has to be done." He grimaced, realizing he wasn't acting natural.

Determinedly, he looked down at her and met her gaze. There. Nothing happened. It was okay. "Besides, eventually I'll probably turn your apartment into more offices," he said, the relief clear in his voice.

She wanted things back to normal just as much as he did, and she made the effort, flouncing past him just as she might have done before. "Over my dead body," she challenged in what she thought was a convincing tone.

He watched her go. "We just might have to arrange something along those lines," he mentioned cheerfully.

She turned back and looked at him, chin stuck out belligerently. "Am I a problem to you?" she asked, then winced, wondering why she couldn't learn to leave well enough alone.

"Yes, Rosemary. You are." Suddenly he smiled at her, shaking his head. "You know you are."

She went very still. "Maybe I should go," she said softly, her eyes luminous in the darkening room. "Maybe I should find another place to live."

Very slowly, he shook his head. "No," was all he said. But it was enough.

CHAPTER TEN

THE ODD THING was Paul really didn't want her to go, and he wasn't sure why.

He'd lived in mud huts and even caves with other people and had ended up forging a bond because of the hard times they had experienced together. He and Rosemary had been through a few material hardships together in the past week and a half that might have started that particular ball rolling. But he didn't think it was their intimate living situation that drew him to her, not really.

On the other hand, he might be reluctant to let her go because of the sensual awareness that quivered between them now. Could it be that, on some level of his convoluted ego, he still hoped to woo her into his bed?

No, he didn't really think it was that. He hadn't been obsessed with passion since he was in his early twenties. He'd like to think he'd matured a little since those days.

So what was it? Maybe it was really something simple. Maybe he just plain liked her. Could that really be it?

Of course, their quarters were shrinking all the time. Now the walls were down between them and at night they could hear each other breathe. Paul lay awake for an hour that first night, listening to her and thinking about how companionable it was to be this close. And then he began to wonder what she thought of it, and the rosy glow dimmed a bit.

Rosemary had suggested that one or even both of them should move to Mrs. Tibbs's place, now that it was vacant. Paul had quickly explained that the interior would be gutted the very next day and they were better off staying where they were.

He knew she wished this entire situation would go away, that she could be back in her precious apartment again, just as it had been before he entered her life. But that wasn't going to happen. Still, he didn't want her to be any more uncomfortable than she had to be.

The one thing he worried about with the walls down were the nightmares. He didn't want to cry out in the night and wake her. The dreams had been fading lately. He'd been hopeful that they would disappear once he got back into some semblance of normal life, and it seemed to be working. But remnants still lingered.

He'd never been one to have nightmares in the past. He'd never even noticed his dreams much. It had only been in the past year in Bosnia, and then in Chechnya, that he'd begun to feel himself falling down into a long black pit as he fell asleep at night. And after that night with the guns firing overhead, that night he'd been carrying the baby from the village, trying to get her to safety...

Ah hell, he didn't want to think about that. He'd stayed away from civilization for a little too long, that was all. He'd allowed himself to overdo it.

"Living like a refugee," he murmured, thinking back. And living among refugees. Too many, for too long.

BUT AT BREAKFAST the next morning, with the sun peeking in through the ferns in the kitchen window, that overseas world seemed very far away. Spring was a radiant force, showering gold over everything and filling Paul with a sense of well-being.

Rosemary poured out cereal for them both, since the stove wasn't working at the moment. She stood in the kitchen with that beautiful morning light coming in all around her, and he watched her in wonder. There was a regal quality about the woman that he'd never seen in anyone else. In another time, another life, she would have been royalty.

Or a tribal leader in some forest. He grinned to himself, thinking about it.

She caught the grin but didn't bother asking what it was all about. "I'm going to pick up a hamburger for myself on the way home for dinner tonight," she told Paul, sinking into her chair and covering her yawn with her hand. Some mornings it was just so hard to wake up. "Shall I pick one up for you, too?"

He hesitated, looking at her sideways, dreams of romping in the forest forgotten. "I can't. I..." He cleared his throat. "I've got a date."

"A date?" The concept was jarring, but she knew it shouldn't be. After all, this was what he'd been aiming for since he'd arrived. She turned slowly and looked at him, and then, despite all her good intentions, said, "What happened? Did Sally drop by?"

He gave her a withering look and took another spoonful of cereal before bothering to answer her. "No. This date is not with Nurse Sally Rogetti."

"Oh." She pushed cereal around in her bowl without taking a bite at all. "Then what is the name of your... friend?" she asked carefully. "Do I know her?"

"Her name." He frowned. What had Ernie said? "Let's see. I think it's something like Nan Buttercup."

That stopped her cold. "Nan Buttercup?" she asked, incredulous.

He gave her a glare that dared her to make fun of the name. "That's it. She's someone Ernie knows."

Rosemary choked back a giggle and pretended great calm. "I'm afraid I don't know her."

That was a relief as far as he was concerned. "There's no reason you should, is there?"

"No. You're quite right there." Her smile was sunny as the morning.

He smiled back, pleased with that. For some reason, he didn't want his date to be someone Rosemary knew. Actually, he didn't want her to be someone anyone knew. He was going out with the woman because Ernie had set it up, and Ernie had been so good to him, making himself and his cab available at a moment's notice whenever Paul needed a ride anywhere, that he felt he owed him this, at least.

Rosemary noted Paul's reluctance to talk about the event, and she didn't want him to feel constrained. After all, they had made it very clear that there was nothing between the two of them. There couldn't ever be. So she should be supportive. She should be happy for him. She pushed her dish away, still smiling, trying hard to be the friend she'd sworn she would try to be. "I'm sure you will have a very good time," she said with dignity. "She's probably a wonderful woman."

He stared at her for a moment, impressed with the way she was acting. Then, throwing caution to the winds, he opted for total honesty over one-upmanship. "I don't know," he said, setting down his napkin. "To tell you the truth, I don't really have a very good feeling about this." He frowned and sighed. "Ernie says she's an animal trainer." He glanced at Rosemary to see her reaction.

She held herself rigid, refusing to give in to the snort of laughter that threatened. Nan Buttercup, the animal trainer. "Oh?" she said evenly. "Dog obedience school?"

He scowled and glanced at her, then away. "No, Ernie says she trains snakes and mongooses for fairs and TV appearances."

The laughter wouldn't be restrained this time and Rosemary giggled uncontrollably. "Okay, this is a joke, isn't it?" she finally demanded, looking at him for confirmation, ready to laugh along with him when it came.

But he wasn't even smiling. "No, I swear it's on the up-and-up. I can only tell you what Ernie has told me."

"Oh." She bit back her grin. "So you go for the exotic type, is that what you're saying?" Her eyes were shimmering with amusement. "This doesn't really jibe with the picture of the perfect little homemaker you were giving me the other night."

He groaned inside, knowing she was right, but he wasn't about to let her see that. "Well, you never know," he said with forced good cheer, pouring himself another glass of orange juice. "Tastes change."

"Overnight?"

He shrugged. "I'm adaptable."

She rose, laughing, and carried her bowl to the sink, then headed out to the car, still chuckling over his crazy situation.

But as she drove toward work, the laughter died and the smile faded. So Paul had a date. His search for the perfect wife was about to begin in earnest. And what was she going to do—sit there at home and wonder what he was up to? Wait to hear his crutch on the stairs and then dive into bed and pretend she was sleeping?

Impossible. She had to make her own plans. As soon as she got in to work, she was going to call Kayla and see if she'd like to take in a movie. Rosemary had to get out of the house. If she didn't, she had a sinking feeling she would spend the evening mooning over Paul and wondering just what one did on a date with an animal trainer.

KAYLA WAS FREE and the two of them went to see a new comedy that had garnered good reviews. It turned out to be even better than they'd hoped and they laughed so hard they both felt the need for refreshment when it was over. Where else would they go but Marge's?

It was only a little after nine and the place was full of people, most of them young and very noisy. The two friends found an empty booth and slid in, then craned their necks to see what all the commotion was about.

Teenagers in blue-and-gold athletic parkas seemed to be everywhere. Rosemary was frowning, trying to pick out someone she recognized, when Patrick Kelsey disengaged himself from the mob and came toward her with a grin, carrying a root beer float in his hand. "Hey, Rosemary! Good to see you." He nodded to redheaded Kayla as well, and she smiled in greeting. A tall, handsome man, Patrick had dark blue eyes, black curly hair and a smile that lit up a room.

"Listen, help us celebrate," he said, raising his glass as though toasting. "We just came back from upstate. The swim team won its first meet of the season. We beat Baraboo, and had two girls qualify for state championships."

Rosemary gave him a welcoming smile. He was one of her favorite people, and not only because he was married to one of her best friends. "That's wonderful. I didn't even know the high school had a swim team."

"Oh yeah."

He ducked as a paper airplane came gliding toward his head and laughed at the grinning kid who'd launched it.

"We just reactivated it, and already we're rolling toward a championship season. Of course, we have a lot of kids who've been swimming on local club teams for years. Hayley has brought it all together. If it hadn't been for her, this couldn't have happened."

Hayley, was it? Ah, yes. The old girlfriend.

"Oh." Rosemary glanced around the room to see if she could spot the wonderful Hayley. "Well, that's great."

"It really is." His face changed as he realized she might not remember his old flame. "Say, do you know Hayley Ingalls? She's related to the Tyler Ingallses—Judson's great-nice, I think—but didn't grow up here."

He pointed her out and she turned and waved. Short and small boned, she looked dainty but strong, like a miniature superwoman. Her face was pretty, but thin, and her flaxen hair hung like a long, straight slash of silk. Patrick smiled at her as though he'd produced her himself out of thin air and was darn glad he'd done it.

"This will bring new pride to the school," he said. "The football team won't be the only winners around here. And the town can really use some good news. Everyone's still so down because of the fire at the F and M and all the dislocation that's caused. This should help lift spirits."

Rosemary frowned, trying to analyze his tone of voice and the way he was looking at the woman. "So you go to the meets?" she said, forcing a light, casual tone. "I never knew you were that much into swimming."

"Oh, sure." He stepped back while Marge, helping out with the crowd tonight, took their order.

"Apple pie à la mode, and coffee," Kayla said.

"Make mine a hot fudge sundae with all the trimmings," Rosemary chimed in. "We've got to celebrate the swim-team victory and we don't want to be chintzy about it."

Kayla laughed and so did Patrick, leaning forward again once Marge had gone to fill in their order. "It's really great to have the swim team up and running this way. I was on a Y team when I was a kid. And now that I'm athletic director, I like to show up at all the athletic events."

That was in answer to Rosemary's question about his traveling with the team, and she noted that he'd wanted to explain. Why was that? she wondered. Wasn't that usually the behavior of a guilty man? She looked back at Hayley suspiciously, wondering.

"I really should support all the teams," he was saying. "And these kids are great. We're having a wonderful time."

She nodded. That was quite obvious. His eyes were shining and his face was flushed with victory. Winning was

"Damn," he muttered, leaning down to begin putting things back. Photographs, old check stubs, coupons and letters made a scattered mess at his feet and he went down on one knee, picking things up as quickly as he could and stuffing them into the drawer.

A picture of Rosemary as a little girl caught his attention, and he paused, smiling at the cute child she'd been. Another picture fell out from behind it and he stopped, staring. It was a wedding picture. He recognized Rosemary, but he also recognized the man standing next to her wearing a slightly bewildered grin. For a moment he couldn't place the name, but he was sure he'd known him years ago. Had it been in medical school?

No, at the Chicago hospital in the last year of his residency. Greg Simmons, that was it. Good old Greg Simmons.

But why was he standing next to Rosemary in a tuxedo? And why was she wearing a wedding dress? A picture was beginning to emerge from the gloom of his memory. Yes. The party at his apartment that last night. The young woman who had come looking for her husband. In his mind's eye he saw her clearly. Rosemary. It had been her.

The memory was vague but persistent. He remembered a lot about that night, because it had been a turning point for him. The next day he'd made the decision that had changed his life.

The party had been his farewell to the playboy life he'd led for too long. He'd been sick of it, sick of himself, sick of his self-indulgence. It had been going on for years and he knew it had to stop, that he had to do something to completely turn his life around. He'd applied to Doctors without Boundaries, giving up a position he'd been offered at a prestigious research hospital to go overseas and work with refugees. It had been the best decision he'd ever made. How different his life might have been if he'd stayed, if he'd gone on searching for kicks the way a junkie went after a fix. Thank God he'd had the strength to pull out of that life.

But Rosemary... He remembered her now. She'd come looking for her husband in the middle of the night. Steering her away from finding Greg with another woman, he'd sent her home, then sent Greg packing as well.

Greg had returned, saying his wife had left him, but at the time Paul hadn't been in the mood to listen to his tale of woe.

To think that that woman had been Rosemary was mind-boggling. Why hadn't she said something? Maybe she didn't realize...but of course she did. That was why she'd acted the way she had from the beginning, why she still didn't trust him. It was clear to him now. And who could blame her?

He wished she were home, wished he could explain everything to her right away. But what could he say? *Hey, sorry I was such a jerk in those days. But look at me. I'm a nice guy now.* The woman who'd come looking for Greg that night wouldn't buy any excuses. And she shouldn't.

As he finished restoring the desk drawer to its original condition, he quickly thought of things he would say, phrases he would use. But when he heard the car door slam and knew she was on her way in, he knew he wasn't going to say anything. Not yet.

He opened the door for her and she came in, looking remarkably happy and pink-cheeked, as though something good had happened out there in the world and she was gratified.

"Hi there," she said, greeting him with a smile. "You're already home."

He nodded, looking into her eyes for any signs of emotions lingering from the past. "I'm already home," he echoed. "It was a quick date."

"Oh?" She hung up her light coat and turned to look at him. "Well, was this the one?"

He knew what she was talking about and he didn't bother to pretend he didn't. "You can't really tell after one date, you know." He followed her into the kitchen, pushing aside the plastic. "Besides, it wasn't 'this,' it was 'these.'" He sighed, leaning against the kitchen counter, watching as she began to fill the teakettle with water for boiling. "There were two of them."

She blinked, not quite getting it. "Two of what?"

He glanced at her and then away again. "There were two women on this date," he said, muttering.

She frowned, not sure she'd heard him correctly. "You mean you doubled with someone else?" she asked, craning her neck, trying to see his face, which he had deliberately turned away from her.

"No." Annoyed with himself for waffling, he straightened and faced her. "I mean Nan and Jan both came. With me. The three of us."

She stared at him for a moment, then smiled, eyes dancing. "Twins," she guessed with amazing accuracy.

He nodded morosely. "Twins. They're here for the convention."

She laughed softly. "No wonder I'd never heard of Nan Buttercup before." She tried to keep a straight face. "Twins. But I thought your type liked that sort of thing."

His gaze sharpened as he looked at her. "My type?" he said sharply. "Just exactly what is that?"

She hesitated, not sure how to respond once she'd heard his bitter tone.

He waited, watching her, and a thousand things ran through his mind like a flickering film. He couldn't hold back: he had to say something. Before she could answer his question, he swore softly and came toward her. Erasing the distance between them with one stride, he took her hands in his and gazed down into her upturned face.

"Rosemary, I know who you are," he said urgently, his blue eyes alight with intensity. "I know why you hate me.

I remember Greg. I remember what happened that night."
He shook his head, his expression clearly remorseful. "If
I had anything to do with destroying your mar-
riage . . . how can I make you believe how sorry I am?"

She turned to stone. So now he knew. She gazed at him,
searched his face, saw the turmoil there and felt strangely
unmoved by it. Now he knew. Was it going to make a difference?

He was still talking, saying things, explaining, apologizing, but she wasn't listening. It had been so long ago. It
had changed her life, and she'd blamed him for a long
time. And now that he knew, knew how she felt, knew
what he owed her, she wasn't sure how she was going to
handle it. Slowly, she pulled her hands away from his and
turned, ducking under the plastic.

"Rosemary, don't go," he said, but she kept going.
"Hey, don't you want your tea?"

She didn't answer. She went straight to her room and got
ready for bed, and though there were no real walls between them any longer, there might as well have been. She
slid in between the covers and closed her eyes to blot it all
out. She didn't want to think. She was determined she was
going to fall asleep, and within minutes, she did.

But she heard his nightmare that night. She was asleep,
drifting, and suddenly a sound shot through her like a
current and her eyes were wide open and she was holding
her breath, listening for what had awakened her. A stran-
gled cry sent her heartbeat rocketing, and then she realized it was Paul.

"The baby," he was muttering, tossing in his sleep.
"The baby . . . get the baby."

She lay listening, but he quieted, falling deeper into sleep
and leaving the nightmare behind.

The baby. What baby? She had no idea, but something
in the way he'd said it made her feel cold, and it was a long
time before she fell back to sleep herself.

CHAPTER ELEVEN

SOMEONE RANG THE BELL before either of them was fully awake the next morning, but Paul went to answer it while Rosemary headed for the bathroom. When she emerged, she found that he had let in a man with two toddlers, and she sighed. Dr. Chambers was at it again.

But the little ones made her smile. Barely walking, they careened into things like miniature bumper cars, and when they finally managed to crash into each other, each fell back on her well-padded bottom with a thump and began to cry.

"What's the problem?" Rosemary asked Paul, after giving the visitor a quick smile of welcome.

Paul looked grim. "This is a tough one," he said solemnly. "I'm not sure we're equipped to handle it." He gave her a sideways glance. "Mr. Hamilton here can't tell his daughters apart."

"You see, we came for the convention," the pale, worried man explained, leaning forward and looking at her earnestly. "Linda—that's my wife—she's about due to have another set of twins any day, so she couldn't come. So I came on ahead. She sent me. She—she trusted me." He seemed on the verge of tears.

"They really are identical, aren't they?" Rosemary mused, looking at them and searching for some little difference. There was none that she could see. Both were dressed in pastel jumpers, their blond curls light and bouncing. With their blue eyes wide, their little mouths forming perfect O's, they were exactly alike.

"How do you usually tell them apart?" she asked, more interested than alarmed.

"Their—their mother takes care of that," the man said plaintively. "She usually puts bibs on them that say their names, Chrissy and Carla. But they ripped those off during the night as we were driving here."

"Just to be sure, his wife put fingernail polish on one set of fingers," Paul added. "Chrissy was the one who got the polish. But Chrissy chewed it off during the trip."

"Why, you little devils." Rosemary laughed as she watched them both climb up on the couch and try to get under Paul's bedding, which he hadn't tucked away yet. "They are cute, aren't they?"

As though to prove the point, they jumped down from the couch in tandem and began trying on Paul's shoes.

Rosemary grinned. "Have you tried calling out their names and seeing who looks up?"

"Of course." Their father sounded at his wit's end. "They both answer to both names."

Hmm. Rosemary turned to look at the men and found them both staring at her. Blinking, she looked into Paul's eyes, then into Mr. Hamilton's. Both had a questioning look.

"What is it?" she asked quickly. "What have I done?"

"You're a woman," said Mr. Hamilton, as though that were enough.

"He thinks you might be able to think of a way to figure out which is which," Paul explained.

"Me?" She was amazed at the ideas men came up with. "What do I know about babies, much less twins?"

"You have to think of something," Paul told her, looking tragic. "He hasn't got a clue."

She looked at the two of them and began to laugh. "What is this? Are you counting on some crazy woman's intuition or something? I haven't got a clue, either."

"But you have to think of something," Mr. Hamilton wailed. "If Linda finds out . . ."

"If we had time, we could get their charts from their hometown and then I could tell," Paul interjected. "But right now, there's nothing to do but . . ." He shrugged.

"Nothing to do but ask a woman, is that it?" she murmured, but she was thinking and it wasn't long before she had an idea. "Okay, let's try this."

Going into the kitchen, she got out a box of cookies and took two. Coming back into the room, she made sure the little girls saw them, then put one on the coffee table, saying, "This one is for Chrissy," and the other on the footstool, saying, "And this one is for Carla."

The girls looked at the cookies, looked at each other and raced for the one on the coffee table, pushing and jostling.

"Well, that didn't work," Rosemary said, laughing softly as they raced for the second cookie, crumbs flying. "Let's try this."

She went down on her knees beside them. "Okay, girls, let's play a game," she said softly. "I want Chrissy to kiss Carla on the cheek. Okay? Ready, set, go. Chrissy, you kiss Carla."

Two sets of blue eyes stared at her, then, very slowly, two little heads began to shake back and forth. Two lower lips came out and their eyes began to cloud up.

"Okay, okay," Rosemary said quickly. "No kissing. We'll have to try something else." Turning to Paul, she made a face. "If I could only think what."

Paul shook his own head. "Is one of them left-handed?" he asked.

Mr. Hamilton hesitated. "Not that I know of," he said. "Now Linda, she would know."

Paul's head came up. "Why don't we call her?"

"No." Mr. Hamilton turned even paler. "She mustn't know about this. I don't want to worry her. She trusted me."

"Well, short of contacting your wife or your own pediatrician..."

"Who would tell my wife immediately. She confides in him completely."

"So that's out." Paul was growing impatient with the situation. "I guess you'll just have to spend the weekend calling them 'hey you.'"

"Wait." Rosemary had another idea. Rather pleased with herself, she hurried into the bathroom and took a bottle of nail polish from the cabinet.

"Who's ready for nail polish?" she asked when she came back, sitting on the couch with the open bottle in one hand and the little brush in the other.

The two little girls stared at her. Then one began to inch her way forward.

"See the pretty polish?" Rosemary said. "Who's ready?"

The little girl looked at her, then plopped her hand down flat on the coffee table, as though she had done this before. Her twin was watching intently, but kept a safe distance.

"Chrissy gets the nail polish," Rosemary said firmly, and began painting the little girl's nails.

"Chrissy?" Mr. Hamilton said hopefully.

The toddler lifted her pretty face and gave her daddy a gap-toothed grin.

"It is you! Oh, miss, how can I thank you? It would have been hell admitting to my wife that I'd mixed them up."

"I only hope you're right," Paul murmured as they waved goodbye to the little family group.

"If I'm not, the mother will figure it out soon enough," Rosemary promised, and then she stopped herself in wonder. How did she know that? Where had all this female intuition about children appeared from all of a sudden? And come to think of it, she still felt a glow from the visit. The little girls had been so adorable. What would it be like to have one of her own?

No, that thought didn't belong in her mental repertoire. It had to go. She was moving in on forty, and as far as she was concerned the window of opportunity for childbearing had closed for her. Checking the clock, she saw that she was running late and began to bustle about, preparing for work.

The visit from the twins had helped launch the day without the tension that might have been present after the night before, but things still weren't normal between Paul and her. There was a new barrier, a new sense of wariness, and Rosemary wasn't sure why. After all, everything was out in the open now. There was nothing to hide. So why the reluctance to meet his gaze, why the urgent wish to get out of the house and go to work?

Then she remembered something. It was her birthday.

Another year older, as if she hadn't already felt blue enough. At least no one knew about it. And she certainly wasn't going to tell anyone.

"Happy birthday to me," she sang under her breath as she drove to the hospital. "Happy birthday to me. Happy birthday, dear Rosemary..."

Her morning was full. She saw five patients, went down to the gym to help another with some changes in his exercises, then headed back to her office to catch up on paperwork. Time was moving quickly and that was the way she liked it. Soon it would be lunch hour and she would meet Kayla in the cafeteria for a nice green salad.

A technician knocked, poked her head in and said in a harried voice, "Ms. Dusold? They're asking for you in the medical library. There's some problem and Mrs. Reynolds said to get you, quick.''

''In the library?'' What kind of emergency could be happening there? She didn't have any idea, but the technician had already rushed off, so she thought she'd better go take a look. She walked quickly down the hall, her shoes marking a smart rhythm on the tiled floor, and turned into the library.

It hit her like a wave in the ocean—the bright lights, the balloons, the faces, the sudden cries of ''Surprise!''—leaving her breathless.

''Surprise parties are really dangerous, you know,'' she grumbled to Pam later on. ''You could give a person a heart attack. It's such a shock to the system.''

''Lucky we did it in a hospital, then,'' Pam said serenely. ''Professional help at a second's notice.''

To Rosemary most of the party was a blur. There were so many people. Pam had assembled half of Tyler, it seemed. Rosemary had to chat with everyone, until she couldn't remember whom she'd spoken to and whom she still needed to greet.

She did get a chance to take Pam aside for a moment. She wanted to warn her, to tell her she'd seen Hayley and thought she was something to worry about, after all. But Pam brushed the subject aside, as though she were afraid to open up a can of worms, and they ended up talking about Paul Chambers instead.

''Wow, what a doll he is,'' Pam said with feeling. ''I have got to admit, I really like him.''

Rosemary groaned. ''Oh, Pam, not you, too.''

Pam shrugged and shook her head as though she really didn't see the problem. ''He's so charming.''

''Of course he's charming,'' said Rosemary with a frown. ''Playboys are always charming. That's how they become playboys.''

Pam laughed and treated her worries as a joke, and Rosemary began to wonder if maybe she was seeing things where nothing existed. Everyone seemed to like Paul so much. Maybe she was the one with blinders on.

She sat opening presents and smiling and saying nice things to people for almost an hour. Someone put a huge cake in front of her and she blew out the candles as everyone sang "Happy Birthday" to her. Later she ate a piece, but didn't taste a thing.

And then Paul was there, looking very handsome in a suit, with his hair slicked down. Rosemary suddenly got nervous, staring into his blue eyes for a moment, then looking quickly away and pretending to listen while Kayla went on and on about something.

Paul didn't see it as nervousness. To him, it looked like dismissal, and he realized how very badly he wanted to see her smile at him again.

"Hello there," said a voice very near his right elbow. "I'm glad you could make it."

He turned and gave Pam a grin, transferring the box he held from one hand to the other. "Wouldn't have missed it. Thanks for calling and telling me about it. If you hadn't, I wouldn't have known it was her birthday."

Pam nodded wisely. "No one would have known. Rosemary is relentlessly private. As one of her friends, I feel it is my duty to force happiness on her."

Paul glanced at Rosemary's face and frowned. Was that happiness he was seeing? "But how can you define happiness for someone else?" he asked softly, almost speaking to himself.

"You can't," Pam admitted, looking at her as well. "You can only do what you think is right for those you love and hope for the best." She glanced up at Paul's handsome face and stifled a smile. "Anyway, I'm glad you came, because I have something I want to discuss with you. A sort of business proposition."

"Oh?" Paul smiled down at her. "You just can't sit still, can you?"

"No, I can't. I did quit coaching and I'm trying to rest as much as possible, but I'm not used to this inactivity. I've got to be in the mix, you know? Otherwise I'll go nuts."

"So you've decided to open a gym for pregnant ladies to work out in. Is that it?"

"No." She chuckled. "Though that's not a bad idea. I'll file that one away for the future. Actually, I wanted to give you the opportunity to be one of the first to test out a new product coming on the market."

He gazed at her warily, almost backing away. "And what might that be?"

"Videotapes. My sister-in-law, Glenna, has produced a line of videotapes of children playing. They would be perfect for you."

"For me?" He gazed at her blankly. "I've seen children playing. In fact, I consider myself an expert at playing. I don't think I need tapes to help me bone up on the subject."

She shook her head, her eyes bright. "That's not it at all. You see, these tapes have a specific purpose. Many studies have shown that children can learn certain things best, especially social activities, by watching other children perform them. Glenna has taped hours of kids playing and has edited them into categories, such as getting ready for school, visiting at someone's house, going to the park. Children are fascinated by them. And I think the perfect place to test some of them out would be in a pediatrician's waiting room."

Paul grinned. "In other words, my waiting room."

"Right. Can't you see the possibilities? Wouldn't it be nice to have something going in your waiting room that captured the attention of the children, keeping them occupied until their turn in the examining room comes up? And they would be learning something at the same time."

"But I don't have much of a waiting room yet. It's under construction."

"You do have your office in the medical building. Why not try them out there? If you find them intrusive instead of helpful, that would be a good thing for Glenna to know." Pam smiled at him persuasively. "Consider it market research. All you'll need is a television monitor and a VCR."

Paul considered, head to one side. "You know, these tapes sound intriguing," he admitted. "Why not? I'll call Supply and have them bring up the equipment this afternoon."

"Good. And I'll have Glenna drop some of her tapes by for you. She can explain what it's all about and what order you should play them in and all of that." Relief showed in her smile. "She's a wonderful woman and you'll like her." She squeezed his arm. "Thank you, Paul. You're a brick."

"Am I?" He glanced at Rosemary and shifted the box he held from one hand to the other again. She was opening presents and he was going to have to hand over his in a few minutes. For some strange reason he was dreading the moment.

"Yes, you are," Pam insisted, studying his face and noticing the shadows in the depths of his eyes. "I still want to get you together with Cliff Forrester," she said. "I think you two have a lot in common."

Paul looked down at her, his smile completely gone now. "I don't need a fellow veteran of the Third World scene to hold my hand," he said, a touch too sharply. "Thanks just the same, Pam, but I can handle my ghosts on my own."

"Sure you can," she said, shaking her head. "That's why you're so sanguine about the past, isn't it?"

He opened his mouth to say something defensive, but she'd already turned away, exclaiming over the last present Rosemary had opened, a set of garnet earrings in a black velvet case.

Paul swallowed hard. He was next. She looked up at him and met his eyes again as he handed her the box, and she gave him the thinnest of smiles. She wished he hadn't come, and she didn't want to open his gift. Something told her this present would tell her too much about what he thought about her, and she wasn't sure she wanted to know.

"I'm not supposed to say happy birthday," he told her, his eyes still questioning. "So how about good luck?"

"Thank you," she said, meeting his gaze only briefly. "I . . . it's really nice of everyone . . ."

"Aren't you going to open it?" he asked.

She nodded and slowly did so. She pulled off the gold ribbon, removed the top from the box and unfolded the violet tissue paper, to reveal a beautiful dress. She stared down at it, not pulling it out of the box so that she could see it all, but staring at the blue flowers, the white lace. She could tell without looking more closely that she'd never worn a dress like this in her life.

"Thank you," she said stiffly, putting the top back on the box and setting it aside. "That was very nice of you."

He watched as she turned to someone else and smiled and began to chat. She hadn't liked it. He'd known it would be a gamble, but he'd had to do it. And now he'd insulted her.

"Damn, damn, damn," he muttered to himself viciously as he left the room. For a man who'd once been known to have a way with the ladies, he seemed to make all the wrong moves these days.

PAUL WANTED to take Rosemary out to dinner later, but she didn't want to go, so he brought home take-out food from the Mandarin Inn and they ate at the kitchen table.

They made desultory conversation for as long as they could stand it and then they were quiet. Finally, Paul turned to Rosemary. "I've said I was sorry in every way I know how. What can I do to make things okay between us? Tell me. I'll do it."

She shook her head slowly. "You don't need to do anything," she said.

He stared at her and sighed. "Yes, I do. Bad behavior needs atonement. I behaved very badly when I was in my late teens and early twenties. I was trying to blot out unhappiness with chasing kicks, and that never works. When I finally woke up, I tried to do things to make it right again."

She nodded, impressed by the sincerity in his words and tone. "Pam told me about your work overseas. Why didn't you ever mention it?"

That was a good question, one he wasn't sure he knew the answer to. "There never seemed to be a need to tell you. I didn't realize at the time that there was a very big need. That you had to know..." He groped for words. "That I needed you to know that I'd reformed. I know it was too late to do you any good, but still..."

"I'm getting to know you, Paul." She managed a smile. "How could I live with you all this time and not see that you've changed?"

And suddenly she knew that was true. There was no use hiding behind the past. He was nothing like the playboy she had known in Chicago. But for some reason, she couldn't be happy about that just yet.

He searched her eyes, but it wasn't there. What he was looking for he wasn't sure, but he knew it wasn't there. "But you still can't stand me," he said flatly.

"That's not true. I like you very much."

She meant it, he thought bleakly as he searched her face, her eyes. She did like him. So what was he looking for? What more did he need? And why did he feel so empty?

He insisted she let him clean up after their meal, and then he went out to check the construction progress in Mrs. Tibbs's place. When he came back, he was scowling. "There's a young hood out here, asking for you," he said curtly.

Rosemary looked up from where she sat on the couch, reading a magazine, her face full of surprise. "Billy Joe?" she asked, realizing immediately who it must be.

"Oh, you know him?" His voice had an edge of irony. "I thought maybe he'd been hired by the mob to kidnap you."

She held her grin down to a small quirk of the lips and rose, smoothing her shirt, ready to go out and see him. "Billy Joe is...a friend." But her eyes were sparkling. This was a nice birthday present—a visit from a younger man who was attracted to her.

"A boyfriend?" Paul said with a dark look. "Or a lover?"

She shot him a scathing look as she walked past him to the door. "I'm a little old for boyfriends."

Then she was gone and it was too late to call her back.

It was too late for a lot of things. Going to the kitchen, he poured himself a cup of decaf and slouched in a seat at the kitchen table. Funny how he'd pretty much told himself all these years that his work overseas was making up for how he'd acted as a young man. He'd been rather proud of himself when he'd taken the time to think about it. And now he had to face the fact that what he'd got out of it was nightmares and not much forgiveness from the one woman who mattered.

But that wasn't fair. He'd spent a lot of years healing— and trying to heal—people who had nothing and were looking forward to a life with even less. He'd helped more people who desperately needed help than most pediatricians could ever dream of. That was its own reward. And if it had left him with a few emotional problems in the depths of his soul—well, that was a small price to pay. In many ways, he had redeemed himself. And that was a good thing.

And then there was Rosemary.

He could hear them outside, hear her laughter. Billy Joe seemed to be quite a comedian.

"Now what would a classy woman like Rosemary see in a car jockey like that?" he muttered aloud, pouring himself another cup.

And the answer was clear. "Maybe a handsome face, a muscular body, youth, excitement . . . a hot car."

"I've got a pretty nice car," he reminded himself bleakly. "Only it's in the garage at the hospital, where it will stay until this damn foot heals."

He heard the loud roar of a high-performance engine, and then Rosemary was back, her cheeks bright, her eyes even brighter.

"Billy Joe had to get back," she said breezily, reaching for the hot water to make herself some tea.

"Do they have a lockup time on his cage?" Paul asked blithely.

She shot him an amused, superior glance. "He's working on his car. But I'm going out with him on Saturday."

"Great. Is there a sock hop somewhere? Or is the gang all meeting at the hamburger stand?"

She stared at him, amazed and gratified by his tone. This really seemed to bother him, didn't it? Why would he feel threatened by Billy Joe? No, it couldn't be that. More likely he was just in a grouchy mood and ready to make sport of anything that came in his path.

"No, actually, we're going to the Iron Mustache, that new country-and-western club out on the highway near Belton."

He tried to bite his tongue, tried to keep his mouth shut, but he just couldn't. Scowling at her darkly, he said, "Rosemary, what are you going out with that jerk for?"

Her return smile was gloriously sunny. "I thought you were the one who wanted me to get out and live a little more. Find new horizons. Dream dreams."

He felt like growling. "I wanted you to aim for something higher than the back seat of a Chevy," he muttered.

"Paul!" She gave him a look of pure outrage, but inside she was chortling. *My my, does he sound jealous, though?* He couldn't actually be jealous. What would be the point? In order to be jealous he would have to feel he had some stake in... well, in something between the two of them. And that was nuts. He couldn't really be jealous. But she couldn't help but enjoy flirting with the concept.

Paul didn't say anything. He was fresh out of caustic remarks, and his depression was deeper than ever. He glowered down into his cup and ignored her as she began to chatter about the party and the rest of her day.

It was just impatience with the rate at which his foot was healing, he told himself. And anxiety over the renovations and why they were taking so long. And...and the fact that he was jealous.

Oh well. The truth sometimes hurt, but you couldn't get anywhere without it.

CHAPTER TWELVE

THE BOX WITH THE DRESS in it might as well have been
made of plutonium. It seemed to burn itself into Rosemary's mind with an evil yellow glow, always there, never
forgotten. As she lay in bed and tried to sleep, the dress
loomed large in the darkened room.

She hated that Paul had given it to her, hated it for so
many reasons that she had to list them to herself over and
over again. It was far too personal a present for a landlord to give a tenant, for one thing, especially once he'd
found out who she really was and what his connection to
her had been. It was not a style she had ever worn, one she
ever would wear. It was a dress for a little dainty thing, not
for her. Was he living in a dreamworld, or did he think that
if you gave a slinky, feminine dress to an athletic woman,
she would turn skinny when she put it on? Or maybe his
reasoning was different. Maybe it was a way of telling her
he hated the way she dressed.

Whatever, she would never wear it. And she would never
forgive him for giving it to her.

About the past—she wasn't sure why that still affected
how she was treating him. It rankled a bit, but as she'd told
him, she knew he'd turned his life around. He was a different person now. He'd done a lot to help a suffering
world and that was a heck of a lot more important than her
complaints could ever be. After all, he hadn't forced Greg
to go nuts. That had been Greg's choice, and Rosemary
herself had been in a better position to do something about

it than Paul ever was. And she had chosen to do nothing, until it was too late. She couldn't blame that on Paul.

She was still in bed and had almost fallen asleep when the call came. She heard Paul answering the phone and she listened, still groggy, but she couldn't make out what was going on.

"What is it?" she asked, sitting up in bed as he hung up the receiver.

He was dressed in pajama bottoms, and when he turned to look at her, the light from the lamp made grotesque shadows across his golden skin.

"That was Sheila Lawson," he told her. "She's the concierge out at Timberlake Lodge where they are holding the twins convention."

"Yes, I've met her. She's great."

"Well, she's not doing so well right now." He turned and began searching for his clothes. "It seems there has been an outbreak of something among the twins. Sounds like chicken pox to me. But I won't know for sure until I get out there."

An outbreak of something at the lodge. Rosemary watched for a moment as he found his shirt and slacks. Then she surprised herself. "Why don't I go with you?" she suggested, and suddenly she was wide-awake. "You'll need someone to drive you. And someone to help you. I'm no nurse, but I've had enough medical training to be useful."

He stood looking at her for a moment, a smile curling his wide mouth. "I'd really appreciate it," he said softly, his blue eyes glowing in the lamplight. "Thanks."

She dressed quickly, throwing on jeans and a sweatshirt, and soon they were cruising through the darkness, heading out of town. The streets were nearly empty. The lights had been dimmed in most of the businesses they passed, and the atmosphere was ghostly.

They took the highway out toward the lodge, then turned on the side road that led to the lake. Rosemary thought of all the other times she'd traveled out here, of the Christmas parties and visits to Liza Baron Forrester. Timberlake Lodge was a relic from a golden age before World War II. It had been built by the Ingalls family and used as a hunting lodge, the site of sumptuous entertainments that drew a few famous people as well as the wealthier residents of this part of Wisconsin. Then it had fallen into disrepair. A few years back it had been sold to the Addison Hotel chain, which had made extensive renovations.

As they rounded the curve near the lake, Rosemary looked ahead at the rustic gables still visible above the trees and smiled. Things hadn't changed all that much.

"I remember coming here once when I was a boy," Paul said as they pulled into a parking spot near the wide steps leading to the entrance. "We had some kind of country fair on the slope leading to the lake. As I recall, little Amy Thistlethorpe, a particularly obnoxious child who enjoyed sticking her lollipop in other people's hair, among other mean-spirited tricks, met with a mysterious accident. Some unnamed crusader for justice put weeds from the lake bottom down her back, stopping her vicious little campaign of terror in its tracks." He smiled blithely. "No one ever identified the mystery boy who saved the town from Amy's shenanigans."

Rosemary laughed, looking at him sideways as she turned off the engine. "Could that be the same Amy Thistlethorpe who is now married to our local state congressman?"

"Ah, still putting her sticky little fingers where they don't belong, is she?"

"So they say." Rosemary gave him a mock sigh. "If only that mystery man would come back and save us once more."

Paul grinned. "You never know," he said, reaching for his medical bag. "He could pop up at the most unexpected times."

She laughed again as they walked up the steps toward the lobby of the lodge. Watching Paul work with children, Rosemary could see his unusual warmth, his empathy, and the more he talked about his childhood experiences in Tyler, the more she saw how the happiness he'd felt here had probably helped shape his adult outlook. He loved kids. And, she supposed, he'd loved being a kid—at least when he was visiting his grandparents.

But her smile faded as they entered the building. A harried Sheila Lawson rushed forward to meet them, her blond hair disheveled, her pretty face strained.

"Disaster. Utter disaster," she muttered, shaking hands and looking from one to the other. "I'm so glad you've come, Dr. Chambers. I called the hospital first, but there's been a pileup out on the highway and Emergency was flooded with crash victims, so they gave me your number. I hated to get you up in the middle of the night, but every time I turn around we have another casualty." Still talking, she led them into a conference room where beds had been set up in rows. With a flourish, she presented the sick children.

They lay on beds and cots, some with anxious parents hovering nearby, though Sheila tried to discourage that, telling them they would do better to get rest themselves and leave the nursing to the doctor and his helpers.

"We have no idea what this is," Sheila whispered to Rosemary and Paul. "Is it some kind of flu? Is it contagious? Is it environmentally produced? We don't have a clue. That's why we've gathered most of the sick ones here, to keep them away from the others and in one place so that you can better evaluate the problem."

Paul nodded, all business. "Is this hitting children exclusively?" he asked.

Sheila put a hand to her temple. "Mostly. There are two adults, but they're still in their rooms. I'll get the room numbers for you. But please start with the children."

The poor things gazed glumly from their beds. Ranging in age from just over a year to teenagers, some were quite green, some had damp hair clinging to their heads, others just looked pale and wan.

"Wow," Paul murmured, taken aback. "This doesn't look good."

He'd said it softly and only Rosemary heard him. She leaned close. "What do you think it is?" she asked him.

He shrugged. "Too soon to tell." Turning to Sheila, he raised his voice. "Who was the first case? What were the symptoms?"

Sheila quickly sketched in the details for him. "At first it seemed to be mainly a group who arrived on a bus this afternoon—the twins from Turner County in Ohio. But now others are coming down with it, children who've been here for days. What do you think it is, doctor?"

He shook his head, his face expressionless, but knowing him as she did, Rosemary felt a quiver of unease. He was worried. She could see it in his eyes. She thought she knew what he was concerned about. In past years various conventions had come down with flulike contagious diseases that had been quite serious. If this were a similar case, not only would it be horrible for the children involved, but the town of Tyler and the future of its convention business were in trouble as well.

She watched while Paul went from child to child, moving quickly, giving each a smile and a bit of encouragement, putting his hand on each forehead, looking into mouths and eyes. He came back in just a few minutes, but he was frowning.

"Offhand, I'd say food poisoning," he said, nodding to Rosemary, then Sheila, who was hovering behind her.

Sheila groaned. "No," she whispered, looking pale herself.

Paul shook his head. "Right now, I'd say the children who are most ill all came on that bus this afternoon. Don't take it for granted it was something they ate here."

"But what about the ones who were never on that bus?"

Paul shrugged. "We'll see," was all he would say.

"We have fifteen beds set up," Sheila continued, trying to keep a stiff upper lip, but showing strain around the edges. "This is big, really big. Do you know how many people we have coming to this thing? Only about half of them have arrived. There are more due tomorrow, and more on Saturday...."

Rosemary grabbed her hand. "We're going to take care of this," she told Sheila firmly. "Don't you worry."

The woman shook her head. "I'm trying to think what I did wrong. Where did we slip up? Should we throw out all the food in the kitchen?"

Paul didn't waste a minute on her outpouring of dismay. He had already gone to the next bed and was taking the temperature of the child resting miserably in it. "We'll need medical histories on every one of these kids," he said. "Did they fill out forms when they registered for the convention?"

Sheila nodded. "I'll get them for you right away, though they are rather rudimentary, I'm afraid. Mainly for consent and insurance purposes."

"We'll need to work up histories, then," he said shortly. "We'll need the address and telephone number of each child's regular physician, as well as drug allergies, food sensitivities, past illnesses and operations, birth conditions. We can't afford to overlook anything that might complicate this in any of the patients." He patted a little girl on the head and smiled at her. "We don't want any nasty surprises."

"I'll help her make up the charts," Rosemary told him. She knew just what to do. "Do you have a copy machine and plenty of paper?" she asked as she left with Sheila. "We're going to need pens as well."

It didn't take long to generate the medical chart forms Paul needed. Sheila had an up-to-date computer programmed to deal with spreadsheets and tables, and they hurriedly filled in information from the applications Sheila pulled out of a file. Very soon Rosemary was back with clip boards and charts, ready to help Paul go from patient to patient, making a thorough diagnosis of each case.

He glanced up. "It's food poisoning," he told her with confidence. "I'm pretty sure we'll trace it back to a sandwich shop they stopped at for lunch."

"But what about the ones who weren't on that trip?"

He gave her a quick, lopsided grin. "Mass hysteria," he told her. "They saw others getting sick and psychology took over."

Rosemary gasped. "You're sure?"

He nodded. "Pretty sure. We'll see, but that's what I would call it offhand."

She shook her head. "You just never know, do you?" she murmured.

Watching him work was impressive. He had a calm, easy manner that reassured even the most frightened of the children. He seemed to know just when to insert a silly joke or to look for elephants in a toddler's ears. His large, long-fingered hand would settle on a shoulder or gently rub a back, and the child seemed to get confidence from his touch.

There were times when Rosemary could hardly believe this could be the Paul she used to know. Was this wonderful healer the same man who had been such a playboy in the old days? How could a man change so much?

Sheila came and went, maintaining control in a trying situation. Three more patients were admitted to their makeshift ward in the next hour. One was a parent.

"Can you imagine if the adults all start to go?" Sheila whispered to Rosemary as she handed her fresh bedding for the newcomers.

By the time they had the new ones settled and checked over, it was three o'clock in the morning. Rosemary's eyes were burning and her feet hurt, but Paul seemed as fresh as when they'd arrived.

"You love this, don't you?" she said to him as they took a short coffee break in the hall. Sheila had sent over a steaming pot and some finger sandwiches and set up a little table and chairs for them.

Paul thought for a moment, a slight smile on his lips. "Yes, I guess, in a way," he admitted at last. "I like the rush, the pressure. And although it may sound corny, I like helping people."

It didn't sound corny at all. Rosemary had seen him at work and she knew it was true. The more she observed him, the more the stories about his work with refugees and the needy rang true as well.

"Tell me about what you did overseas," she prompted.

He stretched out his long legs and took another sip of coffee. "I was abroad for fifteen years. Which year would you like to hear about?"

She wanted to know everything, but they didn't have much time. "Tell me what you did that first year," she suggested, even though that was awfully close to the breakup, to the night she'd gone after Greg at Paul's house.

He turned his bright blue gaze on her and searched her face, wondering why she was bringing this up. "Well, I signed up to go overseas right after I last saw you." He smiled, looking away. "The next day, in fact."

"Did you really?" Her heart beat a little more quickly and she wasn't sure if that was bad or good. "Why?"

He let his mind drift back for a just a moment to the dark depths he'd been in, to the heartache he'd felt. He'd known how far off track his life had gone and he'd finally had the courage to put it to rights. "Penance," he told her lightly at last. "I knew I'd done ya' wrong."

He was joking. She told herself that, and yet the evidence was clear. He'd changed his life the day after she'd confronted him.

She gazed at him earnestly. "Paul, if I had known you felt that way, it would have changed a lot of things for me."

He winced, but went on gamely. "Would it have changed your getting a divorce from Greg?"

She didn't have to think long on that one. "No. If I had been more honest with myself, I would have known our marriage was a mistake from the start. Thank goodness we didn't have children."

He nodded, and a child began to cry in the next room.

"Back to work," he said, rising as though it were a relief rather than a burden, and she followed with a sigh, because although she was perfectly willing to help, it was getting awfully late and she was tired. Where did he get his energy?

From a passion for his work, she decided about an hour later. That had to be where it came from. The only alternative was birth on Krypton with a marked allergy to kryptonite.

"I can't go any longer," she told him at last. "I've got to get some sleep."

"Come with me," Sheila said, overhearing her. "We're overextended, what with trying to separate twins all over the place, but I saved a room for the two of you to get some rest."

Rosemary followed her numbly, falling onto the bed in the room provided without taking off anything but her shoes. Sleep washed over her and she sank into it gratefully. When she surfaced again a couple of hours later, she did so reluctantly, like a swimmer who'd found a magic world and hated to leave it.

The sun was barely creeping in through the blinds. She knew why she was in a strange bed; she remembered that right away. But she didn't remember why there was someone there with her.

She lay very still, hardly breathing, because she knew who it must be. She could feel his breath on her neck. She was curled up, facing the window, and he was sleeping against her back, one arm flung over her waist. Closing her eyes, she took a deep breath and filled herself with the sense of him. It had been so long since she'd felt a man's body against hers, so hard and warm and male, that she wanted to savor the moment, no matter what the risk. Any lingering resistance she might have melted like chocolate in the sun. This was so very good.

She knew her reactions to Paul were dangerous. She'd known that for a long time. If she were younger, she would have thought herself in love. But she was too old and wise for that sort of nonsense. To let that happen would be suicidal. Still, when a man this attractive fell asleep against you, it was only natural to enjoy it for a while. What could it hurt? He was asleep.

Or was he? The tantalizing tickle of his breath on her neck began to change, very subtly at first, until she could have sworn she felt his lips where once air had stirred. Then his arm tightened, pulling her closer, and she gasped as she found herself being turned until she was partly beneath him and he was dropping tiny kisses along the exposed inch and a half of her collarbone.

"Paul," she murmured in protest, but then his mouth was covering hers and she couldn't get another word out.

A strange lethargy stole over Rosemary. She couldn't seem to move, couldn't push him away, couldn't even make her objections known. For some reason, her traitorous arms had curled around his neck and she was sinking into his kiss as though it were a deliciously comforting feather bed.

But the comfort factor fled and a hot urgency quickly took its place, as though a door too long left locked had suddenly opened, and a need too long denied had burst through.

Paul felt her response and he came alive, wanting her with a deep, hard hunger that shook him to his core. His hands moved on her body and his mouth drank her in, filling him with her taste, her scent. He hadn't meant to do this, but now that it was begun, there seemed to be no reason to stop. It felt too good, it felt too real. It felt like the answer to an ache that had been in him for much too long. Other women hadn't filled that void. Maybe Rosemary would. Maybe she would change him again, as she had once before in a very different way. Maybe she would be his salvation.

She moaned softly, moving against him like something made of water, all slippery and supple, fitting neatly into places where he needed her, melting her curves to his angles and finding the perfect match. She loved the feel of his hard flesh, his strong hands, his hot mouth. If she held him closer, she knew she would love it even more, and maybe she wouldn't feel so all alone in the world.

All alone in the world. Had she really thought that? No, impossible. She prided herself on her independence. She didn't need anyone else. Yet an element of truth reverberated through her, and the shock of it filled her with consternation and stunned her, so that Paul's hand slid beneath the hem of her sweatshirt and found her breast and cupped it before she realized what was happening.

And finally she came down to earth with a sharp thump. This had to stop. It was absolutely crazy.

"Wait," she cried out breathlessly, pulling away at last. "Wait a minute. We're not supposed to be doing this."

He closed his eyes and grimaced, knowing from her tone that the delicious interlude was over. He allowed himself a second or two of mourning before he opened his eyes again and grinned at her sadly. "And it was going so well," he said.

She glared at him, feeling foolish. "You tricked me," she muttered, pulling herself together and swinging her legs off the bed. "I—I thought I was still dreaming."

"Ah. Dream about me a lot, do you?" He sat up in turn, his eyes mocking her playfully. "Are we always about to make love? And more important, do we ever actually get to do it?"

"No, no and no," she said, standing and frowning down at him. He was laughing at a situation she felt like crying over. "Are you ever serious about anything?" she asked softly, wishing she could read his mind.

He stared at her, the humor fading slowly from his face. "Yes, Rosemary," he said quietly. "I'm very serious about a lot of things. But I've seen enough ugliness to want to make life around me as happy as possible. It's a defense mechanism."

Instead of stomping off toward the door as she'd planned to do, she sank back down on the side of the bed and studied his starry eyes. "Last night you were dreaming," she said, knowing she was taking a risk in bringing this up. "You cried out in your sleep."

His face was frozen, his eyes watchful. "Oh? What did I say?"

"Something about a baby. You said, 'get the baby' at one point."

His head jerked back as though she'd slapped him. Without saying a word, he rolled over and began to get up himself, but she reached out and put a hand on his arm. "What baby? What happened to it?" she asked.

He glanced back at her and shook his head. "I don't have the slightest idea," he said lightly. "I deal in babies, you know. I see them every day."

He shifted his cast and rose, pulling his clothes together and bending toward the mirror to comb a hand through his hair. She sat watching him. She didn't believe what he'd said for a minute. But she could see that whatever the truth was, it hurt too much for him to talk about it right now. She wasn't going to nag him. But someday he would have to tell someone. He would have to do that in order to let the wound heal.

Once out in the hallway, they found that other health professionals had arrived and they could go home. Sheila, still awake and running on adrenaline alone, came to thank them and see them to the door.

"I can't tell you how grateful I am for the way you two pitched in," she said. "This is a disaster, but no one seems to think there will be any serious medical effects."

"It's just food poisoning," Paul agreed. "And not a very bad strain of it at that. We're lucky it wasn't chicken pox. That's been going around for weeks. Half the children I see in town have it."

Sheila held up crossed fingers. "Please, no chicken pox," she said fervently.

"Give them plenty of liquids," Paul advised. "I don't think you'll have too much of a problem." When Sheila rolled her eyes comically, Paul chuckled. "Food poisoning is not the black plague."

"It might as well be. My reputation has been devoured by it."

Rosemary put an arm around her shoulders and gave her a hug. "It's going to be all right," she promised.

Sheila managed a wavering smile. "I know it will, in the long run. But we're certainly going through a trial by fire here, don't you think?"

"And you're coming through it magnificently," Rosemary exclaimed.

She and Paul left, waving as they walked to the car. A bird sang from a bush nearby. The sun was finally up and the landscape was slowly coming alive. It was a special time of day and Rosemary felt a thrill that she was sharing it with Paul. Turning, she looked into his face. He felt it, too; she was sure of it.

"Let's go home," she said happily.

"Home," he repeated softly.

They were going home together. Now why did something so simple make her heart beat faster?

CHAPTER THIRTEEN

THE FOLLOWING DAY was a Saturday and they slept until noon, when a strange pounding woke them both.

Rosemary raised her head and looked blearily through her invisible walls toward the couch. Paul raised his head and his gaze met hers.

"What is that awful noise?" she asked, her voice hoarse.

He frowned, thinking hard, then his face cleared. "It's Joe and the boys," he said, remembering a conversation he'd had just the day before. "They're working through the weekend to try and get the upstairs apartments finished."

Groaning, she dropped her head back on her pillow. "Tell them to go away," she muttered.

But the hammering went on and on, and soon they both dragged themselves up to sit at the kitchen table and gaze sleepily into their coffee cups.

"I'm getting too old for this sort of thing," Paul said sadly. "I used to be able to stay up for forty-eight hours at a time, dealing with the wounded along with incoming shells. Now a little thing like a food poisoning outbreak gets me down. I'm losing it, Rosemary."

"Well, don't hang up your stethoscope just yet," she advised, holding back a grin at his pitiful tale of woe. "There are little children who need you."

He sighed, and his eyes darkened, as though he were suddenly seeing something much farther away. "That's just the trouble," he said softly, so softly she wondered if he had even meant for her to hear. "There are too many little children who need someone. You can work as many forty-eight-hour shifts as your body will take, and you still won't make a dent in the need."

His tone was deep, his voice filled with pain, and a chill ran down her back. She'd accused him before of not taking things seriously, but it was evident this was something he took very seriously indeed. She could feel his torment, see it in his eyes, and something in her wanted to reach out to connect with it.

But that was foolish. She'd never been in a war zone. She'd never seen atrocities close up and personal. What did she know about it? What did she know about the helplessness of seeing so much suffering, that there was no way to alleviate it?

"Is that why you came home?" she asked him simply.

He looked almost surprised when she spoke, and he gazed at her for a minute before answering. Her eyes were wide and intelligent, and suddenly he knew that she understood in ways most others couldn't. It was like a miracle and he marveled at it.

"Yes," he said. "That was part of it. I was working harder and harder and falling further and further behind. There are too many wars. Too many bombs crushing families. Too many land mines tearing legs off young boys in the fields. Too much malnutrition. Too much disease." He shrugged. "I saw too much. I got to the point where I couldn't take anymore. I looked in the mirror and I noticed time was going by faster than I'd thought. If I was ever going to have a shot at a normal life, it was now or never. So I came home."

She nodded slowly, wishing there was a way to tell him how much she admired what he'd done all those years without sounding as though she were fawning over him. She didn't have to be told that he'd saved lives, that he'd

endured hardship, that he'd been brave and compassion-
ate and effective. It was in his face, in his voice, and the
words weren't necessary. But she couldn't find a way to tell
him so. And she sat mutely staring into her coffee again,
wanting to take his hand and not daring to do it.

THE DAY SEEMED almost over before it had really begun for
them. Sheila called from the lodge to let them know that
things were under control. There had been no new cases
since six that morning, so she was hoping for the best. Paul
called Ernie and went out for a few hours. Rosemary
looked at the clock, saw the time and began to get nervous.

She was going on a date. It had been a long time since
she had and she was pretty excited. The only problem was,
she was dating the wrong man. The truth couldn't be denied forever. She wished it could be Paul she would be
dancing with tonight.

"Face it," she murmured, looking at her reflection in
the mirror as she began to brush on mascara. "You're
falling for the guy."

It was true, but she was bound and determined to keep
it under wraps and not let anyone, especially him, know
about it. Her date was with Billy Joe. She had to keep a
focus here.

She went through her closet looking for something to
wear. There was the dress Paul had bought for her, still in
the box. She hesitated for a moment, but then scorned it
once again. There was no way she was wearing a dress tonight.

In the end, she decided on black slacks and a soft-
collared, peach-colored sweater that made a much more
feminine impression than she was used to. Funny, though,
when she looked at her reflection in the mirror, she really
liked it.

She heard Paul coming in and she glanced at the clock. She was still an hour early, and she groaned. Without walls, it was going to be difficult to hide the fact that she was ready so soon. Steeling herself for the inevitable teasing, she went out to meet him.

He looked up and smiled, appreciating the picture she made. "Hey, you look very nice," he told her casually. He started to tell her he liked her hair down the way she had it, curling softly around her shoulders, but stopped himself before he got a word out. Instinct told him she would go put it up if he said anything. He left well enough alone.

Following her into the kitchen, he got himself a drink of water, then turned, leaning against the counter, and told her calmly, "I think I'll come along with you and Billy Joe tonight."

She whirled, staring at him, not sure whether to laugh or yell at him. "What?" she said in a croaking voice.

He nodded as though it were a good plan. "It's time I got going on my campaign to find a mother for my children," he said playfully. "You're supposed to help me, remember?"

She shook her head, biting her tongue. He was up to something, that was certain. But surely he wasn't serious about coming along on the date. Was he? The very thought made her want to giggle. "What could I do to help?" she asked warily.

His shrug was almost Gallic. "Recommend candidates. Introduce me to beautiful women. Put an ad in the paper. I don't know." He glanced at his watch as though he didn't like what he saw there. "I'm way behind schedule, you know."

"I see." She relaxed a little. He was kidding. He had to be. Well, she could kid along with the best of them. "You thought you'd have a bride lined up about the time the renovations were completed. Is that it?"

His gaze was wide-eyed with innocence. "Why not?"

She wanted to laugh, but instead merely shook her head. "Well, what's stopping you?" she asked archly.

He frowned thoughtfully for a moment, then looked up at her again. "I think it might be you."

"Me?" She looked startled and felt her heart give a little lurch. "Why me?"

"I don't know." He gazed at her speculatively, turning the glass in his hand. "These things are often determined by our basic, primal nature, you know. You're around a lot and that sort of dampens the desire to go out hunting for other women. I mean..." He shook his head. "What's the point when I have a perfectly good woman at home?"

She was going to laugh out loud if she wasn't careful. The laughter was tickling her throat. But she didn't want to let it show. She pressed her lips together, holding it back, and when she finally had it under control, she told him wisely, "Let me point out the flaw in your logic. You see, I'm not yours."

His sigh was heartfelt. "More's the pity." His smile was wide as the Cheshire cat's. "Still, I've thought of a way you can make it up to me."

He was being outrageous on purpose and she knew it very well, but she couldn't keep herself from swallowing the bait. It was just too tempting. "Oh you have, have you?" she challenged mockingly.

"Yes." He smiled at her blandly, his blue eyes twinkling. "That's why I've decided I'll go out with you and lover-boy tonight. That way you can begin to help me in earnest."

This had really gone too far. If he thought he was coming along on her date, he was out of his mind. Rosemary could just imagine herself sitting between the two men, being drowned out on both sides. No, it was an amusing concept, but it just wouldn't work.

"Paul..." she began sternly.

"It's the perfect time for it," he said, being absolutely convincing. "You're going to that country-and-western club. There are bound to be some frisky cowgirls around for me."

She put down her glass and started to turn away. This was too much. "Sorry, friend," she said crisply. "You're going to have to get your frisky cowgirls on your own time."

He sighed. "I was afraid you would balk."

"Balk?" Turning back, she gave a quick, harsh laugh. "You're darn right. And that isn't the half of what Billy Joe would probably do."

Paul's smile was crafty, as if he had just sprung a trap. "You know, I had a feeling you might react this way. That's why I took the precaution of talking to Billy Joe ahead of time."

He took her breath away. The man was a monster. "You did what?" she cried, aghast.

He smiled smugly. "I stopped by Carl's Garage this afternoon and had a chat with good old B.J."

Now she would have to kill him. No two ways about it. This was beyond the pale, way over the line. "Oh you did, did you?" she said, starting toward him and thinking murder.

"Yes." He saw her look and took a quick defensive step backward. "And all the while I was trying to figure out just what you see in the guy."

She stopped and so did he, but her lips were thin and her eyes were flashing cool fire.

"Okay," he continued quickly, his back against the refrigerator. "There are the bulging muscles and the lascivious leer and the daredevil attitude." He tossed his head as though that hardly counted. "And he's young and impetuous. But I'd say he's got a little bit of an ego problem."

Rosemary blinked, disarmed once again. Paul kept throwing her curves, and she wasn't sure whether to be outraged or entertained. Either way, she had to admit, it was hardly ever dull around the man. "What gives you that idea?" she asked incredulously.

He shrugged. "Why else would he feel the need for speed, as we say out there on the racetrack?"

"Maybe because he's good at racing."

"You could be right." He sighed, leaning back again, looking very contented. "However, there are some things he's not that good at. In fact, I pretty much scammed him." He grinned at her with triumph in his eyes. "As far as the date goes, I'm in."

She stared at him. Could he possibly be telling the truth? "I don't believe this." She shook her head slowly, trying to read his eyes, trying to figure out if he was playing with her mind. "And you're trying to tell me he agreed to include you in our date?"

"Sure he did. It took a little persuading, I'll admit. But he saw the light as soon as I told him—" he coughed delicately "—that you were my sister."

She threw up her hands. "Oh brother."

"Exactly." His smile was back. "Your poor, temporarily disabled brother who has been having a lot of trouble finding the woman of his dreams. He felt so bad for me, he volunteered to help." He unsnapped the cuffs of his shirt and gave her a superior look. "I guess I'd better go get ready. I don't want to hold you two up." He straightened and stood very tall. "What do you think? Maybe a little cologne at the temples? At the pulse points?"

She couldn't help it; she was going to laugh, even though she was furious with him at the same time. "You're crazy."

"Probably." He gave her a cheeky grin. "But tonight ought to be very interesting."

He left her and she felt like a deflated balloon, all limp and useless. She usually considered herself a pretty tough cookie, but Paul could run rings around her at times.

"The problem is, he makes me laugh," she muttered to herself. And once she was laughing, anger went out the window. So now she was saddled with a double date—two men and one woman. This would be different, she supposed. And she wasn't sure if she was glad or not.

Paul came out of the bathroom dressed in a white shirt and dark slacks that he'd slit to accommodate his cast. He looked clean and fresh and very sexy. She had to swallow hard and look the other way, try to ignore the way her pulse was racing. Yes, there was no doubt about it—she was falling hard. Why did she always fall for the wrong man?

Billy Joe picked them up in his flashy car, the engine roaring so loudly that pictures had to be rattling on somebody's walls. Paul sat in the back seat, but somehow managed to monopolize the conversation anyway, discussing cars and football and other male pursuits with Billy Joe. Whenever Rosemary glanced back with a dirty look, he grinned at her. From what she could see, he thought he was sitting in the catbird seat.

And he had a right to think exactly that. Coming into the club on a crutch, with his baby-blue eyes shining and his carefree smile in place, he was surrounded by sympathetic females in no time, all anxious to help him to his seat. Once they were back at their own tables, little smiles and waves came thick and fast, each woman wanting to be the one he invited over.

"Which one do you suppose will be my blushing bride?" he murmured softly in Rosemary's ear when they had a moment alone at their table.

"None of them," she told him tartly.

"Why not?" he asked her with laughter in his eyes.

"Because as your *sister*," she said, emphasizing the word, "I will not allow you to marry without love."

He threw out his arms expansively. "I love them all already."

Her smile was plastic and she knew it. But better that than no smile at all. "You do not," she said firmly.

"Come on, give me a chance." He looked disarmingly hopeful, one lock of dark hair falling over his forehead. "I could love them all."

She flashed him a wicked look. "For one night, maybe."

"Ouch." He laughed softly, encircling her wrist with his long fingers. "Sister Rosemary, you'd better watch out or our mama will have to wash your mouth out with soap."

Billy Joe was back before she could answer, and Paul withdrew his hand, smiling at a group of women at the next table. They took the smile as the invitation they'd been waiting for and came over quickly to join him, their drinks held precariously in ruby-tipped fingers.

While Rosemary sat and pretended to be interested in what Billy Joe was telling her about camshafts, Paul had a blonde fetching him drinks, a redhead giving him a neck massage and a dark-haired beauty whispering sweet nothings in his ear. Every now and then he would look up and catch Rosemary's eye and give her a big grin. And she would consider various methods of slow torture she would like to perform on him.

Billy Joe didn't seem to notice. He talked on and on about cars, and finally asked Rosemary to dance. He had a strange, jostling style that made her wonder how easily she bruised these days, but she kept a game smile on her face.

"This is really fun," she lied.

"Yeah," he said with a grin. "Let's dance some more."

Rosemary's smile grew a bit strained. "Uh...don't you think we ought to get back to the table and see how Paul is doing? I mean, he does have a broken foot and all...."

"Ah, your brother's doing fine. He's got women trailing him like a dust cloud behind a dune buggy. I don't think you have to worry about him."

She hesitated, thinking she really ought to tell him the truth about her relationship to Paul. But at this point, it seemed too much trouble. "You don't want go back to the table and have a drink?" she suggested, losing hope.

"Are you kidding? I don't need a drink." He grinned at her, looking handsome but impossibly young and naive. "I'm drunk on you, princess."

Princess? Since when had she been a princess? But then again, maybe he called all his dates that. Everything else he did and said seemed to have a script written for it, an echo that told her it had been said before and probably too often. She began to wonder how long it was going to be before she could go home.

But the music started up again and he grabbed her hand and they were off.

A little later he got her to join in the line dancing, and she had some fun doing that for a while. But when they went back to the table, a short little thing in a cowgirl outfit was sitting on Paul's knee, singing to him, and Rosemary had to make an excuse to visit the powder room, just to calm herself down.

But she couldn't stay in there forever. She had to go back and face them, even though she knew now that she was going to be insanely jealous of every woman who came anywhere near Paul Chambers.

"Am I in love with the man?" she asked herself in horrified wonder.

That couldn't be. It would be so foolhardy. Paul's goals in life were a far cry from her own. He wanted a little woman to tend to his needs, two cats in the yard, children filling the bedrooms. He wanted Little League games and PTA carnivals and braces on teeth and Best Citizen of the Week awards and tennis trophies and Boy Scout meetings. She wanted... wait a minute. What did she want, anyway? She put a hand to her head. For some reason, she couldn't remember.

"Are you okay?" a nice young woman asked, stopping to check on her.

Rosemary jumped up from the chair in front of the mirror where she'd been sitting. "Oh, yes, I'm fine," she said, slightly embarrassed and hoping no one she knew had seen her like this. But it wasn't likely anyone had. This place was pretty far out on the highway for Tyler residents. They liked to stay closer to home, on the whole.

But she had to get her head on straight. They said opposites were supposed to attract, but this was ridiculous. Paul was looking for someone who loved kids. Rosemary hadn't even known any kids until very recently. Coming from the background she had—where her mother had poisoned her opinion toward having children—she'd made big strides in changing her views. She knew a lot more about them now and could handle them pretty easily. And she'd even found she liked them, that a child could touch a chord in her heart no one else could. But that didn't mean she was ready to risk having children.

"Well, don't get all riled up," she told herself. "Because no one is asking you to."

True. And that was lucky, because it just wasn't in the cards for her. But she had to ask herself this question— would she want Paul if he didn't want children? Would that make him okay as a lover and a friend? She didn't know. She didn't know much of anything. Her head was full of conflicting thoughts and images.

She was falling apart. "No," she corrected herself acidly. "You're falling in love. There is a difference." But not much of one, it seemed. She turned unsteadily and started out.

In no hurry to get back to where Paul was the center of female attention, she took the long way around, going through the lobby to the restaurant section and then the bar. She was almost out of the room when a familiar tilt to a head in the corner made her turn around and she found herself staring at Patrick Kelsey—and Hayley Ingalls.

Rosemary's breath caught in her throat. It couldn't be! No. Pam had to be here with them, be here somewhere. Rosemary looked around, looked back at the table, noted the fact that there wasn't a third chair. They were alone. And they seemed very much a couple, their heads together, their attention focused on each other.

"Oh my God," she thought, dreading the ramifications. "No, Patrick, don't do this to Pam."

Turning blindly, Rosemary made her way out of the bar and stumbled back toward the table where her two men were waiting for her. She knew she must have been deathly pale, because Billy Joe jumped up and came toward her.

"What is it?" he asked. "Are you all right?"

"I'm fine," she lied, smiling at him. "No, actually, I'm—I'm not feeling very well. I'm afraid I'm going to have to ask you to take me home."

Paul looked concerned for a moment, but his enchanting ladies soon distracted him, and when he realized Rosemary and Billy Joe were actually leaving, he decided not to go with them.

"Don't you worry about a thing," the girls crowed. "We'll take good care of him and we'll give him a ride home."

"That is, if we don't decide to keep him," the blonde chirped.

They all laughed and Paul looked smug, and Rosemary wished she could think of something cutting to say to him. But her mind was in too much turmoil for that. Billy Joe put an arm around her shoulders and led her out, and she didn't look back to see if Paul was watching.

SHE DIDN'T KNOW what she was going to do about Pam. There was very little doubt anymore that something was going on. She ached for her friend, so alone now with the baby coming. If it hadn't been so late, she would have run over to keep her company at least. But when you came right down to it, there was very little she could do to help her. What went on between a man and a woman couldn't be fixed by sympathy from friends. It had to be dealt with at its roots.

But she resolved to go and see Pam the next morning. At least Rosemary could give her a little moral support, and maybe a shoulder to cry on.

She got ready for bed, taking a long shower, then drying off with her fluffiest towel and putting on a nightgown. She usually wore pajamas, but for some reason she refused to let herself think through, she felt like wearing her old cotton nightgown, the one that tied at the neck and fell in graceful folds around her body. She looked at herself in the mirror, the gown floating around her, her hair falling in waves. *I look really pretty,* she thought in surprise.

Pretty wasn't a word she often attached to herself. It was for bits of fluff like those women at the club who were hanging all over Paul. Rosemary cared about being smart and bright and competent and effective.

But what if she could be all those things . . . and pretty, too? She caught her breath and looked at herself again. "Guess what," she whispered. "I think you made it." A warm feeling coursed through her and for the moment she felt happy.

By that time it was after midnight, and Paul still wasn't home. But why should he be? He was out on the town, as he had every right to be. She hoped he was having a very good time. Let him stay out all night if he wanted. Yes, just let him. She didn't care.

"Time for bed," she told herself with forced cheer. Climbing under the covers, she snuggled down into her pillow and closed her eyes. And immediately opened them again. She wasn't going to fall asleep—that much was perfectly obvious. She was going to lie here worrying until she heard Paul come in.

Worrying? Had she really thought that? What was there to worry about? He was a big boy. He could take care of himself, and had for a long time, under very arduous circumstances. He was a man who'd lived through wars, for goodness sake. She was not going to lie here and worry that he might get into a traffic accident.

But she knew very well her worries had other sources. She'd seen the way that redhead had been looking at him. And the blonde, with her long, redtipped fingernails on his arm...

Rosemary was writhing in agony and hated herself for doing so. This wasn't the way she had meant things to be. This wasn't the way she would allow them to be.

She heard his key in the lock and held her breath. The sound of female laughter filtered in, and then his voice. Outrage coursed through her. Surely he wouldn't bring one of those women in!

But no. She heard him saying good-night, and then the door closed and a car drove off. She lay very still, her eyes clamped shut, hoping he wouldn't look over and notice that she was still awake.

But she heard him moving through the living room, stopping where the walls used to be and then coming into her bedroom space.

"Rosemary," he said softly. "Are you okay?"

She opened her eyes and stared up at him. His blue eyes seemed to glow in the gloom, and his dark hair was falling over his forehead. He was the most gorgeous man she'd ever seen and she ached to hold him. Could he see it in her eyes? Could he read how much she needed him?

"Are you okay?" he asked again, and she nodded, still holding his gaze.

"Good," he said, and suddenly his fingers trailed across her cheek. "Good night."

And then he was gone, turning off the light as he went. For some crazy reason, tears welled in her eyes, and that made her more angry still. She never cried. Never. And she wasn't going to start crying over a man who could never be hers.

PAUL STIRRED in his sleep, muttering. He was back in Chechnya. He could hear shelling a few blocks away. The streetlights had been blown out and there wasn't much of a moon. When he looked down, he realized the baby was in his arms.

Analise was calling him. "Hurry, hurry," she cried. "Bring him quickly. There isn't much time."

He wrapped the blanket around the baby's face and started down the street, dodging from one doorway to the next, staying out of sight as much as possible. A round hit a building across the street and he froze, then went on quickly, trying not to make too much noise as his feet hit the rubble.

"Paul."

Was it Analise calling to him again? He looked around but couldn't see her.

"Paul, wake up."

He was falling. He was falling and the baby was flung from his arms. He turned, desperate to protect the baby, and then she was looking down at him.

"Analise?" he murmured, still half-asleep.

"Paul, it's Rosemary. You were dreaming. You were calling out things...."

He stared up at her and she stared back, and then her hand moved, brushing back his hair, and he grabbed her wrist and pulled her to him.

His mouth took hers and her hair flowed around him like liquid, drowning him in sweet scent and a featherlight touch. Her body came to him in the same way, sliding around him like mercury. She was strong and smooth and intoxicating pressed to him like this, and he became filled with pleasure at the feel of her. She didn't say a word, and when his mouth demanded more of hers, she gave it fully. Her heat was his, wrapping around him and carrying him in the current of a shared urgency. It flowed like a river, and he had to fight to get to the surface again, fight for air. But he went with the force of it, not even trying to resist. He wanted her, needed her, and she was responding in kind.

The light cotton gown she wore might as well have been made of mist. It seemed to evaporate under his hands. And then he saw her in the moonlight that came in the window, and his heart stopped.

She was Venus de Milo with arms, Aphrodite with softer hair. Her body was strong and alive, her breasts as firm as a teenager's, her legs long and taut, her skin moist and slick, glowing like gold. He wanted her as he'd never wanted a woman before, and he'd wanted a few. But this was different. This was so full and rich and strong, his body began to tremble with it. His large, long hands took her and held her, and she clung to him as though she would never let go.

She felt him shaking and a feeling of pure awe poured through her. He was doing that because of her, and she knew it. She'd never felt her power this way before, never known she could overwhelm a man with desire just when she was shaken by the same need herself. This was wonderful in a way that defined wonder, joyful in a way that defined joy. At that moment, she would have done anything he might have asked, given herself completely in any and every way she could.

She was so in love. Her hands slid down his sides, across his chest, reveled in his hot, hard flesh. She pressed her face to his neck, using her tongue to trace a pattern on his skin, and she knew this was going to be the time they didn't stop. She didn't want to stop. She wanted him, wanted his male power inside her, wanted to feel the thrill of victory when he took her.

And he took her quickly, stopping only to find protection, his breath hard and rasping in his throat, as though he couldn't wait, couldn't live without having her that very instant. It was a hunger such as he'd never felt before and he was firm, demanding, and yet he held back enough so that he could be tender as well. It was torture to wait for her, agony to hold on, but when he felt her let herself go, when she let the current take her, he cried out as he let go as well, thrusting inside her as deeply as he could, groaning with the release, grimacing as though in pain, when actually he was in an ecstasy that seemed as though it would never stop.

She lay back, dazed. She'd never felt like this. There had been no groping, no awkward moves, despite his cast. No false apologies. It had gone like a symphony, like a string duet. It had built until it soared, and then had come back to earth like a sweet and very poignant recurring theme.

She was in love. She had never felt for any man what she felt for this one. Every move he made, every gesture, every word, every smile—she adored them all. She wanted to breathe in his breath, taste his skin, hold his body, merge and become one in every way. She wanted to have him, have him all. And at the same time, she knew she would never really reach that goal. It wasn't to be.

She turned and looked into his eyes. Waiting, she searched them, looking for...what? She wasn't sure. Was it a change, something new, something to tell her that he wanted her as much as she wanted him, that everything else had faded in importance now that they had found this together? Was that it? All she knew was, whatever it might be, she didn't find it.

Bitterness welled in her chest and she turned away, sick at heart but determined not to show it. It wasn't his fault that she'd lost her mind along with her heart. She couldn't let him see how far gone she was. She had to keep up a front, for both their sakes. She rolled away from him.

"Well, I'm glad that's over with," she said crisply, pulling her nightgown back over her head and rising from the couch.

He caught hold of her hand before she got away. "What do you mean by that?" he asked her quietly, searching what he could see of her face in the shadows.

She barely spared him a glance. "We've both been wondering what it would be like since you got here," she said, forcing a casual tone. "Now we know, and we can go on to other things."

His hand tightened on hers. "Are you trying to tell me you didn't like it?" he asked, his voice spiked with an element of steel.

Her laugh sounded like pennies falling on a tin plate. "Are you kidding? Of course I liked it." She pulled her hand away from his and rubbed where he'd held her. "But that doesn't mean I'll ever do it again," she warned him, walking quickly toward her bedroom.

She had to be alone, had to savor the moment and hold it to her. Climbing into bed, she closed her eyes and blotted out everything but what had happened and how she had felt; how he had moved her, and she him; how he had filled her with a joy she would never lose again. She replayed it all in her head, protecting it for all time. No matter what else happened, she would always have this in her heart.

Paul pulled the covers up around his neck and stared at the window. The tree outside was blowing in a steady breeze, the branches brushing the house now and then, making a weird sound. His body was relaxed, at peace, satisfied. But his mind was churning, and his soul was unfulfilled. He wasn't sure what he'd done here, why he'd done it. Rosemary was off limits. He'd known that from the first. He should have kept his hands off her. He'd wanted her. God knows, he'd wanted her badly, to the point where it was ripping him up inside. But now that he'd had what he'd been after, he only hoped it hadn't ruined the relationship they had between them. Because, despite its prickly moments, it had become very important to . him. He didn't want to be without it.

Something told him he had gone too far, that he was going to lose this thing he cherished. That was the paradox: to have her was to lose her. What a fool he was. What a jerk.

CHAPTER FOURTEEN

THE MORNING WAS FILLED with unease. They sat together at the kitchen table with sheets of plastic hanging around them, protecting them from the elements, but there was nothing that could protect them from the emotions that were spilling out and tinging the atmosphere.

"I guess I'd better find another place to live," Rosemary said at last, setting down her coffee mug with a thump that denoted a decision made. "That's the only thing to do."

Paul moved restlessly but couldn't think of a logical argument against it. What he'd said yesterday in semijest had turned out to be true. He knew there was no way he was going to find a woman to marry with Rosemary around. While she was here, his mind was filled with her. The trouble was, he wasn't too sure that would change when she was gone. She seemed to be taking over a major part of his brain lately. How the hell had that happened?

"It's lucky everything is already in boxes," she said, trying to smile and failing miserably. "I can move out at a moment's notice."

"You don't have to go," he said, but not convincingly.

She smiled at him and took his hand for a moment, looking deep into his eyes. "I do have to go and we both know it. But I don't want to."

His fingers curled around hers. "Then don't. Stay. We can move you up to the Coopers' place and—"

She was already shaking her head. Pulling his hand to her lips, she kissed it and smiled at him. "Nice try, but no cigar. I've got to go. I've called Kayla, and she can put me up until I find somewhere to move into. I'm going."

She rose and left the room, and he watched her, wondering what he was going to do without her.

SHE DRESSED and went to visit Pam. Funny how falling in love herself had put a whole new light on the dangers Pam faced, and how awful Patrick's current inattention must feel. She approached Pam's cute house with trepidation, not sure what she was going to say or how she was going to say it. There was no doubt about what she'd seen the night before. Patrick had been with Hayley in a bar out on the highway on a Saturday night, later than could ever be excused by the responsibilities of work. Pam had to know about it.

But Pam was seven months pregnant. How could she handle something like this now? Was it better to wait and let her get through her pregnancy first?

Rosemary would have to judge what to do by what she found, by how Pam reacted as she talked to her. There was no other way to do this. But she hated that it had to be done at all.

Patrick was just leaving as she pulled up in front of the house.

"Hey," he called out with a grin. "I'm glad you came. You can keep Pam company. I've got to meet with some disgruntled baseball parents. You know how it is, every dad thinks his kid should be a starter and wants the coach strung up if it doesn't happen." He shook his head, laughing. "Who knows? That disgruntled parent may be me someday."

"Maybe," Rosemary said faintly, studying him. He hadn't spotted her in the bar last night, or surely he wouldn't be able to chat cheerfully like this. But she had seen him, and that made it difficult.

"I've got to go," he sang out, backing his car the rest of the way down the drive. "See you later." With a jaunty wave, he was off.

But off to where? she wondered, shading her eyes as she looked after him. And to whom?

Pam seemed very glad to see her, and Rosemary couldn't detect any heartache lurking in her bright eyes. Samson was barking and Pam had to let him out into the backyard before they could really talk, but when she came back from doing that, she was laughing.

"That dog. I think he'd like to join us for a cup of tea." She started the water without bothering to ask if Rosemary wanted tea, knowing her well enough to know she was always ready for a cup. "But we can't allow that. He'd just dominate the conversation, wouldn't he?"

They chatted inconsequentially for a few minutes, about the latest Tyler news, and then Rosemary tried to turn things in another direction. "I spoke to Patrick outside. He was on his way to a meeting, I guess."

Pam nodded. "Since he's become athletic director, the work never stops. He's always on his way to something."

Rosemary looked down into her teacup. She was beginning to feel a little queasy, and she wondered if it had anything to do with the emotional turmoil she'd been going through since the night before. Not only was she upset about Patrick, she had Paul to think about, and the fact that she was losing him. No wonder she felt as though she had a black cloud hanging over her head.

"Is he still helping that old girlfriend of his establish the school swim team?" she asked Pam.

"Oh sure. They're great friends. I only wish I felt stable enough to join them at some of the meets and the team dinners."

Rosemary looked up, concerned. "Is there something wrong? Have you been having any weak spells?"

Pam hesitated. "No, not really. But I just feel so fragile sometimes. And I'm not used to that. I want to run and do all the things I've always done. But more than that, I want to protect this baby." She held the smooth curve of her stomach, covered by a soft, baggy T-shirt, in her hands. "This wonderful, wonderful baby," she said softly, looking down, her face full of love.

Rosemary bit her lip. "You know, you really ought to make it to some of those things Patrick does with Hayley," she said quickly. "If there's anything I can do to help you, let me know. I could drive you and stay with you...."

"And nursemaid me, and hold my spoon while I slurp my soup." Pam made a face at her friend. "No thank you. I'll get this baby born and then I'll get back into the swing of things."

Rosemary looked at her, feeling uncomfortable. She didn't know if it was right or wrong, but she knew she couldn't tell her about what she'd seen the night before. Still, she felt as though she had to warn her somehow. "About this Hayley person—" she began, but Pam cut her off.

"I can tell by your tone of voice you're suspicious of her," she said with a smile. "And to tell you the truth, I've had a moment or two of unease myself. Especially..." She laughed, remembering. "One day last week I had a doctor's appointment, and when I got to the hospital, the doctor had left on an emergency, so I went home. Who should I see driving away from the house but Patrick and Hayley?"

Rosemary's mouth dropped open and her outrage surged. How could Patrick be such a skunk? In his own home? "You're kidding."

Pam shook her head. "I was feeling a little low to begin with, and my first reaction was pure jealousy. Can you imagine?'' She laughed now, thinking about it, as though that had been such nonsense. ''But once I settled down and thought about it, I realized they must have been going somewhere and had just stopped by the house to get something Patrick had forgotten.''

Oh Pam, are you naive or blind? ''What did he say when you asked him about it?''

Pam gazed at her, wide-eyed. ''Oh, I didn't do that. I wouldn't ask him a thing like that.''

Rosemary gaped again. ''Why not?''

Pam leaned forward and put a hand on her arm. ''Don't you get it, Rosemary? I trust my husband. We are in perfect accord. If he has anything to tell me, he'll tell me.''

''Pam...''

''Anyway, Hayley is becoming a real friend. Her training is in interior decorating, you know. Though she loves coaching the swim team, she doesn't have a teaching certificate and can't combine it with a teaching job like most coaches do. So she's planning to open an interior design studio. Maybe Paul could hire her to put the finishing touch on his renovations.''

Rosemary took a long sip of tea to settle herself before she even tried a smile. Wasn't that just like Pam—to hold out a helping hand to the woman who was trying to ruin her life? It made Rosemary furious. She had to do something about it.

I trust my husband. I trust my husband.

Those words echoed through her head like a drumbeat as she drove toward the high school. Pam was so in love with the man, she had blinders on. Would she be so understanding if she'd been at the Iron Mustache and seen what Rosemary had seen the night before?

The drumbeat didn't stop, and she realized she had a splitting headache. Still, she wanted to get this over with. She pulled up into the pool parking lot. There was only one other car there, and it wasn't Patrick's. It looked as if she just might be in luck. She wanted to find Hayley alone. And as she walked out onto the pool deck, she found her.

"Hello, Hayley Ingalls," she said, knowing she was coming on a bit too strong, but unable to stop. She was upset. This person was threatening one of the best relationships she'd ever seen, and it just wasn't fair.

"I'm Rosemary Dusold, a friend of Patrick and Pam's. I sort of met you at Marge's the other night."

"I remember," the smaller woman said, standing with her head thrown back, her eyes wary. "What can I do for you?"

"You can find yourself a man who's unattached," she said bluntly. "You can respect a good marriage and leave it alone. That's what you can do."

The woman stared at her coolly. "I take it you think I'm some sort of threat to Patrick's marriage?" she noted. "What are you, the town disciplinarian? Or just a nosy neighbor?"

"I'm whatever it takes to fight you on this," Rosemary declared. "You've got to leave Patrick alone."

"And if I opt to disregard your wishes?" Hayley asked evenly, not showing any evidence of backing down. "What happens? Do I get run out of town on a rail?"

Rosemary glared at her. "We don't believe in violence, even when it's deserved. No, if you go on playing with fire the way you are, not only will you get burned, but you will be exposed for the selfish little flirt you are. And that's a promise."

Turning on her heel, she marched back to her car, knowing she'd made a mess of this and wishing she could think straight. She hadn't meant to come on so confrontationally right from the start. She'd planned to chat, to become friends, before she lowered the boom.

Well, it was too late now, and she was feeling worse and worse. Heading for home, she resented every red light that made the trip last longer. When she finally saw her charming Victorian—the house she was about to leave forever—ahead, she almost cried with relief.

"I feel horrible," she said as she entered.

Paul looked up from the sofa, where he was reading, and came to her at once. "Sit down," he ordered, feeling her forehead with his hand. "You're burning up."

She shook her head but sank into the chair anyway. "I can't be," she said hoarsely. "I just need dinner or something. I'll be all right. I have to move out tonight."

He looked at her eyelids, then lifted her sweatshirt to look at her torso. She closed her eyes, enduring this because she didn't have any choice. He pulled her shirt back down and rose to stand above her.

"Rosemary, my dear, you're not going anywhere," he said. "You've got chicken pox."

CHAPTER FIFTEEN

THE NEXT FEW DAYS were a blur of drinking fluids, rubbing on calamine lotion and lying in a darkened room feeling miserable and lethargic. Under such circumstances, Rosemary's conversational range tended to be limited.

"I can't have chicken pox," she insisted by the hour. "I had it when I was a kid."

"You thought you had it as a kid," Paul would respond cheerfully. "You probably had something else. This is real chicken pox, Rosemary. Believe me. You've got a classic case. You probably caught it from one of my patients. Maybe little Jennifer Sullivan."

Rosemary gazed up at him resentfully, wondering why he looked so happy about it. "This is a power thing with you, isn't it?" she muttered.

"What gives you that idea?" he responded, handing her the medicine he'd prescribed and setting out the liquids he wanted her to get down.

Actually, he wasn't happy, just accepting. It was always serious when an adult contracted a children's disease, and he watched her carefully. Luckily, the upstairs apartment needed only a final coat of paint, which could wait. After cleaning and vacuuming and airing out the place, he moved a bed up there and put her in it, away from the stream of visiting children that seemed to grow by the day. He was getting quite a reputation in Tyler. Children loved him and their parents trusted him.

"Hey, you were made to be a pediatrician in Tyler," Joe Santori told him. "A small-town doc, that's what you are. You've got the personality for it, you've got the skills. You made a good choice."

That was nice to hear, but there were times when he still wondered. He had spent too many years trudging through trenches and living through Third-World crises not to feel withdrawal pains at times.

And guilt. Why the guilt, he wasn't really sure. Maybe it was because he hadn't done enough. Maybe it was because he'd stayed too long. Or maybe it was just the human condition to never be satisfied with anything.

Caring for Rosemary, helping to pull her through the misery of chicken pox, reminded him of the old days, of watching children fight fevers in the jungle, and he was grateful for the clean conditions he had here, the infinite resources. If anything went wrong with Rosemary's case, he wouldn't have to watch helplessly while medicine ran out and the hospital was bombed.

But caring for her did more than remind him of the past. It deepened the bond he felt with her and made clear that this was more than sexual attraction at work between them.

On the third day, Joe brought her some chicken soup his wife, Susannah, had made for her, along with a present. Paul joked with him as he led him up to the room, then left him with the cranky sick lady, hoping the visit would raise her spirits a bit.

"Hi, Joe," she said grumpily, looking as Victorian as the house in the ruffled nightgown Kayla had brought her to wear for visitors. "This isn't chicken pox, you know."

"It isn't?" Joe looked surprised. "What is it, then?"

"It's some crazy tropical disease Paul brought with him from the wars." She struck a tragic pose. "It pretends to be chicken pox, but it's all a sham. I'm going to die soon."

Joe laughed, glad she still had her sense of humor. "My, aren't we the fatalist," he teased. "There's nothing you can do about it, right? Just lie there and die."

"That's the plan," Rosemary said, actually growing a little more cheerful at the thought. "I could go at any minute."

"Nah, the soup Susannah made for you will fix you right up. And guess what? She went out and got you a present." He handed her the large, gaily wrapped package. "Go ahead. Open it up."

She pulled off the paper impatiently, and out popped a large, soft teddy bear with shoe-button eyes and a bashful smile.

"It's a teddy bear," she said, holding it out so that she could look at it.

A teddy bear. What kind of crazy man would bring a teddy bear to a grown woman? She frowned, gazing at the bear and then gazing at Joe. Slowly, she pulled it close and wrapped her arms around it, and a feeling of peace came with it. It was something to hold, something to love, something to keep her company during the long, lonely, achy afternoons.

"I love it," she said earnestly, holding it tighter. "Oh Joe, tell Susannah it's just what I needed. Thank you so much."

When Paul came up a little while later, she was still holding it, and as he came into the darkened room he was startled. At first glance, it looked as though she had a baby in her arms, and his heart raced before logic took over and he realized what it was.

"Isn't this silly?" she said, not letting go. "Here I am with a teddy bear. But you know what? It feels so good to hold on to something, and I'm so miserable."

He smiled and stroked her hair and held her, and she sighed and relaxed and let him. He was being so good to her. She loved him so much. She didn't let herself think about how, when she got well, she would have to leave. All she could think about was how sick she was and how glad she was he was the one taking care of her.

The twins convention was over. In Sheila's eyes, it had been a disaster, but there were already plans afoot to hold the second annual twins get-together next year at Timberlake Lodge. Paul helped oversee the last of the stragglers to head for home, contacting their hometown physicians and checking the children over to make sure each was ready to travel.

Once he'd completed that task, he went back to his office in the medical building to go over some paperwork and see a couple of patients. He had the videos of children playing running in his makeshift waiting room, and they were working quite well. In fact, he'd found that children passing by in the hallway were attracted by the sound of the videos.

He'd finished with his patients and was going over some forms when he realized he'd left the tape running. Going out to turn it off, he found a little blond girl with ringlets sitting cross-legged on the floor in front of the screen and watching it intently.

"Hi there," he said.

She looked up at him and gave him a quick once-over. "Are you the doctor?" she asked in the chirping, child-like voice of a four-year-old.

"Yes, I am. Did you come to see me?"

She shook her head emphatically. "I like the babies," she told him.

"We don't have any newborns today," he told her. "You'll have to go over to the maternity wing."

"I know," she told him, her self-possession evident in her confident smile. "We already went there. We saw the new babies. And now, I have to watch this movie."

Standing back, he looked at what was interesting her. A group of children were putting on costumes. "Do you like it?"

"Uh-huh. Look." She pointed out a little girl on the screen. "That's me."

At first he thought she was kidding, but on closer examination, he realized she was absolutely right.

"Wow," he said, smiling at her. "I didn't know you were a movie star."

She nodded as though it were no big deal. "They took us at school," she told him.

So that was the connection. He chuckled. "What is your name, Miss Movie Star?"

"Margaret 'lyssa Forrester."

Forrester. He frowned. The name had a familiar ring but he couldn't quite place it. "Where is your mother?"

"Home."

But someone had to be here with the child. "How about your dad?"

"He's coming." She cocked her head to the side and a smile lit her face. "Here he comes!"

Just as he finished the words, the sound of a male voice could be heard in the hallway. "Maggie? Where did you get to?"

"I'm in here, Daddy," she called without getting up. "I'm watching my movie."

A tall, wiry, handsome man filled the doorway. He glanced down at his daughter, then looked at Paul.

"You're Paul Chambers, aren't you?" he said, putting out his hand. "I'm Cliff Forrester."

The name clicked in Paul's brain and he returned the handshake. "Ah yes, Pam Kelsey told me about you."

Cliff's face took on a wary expression. "Yeah, you can make that mutual." His gaze met Paul's, then he turned away and shoved his hands into his pockets, looking uncomfortable. Pam had been after him, and so had his wife,

Liza. They thought he ought to talk to this man who'd supposedly had similar experiences to his own. But talking to others wasn't one of his talents, and he wondered if just shaking hands with the doctor would be enough to satisfy the women.

"That's one great little girl you have there," Paul noted.

Cliff nodded, and the two of them stood in the back of the room, arms folded, watching Maggie watch the television screen.

"Yeah, she's pretty much the center of attention in our family," Cliff added at last.

Paul nodded, enjoying her enjoyment of the video. She looked like quite a handful to him. Probably a lot like her mother, Liza, who he'd heard was a real firecracker of a woman. "I imagine she is."

Cliff shifted his weight restlessly from one foot to the other. "You have any kids?" he asked.

"No, not yet," Paul replied. "But I'm hoping to have some soon."

Cliff turned and looked at him, surprised. "I didn't know you were married."

A sheepish grin lit Paul's face. "I'm not. I've got to find someone to marry, first."

Cliff laughed. "Then you've got your work cut out for you."

Paul nodded, and the two of them were silent for another moment, watching the children play in the video.

Cliff moved nervously. Pam was going to ask him what he'd said. Liza was going to put him through the wringer if he didn't have a good answer. And the guy was nice enough. Looking away so that he wouldn't have to meet Paul's eyes, he said gruffly, "So I hear you've been overseas."

Paul nodded. "Yes. I've spent the last fifteen years overseas."

"Whereabouts?" he asked, risking a look at his face.

"Everywhere." Paul gave him a crooked grin. "The last few years were mostly in Bosnia and Chechnya."

Cliff nodded. "Rough places these days."

"You bet."

Cliff shuffled his feet. Surely that would be enough to satisfy them. He'd made an effort. Maybe if he just called out to Maggie and got out of here . . .

"So you were in 'Nam?" Paul queried. He'd heard the stories by now—knew all about how Cliff had come back a basket case; how he'd lived like a lonely, tortured hermit in the woods by Timberlake Lodge; how it had only been a few years ago that he could face coming near others in Tyler. How Liza Baron had changed his life and become his wife.

Cliff nodded slowly. "Yeah, I was in 'Nam," he said.

"That was even rougher," Paul said quietly. "I had an uncle who got pretty messed up by his experiences there."

Cliff nodded. "Sometimes . . ." he began, and then he cleared his throat. "Sometimes the hardest thing is to forgive yourself."

Paul frowned. "I'm not sure I know what you're talking about."

Cliff shrugged. "Different people get hung up on different things," he said, and suddenly he was rolling, surprising even himself. "Sometimes you feel guilty because others died and you didn't. You start to wonder what was so damn special about you. Why you and not that nice girl selling flowers on the corner, the one about to get married? Why did the bomb kill her and miss you? You know what I mean."

Paul nodded slowly. "Yes," he said softly, his eyes a little glazed. "I know what you mean."

Cliff grimaced and rubbed the back of his neck with his hand. "One of the hardest things to face is that there are things your loved ones may never understand. Things you'll have to keep to yourself forever."

This was a dilemma Paul had been wrestling with. How much to tell about? And did anybody care? "But doesn't that eat away at you inside?" he asked, looking at Cliff.

Cliff shrugged. "If you feel the need to tell all, go get a therapist to spill your guts to. Don't lay it on the people who love you until you're sure it won't hurt them more than it hurts you."

Paul nodded slowly, wondering what was behind the exquisite pain he could read in the depths of Cliff's eyes. He knew he hadn't been through anything as bad as what Cliff was talking about. He had, after all, mainly been on a mission of mercy overseas. But he'd seen things he wished he could erase from his mind. And Cliff was right. There was no reason he should put that burden on . . . say, Rosemary. If he were in love with her. What would be the point? To be open and honest and give the other person a good idea of what you'd gone through—that was important. But to transfer nightmares from your shoulders to hers . . . no, that wouldn't be right. His nightmares were his own. After all, what was it they said? Living well is the best revenge. Well, living decently was the best way to blot indecencies from the past. It had to be.

"Well, we've got to go." Cliff held out his hand again, and this time his face was shining with virtuous relief. He'd done it. He'd had a talk with Paul Chambers, and he wasn't going to have to hedge about it at all.

"It's been nice talking to you," Paul told him, pretty sure he understood the man and what it had cost him to do this. "And you can tell Pam, mission accomplished."

Cliff flashed a quick look at him and grinned. "Thanks for everything," he said heartily, taking his daughter by the hand. "We'll see you later."

"Bye, Mr. Doctor," Maggie cried, skipping alongside her daddy.

Paul watched them go, alternately amused and touched. From the description he'd had, Cliff Forrester seemed to have made an amazing transformation. Paul's own problems seemed trivial compared to those of the Vietnam veteran, but he did have his own ghosts. It would be a good thing to clear the air and get them out of his system. "Clear the decks for something new," he muttered to himself.

He'd thought it would be so simple. All he had to do was find a nice woman, fall madly in love and marry her. But things had become confused. The only woman he'd seen that he wanted was bound and determined not to have children. And that was a real-life problem, one you could touch and taste and get your arms around.

But he needed to get some more work done, more forms filled out. Paul worked for another hour, then stopped for a break and gave Rosemary a call, just to check on her.

"I promised myself I wasn't going to whine the next time I talked to you," she said, actually sounding better than she had that morning when he'd left her. "I'm getting better. Honest. I may live after all."

He laughed, but a tentative knock on the door interrupted and he asked her to hold on while he responded. "Come in," he called, looking up and holding the receiver against his shoulder.

A beautiful young woman entered, her black hair wrapped about her head in an elaborate French twist, her face exquisite, her bearing regal—and her form very pregnant.

"Paul, darling," she said, her smile both gentle and knowing. "I've found you at last."

Paul stared at her, the telephone forgotten. "Charmayne," he said. "My God. I haven't seen you since Paris. What are you doing here?"

"Looking for you." Her laugh was like a run over piano keys. "And look," she said, pointing out the obvious. "I'm going to have a baby."

Paul stared at her numbly, then lifted the receiver slowly and spoke into it haltingly. "Uh, Rosemary? Listen, someone is here. I'm going to have to get back to you."

Rosemary leaned against her pillows, stunned and filled with a strange sinking feeling. She'd heard every word, and every word had cut like a knife. The connection had been lost, but she still held the phone to her ear as the dial tone droned on and on.

Who the heck was Charmayne? And why was she pregnant? Rosemary had heard the exchange between them, but she hadn't seen their faces, hadn't been able to read the nuances, and now more than ever she was filled with frustration at being tied to a bed when things were happening out there in the world. Thinking quickly, she dialed Kayla at her office in the finance department of the hospital.

"Run to Paul's office, quick," she demanded without preamble. "Take a look at the woman he's got in there with him. Soak up everything you can about her, about their relationship, the way they deal with each other. And call me right back."

"What am I going to say about why I'm at his office?" Kayla wailed in protest.

"I don't know. You'll think of something. Tell him you want to give me a get-well card."

"But I don't have a card to give you."

"Tell him you're going to be getting a card and would he deliver it to me."

"Weak, Rosemary. I'll think of something better on my way."

Rosemary fretted while waiting for Kayla to call back. Each minute seemed an hour long. Meanwhile, she tried to think of innocuous reasons Paul might have a female friend—an apparently close female friend—who was pregnant at this time. She couldn't think of one.

Finally, the phone rang.

"Kayla?" she said, jamming the receiver to her ear. "What did you find out?"

Kayla let out her breath in a sigh. "Are you sitting down?"

"Of course, my dear little spy. I'm sick in bed, remember?"

"Oh. That's right. Sorry. Well, okay. Here goes. She's gorgeous."

Rosemary groaned. "That was something I didn't need to hear."

"The truth always hurts. She's one of those tall, elegant European types in designer clothes."

Rosemary's jaw set. "In designer maternity clothes, you mean," she said bitterly.

Kayla gasped. "How did you know that?"

"Psychic powers. Tell me more."

Kayla hesitated. "You're not going to like this," she warned.

Rosemary's fingers tightened on the receiver. "That's why I made you check it out. Tell me."

"They were holding hands across the desk."

Rosemary sat in stunned silence. Somehow that was the last thing she had wanted to hear. A friendly kiss, a hug, laughing together she could have handled. But holding hands was just so intimate, so caring. Her heart lurched and her throat felt raw and horrible.

"Anything else?" she asked hoarsely.

"The only thing I heard him say was, 'Don't worry. I'll take care of everything.'"

Rosemary closed her eyes and nodded. That was what she'd been afraid of, and what she would expect him to say. This was a new Paul, not the irresponsible profligate of old, an image she hardly thought of any longer. She'd seen Paul in action too many times. He was a wonderful man, the most trustworthy one she'd ever known. She didn't have a second thought about that.

"Thanks, Kayla," she said dully, ringing off. "You're a good friend."

She'd been feeling better, but she felt a relapse coming on. An old love had turned up from Paul's past. Well, what did she expect? With a man like Paul, there would always be old loves coming out of the woodwork. Responsible he might be, but women flocked to him, and he had often responded in kind. That was as much a part of him as his good nature, his handsome face, his tender touch. A woman would have a hard time dealing with that sort of thing if she were serious about the man.

Rosemary closed her eyes, laid her head back and tried very hard to go to sleep. What she had to do was get better so she could go out in the world and take care of these things, see what was happening for herself. Being sick was no fun. She wanted to sleep until it was over.

THE NEXT DAY she was well enough to get up and walk around.

"Take it easy," Paul advised. "You don't want to take it too fast. You might end up back in bed for a week."

"Not me," she said stoutly. "I won't be an invalid, no matter what. I've got to be free."

He grinned at her. "The classic cry of the oppressed around the world."

She nodded, sinking to her seat at the kitchen table, where he'd prepared a nice lunch for her. "That's what I am," she claimed, poking at the shrimp salad he'd made. "Oppressed."

He nodded to show his deep compassion for her pain. "Who's oppressing you at the moment?" he asked with interest.

She thought for a few seconds, fork poised in the air. "Males," she decided at last. "It's got to be the male-dominated society."

He chuckled. "Why? Because you can't think of anything else?"

She threw him a mock glare of resentment. "You're too busy oppressing me to understand."

"I'm an oppressor all right," he said carelessly.

But at the same time, she saw his face change and he looked away, and she regretted having made light of something he'd experienced. After all, he had spent a lot of years working against real oppression. She thought about the dream he'd had the other night, how she'd heard him cry out. What was the name he'd called? Analise. Was she a lost love? She was surely someone he felt deeply about, or why would he dream about her? And then there was the pregnant lady, Charmayne. Rosemary closed her eyes and winced. There were too many questions. She had to have some answers.

"Paul," she said, watching his reaction. "Who is Analise?"

"Analise?" He looked up at her, startled. "Where did you hear that name?"

"From you." She hesitated, then took her courage in her hands and went on. "The other night, when you were dreaming."

"Ah, the other night."

They were both silent for a moment, both remembering what had happened shortly after that dream. Somehow such a response between them seemed almost impossible now. They had both drawn back into defensive mode, and with her being sick, the wall between them had thickened somehow. At least on the sensual level. The friendship level, however, seemed stronger than ever.

"She was a woman I knew in Chechnya," he said, and he could see by the look on Rosemary's face what she was thinking. And why not? She, of all people, knew what his reputation had been. But there was more to him than that. He hated having her think of him that way again.

And that was why he decided to tell her the whole truth.

"It's a long story," he said quietly. "I'll give you the abbreviated version. I was with a team of medical workers in Chechnya, when that country was trying to break away from Russia. There was a lot of fighting in the streets. A lot of ordinary people being killed. A lot of children being hurt."

He winced involuntarily, sitting back as though to avoid something painful. But the pain was in his mind, in his memories, and the only way to avoid that was not to think at all.

"We were doing all we could, but hospital conditions are pretty primitive in that part of the world and we saw horrible tragedies every day. I had to watch children die just because we couldn't get enough antibiotics to save them," he said, his voice growing harsher and harsher, "when you knew damn well there were planes filled with supplies just sitting on runways...." He swore softly and forced back his anger, regaining his composure. Glancing at her, he tried to smile and failed. "Anyway, it was bad. Analise was a local woman, a translator who was helping us. We became...friendly."

Rosemary nodded. She'd expected that.

"Analise had a baby, eight months old. Her husband had been killed by the Russians. The baby had spinal meningitis and there was no way I could save it there. We had to get the baby to a real hospital."

His eyes glazed over for a moment, and he was back there. He remembered running through the night with the baby in his arms, dodging soldiers, trying to get across town on time. They were about to close the airport; the last plane for Berlin was about to leave. He had no idea if he was going to make it in time, but he had to try. Running through the dark, falling and dropping the baby, bribing a group of soldiers when he didn't know for sure who they were allied with, screaming for them to hold the plane as he ran out onto the tarmac, not sure if the baby in his arms was even still alive after all it had been through...it was all a nightmare that lived on in his head, but there was no way he could tell her all about it.

"Did you get the baby out?" she asked, and he looked at her, wondering at the way she put it, as though she already knew the story, could sense it without having to be told.

He nodded slowly. "I got her out. We got her to a wonderful hospital in Berlin. We saved her, and got her mother there about a week later."

Rosemary nodded, her eyes shining as she watched him. She knew he'd been a hero. He didn't have to tell her as much. "So you succeeded. Why the nightmares?"

He shrugged. "Good question. I used to think it was guilt for leaving. There is still so much to do in those countries, so many people who need help. But I've decided that wasn't it." He smiled at her. "I think it's because of the baby angle. I have a deep, abiding need to have children. Something in my soul is telling me to hurry up and get with it or risk missing out."

Rosemary bit her lip. She wasn't crazy about that explanation. "Do you still hear from Analise?" she asked.

He shook his head slowly. "She went back to Chechnya, from what I've heard. And her baby is doing well."

"And you decided to come back home yourself," she said softly.

He smiled at her. "I did. And now I'm dealing with chicken pox and splinters instead of missing legs and malaria."

Reaching out, she put a comforting hand on his arm. "These kids need doctors, too," she told him. "I think you've done your share to save the world."

"Do you?" He searched her eyes as though he could find out for sure if he just looked hard enough. But she didn't know. She couldn't know. The answer would have to come from inside him.

Rosemary couldn't finish her salad, but she felt much better for having ventured out into the world again, even if for just a little while. It had been a relief to hear the story of Analise. She could see by Paul's reaction that, though the woman's life had touched him in many ways, he hadn't been in love with her, and he wasn't in love with her now. Rosemary had no right to care about that, to feel a sense of relief. But she did just the same.

Now there was the puzzle of Charmayne. But somehow the woman was too close, too immediate, and Rosemary was afraid to ask him, afraid of what she might find out. So she went back up to her bed and lay alone and stared at the ceiling and wondered.

CHAPTER SIXTEEN

IT WAS TIME she left. It was, in fact, way past time for her to leave. The chicken pox was gone, though the spots not quite forgotten. Still, there were no excuses any longer. She had to go. Staying here, she was just delaying the agony.

Rosemary packed what few things she still had left to put away. She had an apartment waiting for her, a place in a new building out on the highway. It was evening, but she knew she should go ahead and get out now, while she still had the will to do it. Sadly, she walked through the house that she had loved, touching things, remembering. Not so long ago, keeping her home here had been the most important thing in her life. Now all that seemed superfluous. All she cared about was Paul.

She'd never felt this way before, not even when she'd been married to Greg. They had been so young and so wrong for each other. She'd loved him, but in a different way. This feeling she had for Paul was deeper, stronger. Inside her was a fierce determination that he should be happy, that he should have the way of life he'd wanted for so long and deserved.

She had to get out of his way and let him get on with his search for love and family. It was probably the hardest thing she'd ever had to do, but she had to do it. And why? Because she loved him.

She wasn't sure just how he felt about her. She knew he wanted her, that he liked her, that they got along awfully well. Beneath everything, they were friends. And sometimes something smoldered in his eyes when he looked at her, something that made her heart beat faster and reminded her of the night they had made love. She held that memory close to her heart. Nothing would ever make her let it go.

It all seemed so simple. She loved him; he wanted her. Why not just go with the flow? Why not let nature take its course?

Because...because it was too dangerous, too crazy. He'd been very open about what he wanted from the very first. He wanted children. And for that, she was just too old.

"Thirty-eight isn't ancient, you know," one side of her would argue. "What if...?"

"It's too late," she would respond angrily. "I've never wanted children before. I can't start now, just because I want to hold on to a man."

Ah, but what a man. Her toes curled and her shoulders went limp when she looked at him. His face was as chiseled as the profile on a coin and his body could have served as a model for Greek statues. But better than that, he was good and generous and kind. You didn't find such a man every day.

When she thought now about how she'd pictured him and resented him all these years, it made her smile and shake her head. She'd deluded herself because she'd been so desperate to blame the failure of her marriage on someone other than herself. Now she knew where it belonged.

One thing she had learned was this: Paul Chambers was, indeed, the same man she'd known all those years ago. Of course he was. Deep inside, he had never been as careless and cruel as he'd seemed. Chasing his own ghosts, he had acted in ways he thought might blot out things in his past and in himself that he didn't like. But she was pretty sure he'd learned you couldn't do that. You had to accept yourself and build on what you had. And that was exactly what he had done.

Could she really turn her back on all this? She knew she had to.

She was upstairs in the apartment that was to have been hers. Everything looked so fresh and new. It would have been wonderful to have decorated it with her things. But now that wasn't going to happen. Yes, the sooner she got out, the better.

She heard him come in downstairs. Sinking down onto the bed, she listened to his footsteps, heard him go into the kitchen and then head for the stairs. But it wasn't until she saw him in the doorway that she realized something had changed.

"They took your cast off," she exclaimed, delighted. "Oh, Paul, you can walk again."

He grinned, stepping gingerly. "I've still got a wrap on it, but the cast is gone and I hope to keep it that way." He cocked an eyebrow in her direction. "I'm a fully equipped man again, you know. Maybe we ought to test me out."

She smiled, but shook her head, and he noticed the sadness in her eyes. Looking around, he saw the suitcase and the boxes. He turned back to her, his own blue eyes suddenly dark and stormy. "I wish you wouldn't go," he said, his voice husky. "Not yet."

She could hardly bear to meet his gaze. It hurt to think of what she was about to lose.

"I have to go," she said shakily, her hands locked together in her lap. "I have to get out of your way so that you can find a woman who can share your life the way you want it to be."

Sinking onto the bed beside her, he gently disengaged her left hand and took it in his own. "You could take care of that," he said, his voice playful. "You could marry me yourself."

She knew he was kidding and she threw him a fleeting smile, then couldn't look away from his beloved face. Her gaze took in every aspect, every feature, loving his flaws along with his attributes. "I thought we'd settled that a long time ago," she said quietly.

He shook his head, his blue eyes filled with an exquisite agony even as he smiled at her lovingly. "I don't think we have," he told her, searching her face. "I don't think you've listened to my side of the issue."

"Your side of the issue?" She couldn't help but match his smile. He was irresistible.

"I have a side, you know. And I have some very good points on it, too."

"I'll just bet." She laughed softly, looking at him. "Okay." She held up her wrist so that she could see the face of her watch. "I'll give you five minutes to present your case. Ready, set, go."

She looked up at him expectantly, but he didn't say a word. Instead, he slid his arm around her shoulders and began to kiss her neck.

"Oh, Paul," she said, laughing. "Wait. This isn't fair." But she arched her head, giving him better access.

"Fairness," he murmured, tugging aside the collar of her shirt to find a more fertile field for his kisses, "has nothing to do with it."

She tried to push him away, but for some reason her muscles seemed to have lost all strength. "Paul," she murmured again, though this time her tone was less defensive, more a moan of pleasure. But this was wrong. She had to fight this overwhelming temptation. "Paul, we can't do this," she muttered breathlessly as her pulse began to pound in her ears.

"Can't we?" He took kisses from her lips, took them quickly and then buried his face in the cradle of her neck. "This is my argument," he said between caresses. "You said you'd give me a chance. When I'm done, you can refute everything I present, if you dare."

Her head fell back, her eyes half-closed as she began to lose her grip on sanity. "This isn't an argument," she whispered, her hands plunging into his hair, holding his head to her. "This is bribery."

"Call it what you will," he muttered, pushing her gently back against the pillows. "Just tell me if it's working."

She laughed very low in her throat as her blood began to pound through her veins with new intensity and purpose. His body was hard and long and made of the most intoxicating substance on earth. How could it not work?

She gave in then, let his lovemaking melt her resistance and turn them both into lovers. It was what they longed most to be, and it happened so naturally.

He had a magic way with clothes. Hers seemed to disappear without her really being aware of what he'd done to cause it. And then his were gone, too, and she was able to run her hands along the solid hardness of his beautiful body, trailing fire wherever they went. And as his hot, liquid mouth covered her full, erect nipple, she cried out and felt her hips lift, a natural invitation she couldn't have held back if she'd tried to. She pulled him in to where her need was most intense, demanding satisfaction, and he gave her everything he could. It came upon them like a flash flood, roaring and tearing up everything in its path, tumbling them in the raging waters, turning their lives and bodies inside out, only to leave them spent and breathless in its wake.

He pulled her back into his arms and held her close against him. "Don't go now," he whispered into her tousled hair. "Give me one night."

She nodded, with tears in her eyes. "One night," she whispered in return, and she sank back into the cloud of love he'd created around them.

SUNSHINE CAME SOFTLY through the window as Rosemary danced through the area where the kitchen had been the next morning. A lot of the remodeling had been finished and the place was no longer draped in plastic. It was going to be the hottest day yet of the late spring. The morning was already heating up and she hummed as she set out things for breakfast. A warm, happy glow filled her. There was a "maybe" in the air. Maybe they could work things out. They were so darn good together. Maybe, just maybe...

The doorbell rang and she groaned. What was this, another set of twins? At least she'd put on a pair of shorts and a tank top instead of her Victorian nightgown. Paul was in the shower, enjoying it to the hilt now that his cast was off. Rosemary went to the door, expecting someone with a sick child.

What she found instead was a tall, beautiful woman in a cashmere suit who looked as though she were expected for a fashion-photography magazine shoot and had lost her way. "I'm looking for Dr. Chambers," she said, speaking carefully, as though she were afraid Rosemary might not be too bright. "Can you tell me where I might find him?"

"He lives right here," Rosemary replied evenly. "With me."

She didn't know why she'd said that, and the moment the words were out of her mouth, she wished she could take them back. But the woman wasn't shocked. In fact, she seemed to find the fact amusing.

"With you?" she echoed, giving the impression of rolling her eyes without actually doing it. "Yes, Paul is such a rascal, isn't he? My name is Charmayne Allredo. Paul and I are ... old friends. Is he here?"

Rosemary nodded slowly, taking her time. It was obvious this woman liked to put people at a disadvantage as quickly and as thoroughly as possible. She wasn't going to let that happen. "He is here," she said. "If you would like to come in and wait for him, I'm sure he'll be down soon."

"Thank you." Charmayne entered, looking around with interest, but with a sense of superiority that said she'd never seen anything so quaint in all her life. "You seem to be remodeling."

"Yes. Paul is transforming this lovely old Victorian into his new pediatric office."

"Oh, yes, that sounds like Paul." Her laugh was meant to be charming, and to Rosemary's chagrin, it succeeded. "We met in Paris some months ago. He was trying to decide whether or not to come back to live in the States at the time. He does so want a stable home and his own children." She smiled and pressed a jeweled hand to her very pregnant belly. "I'm just glad I'm going to be able to give that to him."

The earth fell away beneath Rosemary's feet. The sky went black, and there was a strange buzzing in her ears. She continued to chat inconsequentially, even offering Charmayne a cup of coffee, but she was running on automatic pilot. Her brain was not really engaged, and her soul was shriveling into a corner of her heart.

When Paul finally showed up in the living room, she left as quickly as she could, moving blindly. She couldn't stay to watch their meeting. She didn't want to see the look in his eyes, see how he looked at the baby Charmayne was carrying.

This was what he wanted, after all. A baby. Something she could never give him. Staying here at a time like this would only be standing in the way of his happiness. She had to leave, to remove herself from the equation.

Just moments before, she'd thought there might be hope. Now she knew there was none. Moving like a zombie, she finished her packing and began to load her possessions into her car.

ROSEMARY'S NEW APARTMENT was very nice. Upstairs in a redbrick, two-story building, it overlooked a greenbelt, and there were plenty of trees around. It wasn't far from the park, and she was getting in lots of hiking.

It was more than a month since she'd moved out. Spring was fading, giving way to summer, which was coming in with a vengeance. Heat wave after heat wave left everyone limp, despite the air-conditioning, and the summer thunderstorms seemed more frightening, more severe.

But maybe it was just this apartment, so different from the home she was used to, where the tree in the front yard kept it cool in the summertime and the solid construction kept things warm in winter. It wasn't like that here. The walls seemed thin and central air-conditioning prevailed.

Rosemary missed the house. She missed the neighborhood. But most of all, she missed Paul. During the day, she kept herself busy and she managed not to think about him too much.

But nights were another matter. As soon as her head hit the pillow, as soon as she'd turned out her light, he was there with her, every part of him, every sound, every scent. She'd never been so sweepingly in love before, and she wasn't sure if it was something that would pass, like loss, like grief, or if it would go on forever and be a part of her. She was beginning to be very much afraid that the latter was happening.

She'd begun doing something strange. Every evening, she put on the dress he'd given her. She only put it on for a few minutes, and then she stood in front of her full-length mirror and stared at herself in it. At first she felt awkward and thought it looked out of place and out of character. But little by little, it was beginning to grow on her, and finally she began to dance in front of the mirror when she had it on, enjoying the way the lace looked against her tanned skin, the way the fabric swayed against her legs, the fit of the bodice, how it showed off her figure.

"Darned if I don't look sort of pretty," she admitted to herself at last. And then she wished she could wear it somewhere, so Paul might see her in it.

"Traitor," she said to herself. But there wasn't much conviction in her voice.

She'd tried to decorate the apartment in a similar fashion to the way she'd had her place in the Victorian, but it just didn't work out in this sterile environment. Rosemary had bought some of her favorite antique pieces from Paul, unable to give them up, and they helped to a degree. But the small touches that had worked so well on Morgan Avenue looked out of place here, and they just weren't satisfying. The teddy bear Susannah and Joe had given her sat on her bed, but it was the only thing she'd brought along that comforted her at all.

She'd driven past the house. The remodeling was finished and the outside looked gorgeous, a real showplace. She'd ached to go in, to see what he'd done, to see him again. But she couldn't let herself do that. She couldn't tempt fate. Besides, if Charmayne was living there, she didn't want to know.

"I don't think she is," Kayla told her. "She comes in to see Dr. Garza, the new ob/gyn, every week or so, and I checked out her address. She lives in Sugar Creek. And she has a Sugar Creek telephone number."

"That's odd," Rosemary mused. "I would have thought he would want to keep on eye on things...."

Pam wasn't much for subterfuge, and when Rosemary confided her story, Pam went right to the source. "Paul," she said, stopping by his office in the hospital medical building. "I have a few things I want to ask you."

"Ask me quick," he told her with a welcoming smile. "I'm packing up the last of my belongings. From now on, if you want to see me, you're going to have to come over to Morgan Avenue.''

"Wonderful. I'm glad for you." Pam lifted her chin and gave him a steady look. "But I want to know if you're going to marry this Charmayne person."

"Marry?" Paul looked annoyed. "Whoever said anything about marrying her?"

"She did, I take it." Pam fixed him with a glare that could have pinned small animals to the wall. "Isn't she having your baby? And doesn't that fit in perfectly with your plans?"

His gaze glinted like steel and a white line outlined his lips. He stared at Pam so long before answering, she began to get nervous. "You can tell Rosemary she should come talk to me herself," he said coldly at last. "She doesn't have to send her friends if she wants to find things out."

Rosemary had groaned when Pam reported what had happened. "Now he thinks I'm sending spies. Oh, Pam, why did you do that?"

"Because I wanted to know," Pam retorted stubbornly. "And because you need to know."

Rosemary hated that Paul thought she was a sneak, but she had to admit it was intriguing to wonder what Charmayne was up to and why Paul didn't seem to be marrying her yet. In fact, he seemed to be busy doing other things.

"Okay, here's the latest," Pam told her in a hurried phone call one afternoon. "He's spending all his free time at that old duck pond. They say he's been helping that old man who runs the place clear some of the land and build shelters for animals, stuff like that. Isn't that a kick? And you thought he was out partying with Charmayne."

Actually, Rosemary never thought of him partying anymore. But she did wonder what he was up to. She saw him from afar a few times, in the hall of the hospital or down in the parking lot. She had fantasies every night about what she would say to him when they finally did come face-to-face again. But when it happened, things didn't at all go as she'd planned.

She and Glenna Kelsey Nielsen were planning a baby shower for Pam, even though Glenna was busy preparing for her own wedding in July. Rosemary had gone to Gates Department Store to pick up some supplies for the celebration. As she walked out through the large glass doors, there he was, coming in.

"Hi," she said, stopping dead and staring at him, drinking in every beloved feature like a thirsty person who'd found a canteen full of sweet water.

"Hi, yourself," he said, stopping as well, his hands in the pockets of his light jacket. A small storm had just swept through and water was still dripping from the trees in the town square behind him. His eyes were blue as ever, but they looked at her warily, as though he wasn't sure what she might say to him.

"How are you?" she asked, really wanting to know.

"Lonely," he answered shortly. And he held her gaze, not saying another word.

She swallowed, wondering why he was acting like this, as though he blamed her for something. "How—how's Charmayne?" she asked, then wished she hadn't.

He grimaced and his hands balled into fists in the pockets of his jacket. "Charmayne is just fine," he said, his voice harsh. His blue eyes sparked as he glared at her. "That isn't my baby she's carrying, Rosemary. In fact, she isn't here because of me at all. She's staying with her aunt in Sugar Creek until the baby comes. As an old friend, I'm helping her find a good couple to adopt her child. That's what she came to me for."

Rosemary's fingers had gone numb. "Oh," she said in a tiny voice. "But, she implied . . . I thought . . ."

"She had some hopes when she first arrived," he admitted. "She was grasping at straws. Her marriage fell apart a long time ago and her lover left her when he found out she was pregnant. She had no money, no one to help her, so she came back here to Wisconsin, where she grew up, and she thought we might get together." He shrugged. "She was pretty desperate. But she's okay now." He gazed at Rosemary for a moment.

"So you lose that excuse," he said coldly. "Now I guess you'll have to think of another."

His gaze held hers for a long moment, and she couldn't think of anything to say. Swearing under his breath, he pushed past her, going into the store, and she turned, her hand out to stop him.

"Paul..." she began, but he was gone.

He was angry with her, hurt that she'd left the way she had after the night they'd spent together. She couldn't blame him. She wanted to run after him, to explain, to make him smile at her...but what would be the point? She would just have to leave him again. She went on home and sat in a darkened room and cried.

She seemed to be crying a lot lately. In fact, other odd things were happening. At first she'd attributed them to her sadness, and to the changing seasons. But finally she had to admit to herself that something was wrong. And the signs were very scary.

Her breasts were tender and seemed swollen. She was nervous and got upset easily. Sometimes in the afternoon, she was so hungry she felt as though she had to have food right away or she would pass out. And then in the mornings, the queasiness in her stomach...

She couldn't be. Could she? Could she really? The thought froze her like a deer caught in headlights.

No, it was impossible. After all, Paul had used protection. Except for those last two times, in the morning that final day...

"Oh my God," she moaned, clutching herself in a desperate embrace. "This can't be happening."

She drove all the way to Madison where no one knew her, to buy a pregnancy testing kit. And even then, she wore huge dark glasses and a scarf over her hair, just in case.

Driving home, her foot kept pressing harder and harder on the accelerator and she got stopped for speeding just outside of town. But she didn't care about that, didn't care about the ticket or the day in traffic school that lay ahead of her. All she cared about was the time it ate up. She just wanted to get home and take the test.

And then, finally, she was in her own bathroom with the test kit. She closed her eyes, she held her breath, and when she finally let herself look at the panel, the pink dot had turned blue. She was carrying a child inside her. Paul's baby.

A thousand conflicting emotions and thoughts raged through her for the next few hours. She didn't know what she was going to do. Abortion? Adoption? Going off somewhere and raising the child on her own? There were pros and cons to everything. She needed help in making a decision. She needed real advice.

She took a trip to Chicago and went to the doctor she had trusted for years. After a thorough examination, he took her into his office and closed the door.

"Well, my dear," he said, his kindly eyes shining, "you are definitely pregnant. Congratulations. I'm sure you'll have a wonderful baby."

Her last hope had crashed and she didn't know where to turn. "But...doctor, I'm almost forty years old. Isn't that dangerous? Wouldn't I be crazy to go through with this?"

He looked shocked. "My dear, it is true that the risk of complications goes up as a woman gets older. But you are hardly in a category for panic yet. These days, I have many patients who have babies in their early forties. I don't recommend it much beyond those years, but a woman who is careful of her health and exercise and is cautious has a very good chance of a successful birth. You're healthy as a horse. I wouldn't give age another thought.''

His words were a revelation to Rosemary. He showed her pictures of older mothers and their children, and a small spark of hope began to grow in her. Could she really go through with this?

She held the information in strictest privacy, not telling even her closest friends. She couldn't possibly talk about it until she knew what she was going to do.

Her baby. It overwhelmed her. She went back over her own childhood, brought up all the bitter things her mother had ever said, sifted through the past, looking for answers. But all those old ideas seemed dusty and trivial. She knew children now. She wasn't swayed by her mother's anger any longer. A child seemed a golden thing, a wonder.

Her baby. The idea was so new, it took days to get used to it, and by that time, her wonder had matured into determination. This child was going to have the best, one way or another. And if that meant putting the baby up for adoption so that he or she could have the advantage of a two-parent home, that might be what she'd have to do.

Paul's baby. A new area of her heart opened up and filled with love.

CHAPTER SEVENTEEN

SHOULD SHE TELL PAUL? She agonized over that for days. How could she tell him? Wouldn't she be doing exactly what she'd despised Charmayne for supposedly doing—trapping him? How could she go to him and say, *I'm carrying your baby. Marry me.*

Rosemary wasn't even sure he would want to marry her, baby or not. He had kidded about it, but he'd never actually asked her, had he? And right now, he seemed to detest her.

She and Glenna had the baby shower for Pam at the Kelsey Boardinghouse. The room was full of chattering women. Streamers hung from the ceiling, balloons bobbed in every corner, lullabies played from the stereo. And the gifts were adorable—tiny baby suits, bonnets, toys. Rosemary found herself in raptures over every detail. Funny, these things had never interested her before, but suddenly she charmed with every baby item she saw.

Pam looked very happy. The problems with Patrick seemed to have faded. Rosemary had tried to have a talk with him at one point, but he'd brushed her off. Still, ever since that day, Pam seemed to think he'd made more of an effort to be at home with her when she needed him.

Rosemary wasn't sure. Hayley Ingalls was invited to the shower and she came, acting very friendly. In fact, Rosemary and she had a chat and Rosemary came very close to apologizing for her outburst at the pool a few weeks before, explaining how ill she had been at the time. But she stopped short of a complete change of mind. After all, she still didn't know for sure how guilty Hayley actually was.

It was just a few nights later when Pam called and asked Rosemary to come over. A storm was brewing. The rain had already begun and there was electricity in the air, a sense of something big coming. Rosemary felt the unease even before she got the phone call, but once Pam asked for help, she was more than ready to comply.

"Patrick's out of town at an educators' conference. I don't know, I just feel sort of strange, and I'd be more comfortable if I had someone with me."

When she had first come to Tyler, Pam had stayed with Rosemary in her apartment in the Victorian. They'd been friends before that, but the close proximity, plus the fact that as a physical therapist, Rosemary had been able to help Pam deal with her MS symptoms, had strengthened the ties between them. Those symptoms hadn't been in evidence lately, but something in Pam's voice made Rosemary think of them.

"You aren't having any problems, are you?" she asked sharply.

"With my MS?" Pam paused, and when she went on, her voice was strained. "I don't really know. There is a fluttery feeling, a weakness, that sort of reminds me of those old symptoms."

Rosemary's heart sank. Things had been going so well, and Pam had been told her disease was in remission. It would be a tragedy if it came back now. Pam didn't deserve that. "You hold tight. I'll be right over."

It took twice as long as usual to get to Pam's house. The wind was whipping down the streets and sheets of rain pelted the car. Rosemary breathed a sigh of relief as she pulled into the driveway, then put up the hood of her jacket and ran for the front door.

She found Pam inside, looking a bit pale and shaky. "Let's get you to the doctor," she urged.

"No." Pam was adamant. "I don't want to go to the doctor. I'm okay, really I am. But I did want someone here with me just in case."

Rosemary hesitated, then shrugged. "Okay. But you'll tell me right away if you start feeling worse?"

"Of course."

They popped popcorn and watched an old movie and chatted about the past, laughing over memories. Outside, the wind was getting wilder, blowing hard against the roof. Gusts seemed ready to snatch it right off. And then the lightning came smashing down, as though it could open up the sky.

"This is some storm," Rosemary commented, and the moment the words were out of her mouth, a ground-shuddering crash came from the front of the house and the electricity went dead.

They both headed for the front window, pulling back the drapes. The rain slanted against the windowpane, making it hard to see out, but they could tell that there was a very large gap where the old oak tree had stood.

"My car," Rosemary moaned, running for the front door and flinging it open. There was her car, all right, and there was the oak tree, lying right on top of it.

"I don't believe this," she said, letting the door close again and staring out the window at the dark night. "The tree took out my car!"

"Rosemary..." Pam sank into a chair.

Rosemary spun around, her face full of horror, full of outrage, and with no one to blame but Mother Nature herself. "It's totaled. I'm sure of it. I just hope insurance will cover—"

"Rosemary!"

Pam's tone of voice finally penetrated Rosemary's anguish, and she turned, moving toward where Pam was sitting in the dark. "What is it?" she asked quickly, reaching for her hand.

Pam took a deep breath and tried to sound calm, though she was feeling anything but. "Something's happening. I'm not sure what."

"Hold on." Rosemary groped her way to the kitchen and found candles and matches in a drawer, coming back with two sources of flickering light in her hands.

"Let's see." She had Pam stretch out on the couch and took her pulse and then felt her rounded belly. It was hard as a rock. "Any contractions?" she asked shortly.

Pam nodded. "Just practice ones, I think. I've been having them on and off for days."

Rosemary paused a moment to steady herself and tried to keep her heart rate calm. "I think you're going to have this baby," she said at last, in a solemn voice.

"No," Pam groaned. "No, it's not time yet. It's not due for almost a month."

"Tell that to the baby." She jumped to her feet. "We need to get you to the hospital." Going quickly to the phone, she lifted the receiver to her ear. No dial tone. "The phone's dead. Lines must be down."

This was not good. How was she going to get Pam to the hospital if her car was ruined, Pam's was blocked in the garage by the fallen tree and there was no way to call a cab, or anyone else, for that matter.

She stopped to think. "How about a neighbor?"

"The Kenneys are out of town, but the Sinclairs might be home," Pam offered, breathing quickly. "Oh, hurry, Rosemary. This feels so strange."

Rosemary kept panic at bay by hurrying. She went to the neighbors' and pounded on the door, but there was no answer. Now what? Hurry. She had to hurry. But where?

Putting a hand to her wet hair, she tried to think. Paul. His house was only two blocks away. If she raced....

She began to run. Lightning flashed ahead of her, making her jump, but she kept running, running in the rain. She reached the Victorian and ran up the steps, banging hard on the door. It opened almost immediately and Paul looked out, his face as handsome as ever, his eyes full of surprise.

"Rosemary," he cried, taking her into his arms, wet hair, wet clothes and all. "What is it? What's happened?"

"It's Pam." She stumbled over words, trying to get them out too quickly. "Either she's having a baby or something has gone very wrong. A tree hit my car. Can you come?"

Paul had been living in emergency situations half his life and this didn't faze him. It was as though he'd always been in training for exactly this moment.

"Sure," he said. Reaching back to grab his raincoat and a flashlight, he came without hesitation. "Let's go in my car."

They drove slowly through the streets, dodging branches that had sheared off in the wind. He pulled up in front of Pam's house and gave a low whistle when he saw the tree and what it had done to her car. But that was for another time. Right now, Pam was on their minds.

"She's having the baby, all right," he said after a cursory examination. "We don't have much time. But I do want to get her to the hospital. This baby is coming early and I want a trained ob to handle it."

Rosemary nodded. Paul was cool and calm in an emergency, and she liked that. She helped bundle Pam up and take her to the car, then sat with her in the back seat while Paul raced toward the hospital, calling in their arrival on his cellular phone. Nurses were waiting as they drove up to the door. They took Pam quickly and efficiently, plopping her into a wheelchair and whisking her through the double doors to the elevator that would take her to Maternity. Rosemary watched her go, her shoulders sagging, and then turned to smile at Paul.

"Thanks," she said, smiling at him shyly. "I couldn't have done it without you, you know."

He didn't say a word. Instead, he reached out and touched her cheek, then took her hand, and they went together to the maternity ward on the regular elevator.

Rosemary used the telephone to call Pam's many in-laws and friends, and soon the waiting room was full of people. Even Patrick showed up just about dawn, rushing past everyone and on into the labor room. When he came back out a little later, he was all smiles.

"She's beautiful," he cried out to them all.

"We know that," his father responded. "But how is she?"

"I mean the baby," Patrick said. "Six pounds four ounces of bouncing baby girl. She's a little early but the doctor says she seems to be in good shape." He shook his head, overcome by emotion. "Everything—everything's okay."

His relatives gathered around him, laughing and calling out questions. Rosemary and Paul hung back, watching them, smiling, sharing their joy.

"We're naming her Johnann," Patrick said. "After a couple of pretty great grandparents."

Johnny Kelsey, an older version of his handsome son, had tears in his eyes. Turning, he took hold of his wife, Anna, and hugged her.

"Wow," said Patrick as the hubbub died down. "What a great day." Turning to Rosemary and Paul, he gave them each a big bear hug as well. "Thank you so much for taking care of her," he said, his voice breaking. "If only I'd been here. I hate to think of her all alone and feeling strange...."

"Did you arrive in time for the birth?" Rosemary asked him.

He nodded. "Yes, thank God. This is the greatest day of my life. I would have hated to miss it." His face changed. "Oh my God. I forgot. I've got to call Hayley."

Spinning on his heel, he headed for the bank of pay phones along the wall.

Rosemary stood where she was, unable to believe what she'd just heard. "Did you hear that?" she demanded.

"Leave it alone, Rosemary," Paul advised. "It's none of our business."

"None of our business?" She looked at him fiercely. "Pam can't defend herself at the moment. Someone has to do it for her."

Outrage poured through her, and she marched right after Patrick, catching him before he'd dialed. Grabbing his shoulder, she pulled him around.

"How dare you," she said through gritted teeth, her eyes cold with her anger. "How dare you? After all Pam's been through, and the first thing you want to do is call Hayley?"

Patrick looked at her in surprise, then realization filled his eyes and the surprise turned to anger. "Are you through?" he asked her.

"No, I'm not through. You've got to get rid of her, Patrick. Drop her right now. You owe as much to Pam. It's not fair to her or to your new baby to keep up this—this sick relationship...."

"Hold on, Rosemary." He grabbed her by the shoulders. "You don't know what you're talking about."

She tried to twist away from his grip and failed. "I know exactly what I'm talking about. I saw the two of you head-to-head at the Iron Mustache last month."

He stared at her for a long moment and then slowly began to laugh.

She shoved him, furious. "It's not funny, Patrick."

He sobered slowly. "No. You're right. It isn't. It's pathetic." He shook his head. "Rosemary, Rosemary, how could you be so wrong? You know me. You know how much I love Pam." He shrugged, his hands tightening on her shoulders as though he could get through to her that way. "Hayley is a friend. That is all."

"I've heard that one before," she scoffed.

"And you'll hear it again. Because it's true." He gave her a gentle shake. "Listen to me, Rosemary. I spent a lot of time with Hayley because starting the swim team was my first big project as the new athletic director and I wanted to make sure it went well. That was it. I had to make that come out okay for my own sake. Don't you get it?"

She stared at him, not convinced.

"Then I had a great idea of a surprise for Pam. Hayley is an interior decorator. Pam's been frustrated about the house for a long time, not sure what to do to improve things. I've been having Hayley come in and take measurements when Pam wasn't there, and I've met her a few times out of town to go over plans."

Rosemary's face was changing. Could this really be all there was to it? She frowned, not ready to concede, but beginning to realize she could have been wrong.

"This has been in the works for months. While Pam is in the hospital having our baby, Hayley will be decorating our house. That's why I was in a hurry to call her. When Pam comes home, it will be done. Everyone will be happy." He gave Rosemary another little shake and smiled at her. "Except you, who will harbor doubts until your dying day, won't you?"

"No." Lord, how could she have been such a patsy for the dramatic instead of the truth? Rosemary felt her cheeks redden, and it was an unfamiliar feeling for her. "No, I won't. Oh Patrick, I'm so sorry."

Pulling her closer, he gave her a kiss on the forehead. "Never mind, Miss Busybody. I know you were concerned because you love Pam, too. But have a little faith in me next time. Okay?"

She was going to grow teary again. She was doing it all the time lately. Trying to smile at him, she whispered, "Okay," and he hugged her.

"Okay," he said, and he turned to make his call.

She moved away, then found Paul watching. Laughing softly, he came up and took her hand in his. "When are you going to learn to stop jumping to conclusions?" he asked her.

"Probably never," she admitted, half laughing, half in despair.

"You'll be okay as long as you have a backup system," he told her wisely, pulling her even closer. "If you have someone around who can tell you when you're going off the deep end, when you should stop and rethink an issue, you'll be okay."

"Oh?" she said archly, beginning to see where this might be going. "Who did you have in mind?"

He smiled down into her eyes, his own the brightest shade of baby blue she'd ever seen. "I think you know."

"Paul..."

"I love you, Rosemary," he continued, not letting her stop him. "I've loved you for weeks. Maybe longer."

"Paul..." The tears were threatening again and she blinked furiously, trying to stem them.

He kissed her hard, then drew back and gazed down into her face again. "I've been so damn lonely without you. I don't want to be that way anymore. I want us to get married."

"Paul..." The tears were coming in earnest, filling her eyes.

But he still wouldn't let her speak. She'd said too much in the past, and he wasn't going to let her ruin this. This time, he would win. His way would prevail. "I don't want to hear any more lame excuses, Rosemary. I want you in my life. I want to be in yours. And that's it. That's the final word."

"Paul," she said, sniffing, teardrops making silver trails down her cheeks, "about children . . ."

He held her tightly, caressing her. "It's okay," he said, stroking her hair. "I don't care about that anymore. I've got plenty of kids around because of the work I do. That will be enough for me. I can live without a child of my own. But Rosemary—" he held his head back so that he could look into her eyes "—I don't want to live without you."

"Paul, will you be still and let me speak?" she demanded, pulling back. "I love you, too. I just want you to be sure—"

"I'm sure. I'm so sure, I've never been any surer about anything. You are mine, Rosemary. And I'll fight to keep you this time."

"Oh, Paul."

She was in heaven, had to be. She had to tell him about the baby, had to finish the story for him. But not yet. Not here, not like this. She wanted to go home first, to put on the dress he'd bought her, to put candles on the table and pour a glass of wine for him. And maybe sparkling apple juice for her, now that she couldn't drink alcohol. And then she would take his handsome face between her hands and tell him she was carrying his baby inside her, and he would press his cheek against her stomach to listen for his child. She sighed, melting into his arms.

"Is it still raining?" she asked dreamily.

"Just a little," he replied, his arms tightening around her.

"It can rain all it wants," she said, snuggling closer. "I've got my own sunshine from now on."

HOMETOWN REUNION

continues with

Daddy Next Door

by Ginger Chambers

It's a good thing there's a new pediatrician in Tyler,
because all anyone can talk about these days is babies—
especially when Raine comes home from New York...
pregnant. No one's fooled for a minute when she and her
best friend, Gabe Atwood, suddenly get married, but the
question remains—is the baby really his?

Available in February

Here's a preview!

DADDY NEXT DOOR

"TELL ME, RAINE," Gabe urged her. "I can help."

She shook her head, denying him closeness. Tears had started to gather on her lashes, and the sight of them made Gabe's stomach twist with fear.

"Has someone hurt you?" he demanded. "You haven't been ..."

"No," she whispered tightly, instinctively understanding. "I haven't been raped."

Relief surged through him, but something was still terribly wrong. "Are you in some kind of financial trouble? I've got some money saved ... whatever you need, it's yours."

"It's not that," she said.

"A man. A boyfriend." The words hurt him, but he had compromised with reality a long time ago.

She laughed, the sound hollow. "In a way," she admitted, then looked away. "I'm pregnant, Gabe. The father of the baby says he loves me, but he doesn't want the child. He wants me to ..."

"He wants you to have an abortion?" he demanded, his emotions hardening into anger against this unknown man.

"It wasn't his idea that I should get pregnant."

Words burst out of him. "What kind of a man doesn't want his own child?"

She recoiled as if he'd hit her, and he instantly reached out, dragging her against him, pressing her head to his chest.

"I didn't mean that," he swore brokenly, filled with remorse. "I didn't mean... You have a big decision to make, Raine. And I can't... I shouldn't—"

Finally she said, "I should get my things."

"Are you sure you want to do that now? Should you be alone?"

"It's what I want," she said softly.

All he could do was nod. All the years, all the time they'd known each other... He couldn't remember the actual day he'd fallen in love with her. There was no way for him to pinpoint the moment. The feeling was just there, like the air he breathed.

His private agony was that to this day Raine had never reciprocated his feelings. She continued to look upon him as good old Gabe, friend for life. Almost closer than a real brother.

"I think that's everything," she said as she returned to the kitchen, carrying her suitcase.

"Call me if you need anything," he directed her. He saw her to the back door of her mother's house and turned away.

What she had told him made no difference to his love for her. He would love her forever, child or no child.

At his kitchen door he paused to look back. She continued to stand in the doorway of the other house, staring at him but not seeing him, a fact he discovered when he lifted a hand to wave and received no response.

She was thinking of *him*—that man in New York. The father of her baby.

As Gabe's hand fell back to his side, it tightened into a fist.

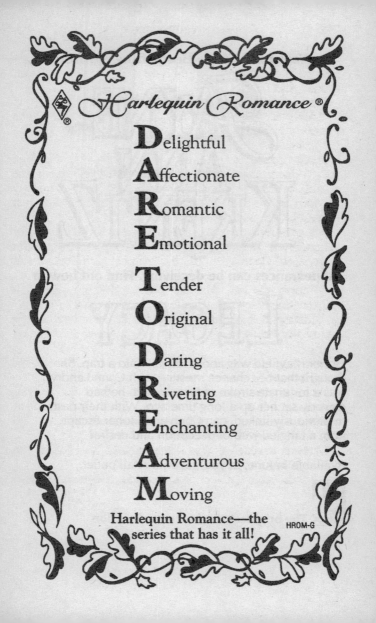

Harlequin Romance ®

Delightful

Affectionate

Romantic

Emotional

Tender

Original

Daring

Riveting

Enchanting

Adventurous

Moving

Harlequin Romance—the
series that has it all!

HROM-G

New York Times **Bestselling Author**

JAYNE ANN KRENTZ

Appearances can be deceiving. Find out how in

LEGACY

Honor Mayfield was about to walk into a trap. She thought that her chance meeting with Conn Landry was a fortunate stroke of luck. In fact, he had cleverly set her up a long time ago. With their pasts mysteriously linked, can Conn and Honor escape from a tangled web of deception and desire?

Available in June, at your favorite retail outlet.

WAYS TO *UNEXPECTEDLY* MEET MR. RIGHT:

♡ *Go out with the sexy-sounding stranger your daughter secretly set you up with through a personal ad.*

♡ *RSVP yes to a wedding invitation—soon it might be your turn to say "I do!"*

♡ *Receive a marriage proposal by mail— from a man you've never met....*

These are just a few of the unexpected ways that written communication leads to love in Silhouette Yours Truly.

Each month, look for two fast-paced, fun and flirtatious Yours Truly novels (with entertaining treats and sneak previews in the back pages) by some of your favorite authors—and some who are sure to become favorites.

YOURS TRULY™:
Love—when you least expect it!

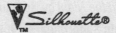

YT-GEN

UNLOCK THE DOOR TO GREAT ROMANCE
AT BRIDE'S BAY RESORT

Join Harlequin's new across-the-lines series, set in an exclusive hotel on an island off the coast of South Carolina.

Seven of your favorite authors will bring you exciting stories about fascinating heroes and heroines discovering love at Bride's Bay Resort.

Look for these fabulous stories coming to a store near you beginning in January 1996.

Harlequin American Romance #613 in January
Matchmaking Baby by Cathy Gillen Thacker

Harlequin Presents #1794 in February
Indiscretions by Robyn Donald

Harlequin Intrigue #362 in March
Love and Lies by Dawn Stewardson

Harlequin Romance #3404 in April
Make Believe Engagement by Day Leclaire

Harlequin Temptation #588 in May
Stranger in the Night by Roseanne Williams

Harlequin Superromance #695 in June
Married to a Stranger by Connie Bennett

Harlequin Historicals #324 in July
Dulcie's Gift by Ruth Langan

Visit Bride's Bay Resort each month wherever Harlequin books are sold.

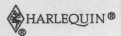

BBAYG